"Feeling better?" asked a deep voice in the dark.

Julia screamed, her arms jerked, and she banged the drinking glass on her front teeth. Cold water flew into her face and onto her T-shirt.

"Sorry about that. I didn't mean to scare you." The voice came closer, and then Aidan was there, turning on the lamp beside her bed. "You okay?"

"No. You scared the life out of me." Julia pressed her free hand to her saturated chest and her terrified heart. "What are you doing here? I thought you left after you brought me the prescription."

"I didn't want to leave you alone. Here." He handed her the pills. "Take these. We'll talk after your shower. Trust me, you'll feel better."

She got a lump in her throat. Aidan Gallagher was a big faker. He acted all dangerous and badass, but underneath he was all caring and kind. She'd seen a hint of his sweetness with his daughter, and now she had proof. The man was a marshmallow.

PRAISE FOR DEBBIE MASON

Sugarplum Way

ALSO BY DEBBIE MASON

THE HIGHLAND FALLS SERIES

Summer on Honeysuckle Ridge
Christmas on Reindeer Road
Falling in Love on Willow Creek
A Wedding on Honeysuckle Ridge (short story)
The Inn on Mirror Lake
At Home on Marigold Lane

THE HARMONY HARBOR SERIES

Mistletoe Cottage
Christmas with an Angel (short story)
Starlight Bridge
Primrose Lane
Sugarplum Way
Driftwood Cove
Sandpiper Shore
The Corner of Holly and Ivy
Barefoot Beach
Christmas in Harmony Harbor

THE CHRISTMAS, COLORADO SERIES

The Trouble with Christmas
Christmas in July
It Happened at Christmas
Wedding Bells in Christmas
Snowbound at Christmas
Kiss Me in Christmas
Happy Ever After in Christmas
Marry Me at Christmas (short story)
Miracle at Christmas (novella)
One Night in Christmas (novella)

Sugarplum Way

DEBBIE MASON

A Harmony Harbor Novel

FOREVER
New York   Boston

Copyright © 2017 by Debbie Mazzuca
Excerpt from Mistletoe Cottage © 2016 by Debbie Mazzuca
Cover design by Daniela Medina. Cover art by Tom Hallman. Cover art by © Shutterstock. Cover copyright © 2022 by Hachette Book Group, Inc.

Forever
Hachette Book Group
1290 Avenue of the Americas, New York, NY 10104
read-forever.com
twitter.com/readforeverpub

Originally published in mass market and ebook by Forever in October 2017
Reissued: October 2022

Forever is an imprint of Grand Central Publishing. The Forever name and logo are trademarks of Hachette Book Group, Inc.

The publisher is not responsible for websites (or their content) that are not owned by the publisher.

The Hachette Speakers Bureau provides a wide range of authors for speaking events. To find out more, go to www.hachettespeakersbureau.com or call (866) 376-6591.

ISBNs: 978-1-5387-2287-9 (mass market), 978-1-5387-4414-7 (ebook)

Printed in the United States of America

OPM

10 9 8 7 6 5 4 3 2 1

This book is dedicated to my granddaughters, Lilianna and Gabriella, who remind me every day that we live in a beautiful and magical world. Don't ever stop looking for the beauty and believing in the magic, my sweet girls.

Acknowledgments

A few weeks ago, Facebook reminded me of this post I shared: *I've been walking on air since Friday and now can finally share. I have a three-book deal with Grand Central/Forever for my small-town contemporary romance series set in Christmas, Colorado!!! I am beyond excited!!*

The post was from five years ago, and I truly did feel like I was walking on air. Grand Central/ Forever was my dream publisher, so I was beyond thrilled that they would be publishing my series. Four contracts, two series, and eleven books later, I still feel exactly the same way. And I couldn't be more grateful to Team Forever. My heartfelt thanks to Beth deGuzman, Amy Pierpont, Leah Hultenschmidt, Lexi Smail, Jodi Rosoff, Michelle Cashman, Monisha Lakhotia, Tareth Mitch, Luria Rittenberg, Carrie Andrews, Elizabeth Turner, Tom Hallman, and last but certainly not least, my incredibly talented and hardworking editor, Alex Logan, who goes above and beyond for me and my books and never fails to make them so much better.

Many thanks to my wonderful agent who has represented me for nine years, Pamela Harty. My thanks also to members of Pamela's team at the Knight Agency, Deirdre Knight, Elaine Spencer, and Jamie Pritchett.

Special thanks to my cousin Rhonda Lamourie, my sister-in-law Connie Simpson, my niece Kelsey Mazzuca, and my son-in-law Shariffe Ghadban for shamelessly pimping my books!

To my husband, children, and grandchildren for always supporting me and encouraging me to go after my dreams, *thank you*. I love you all more than you'll ever know. Additional thanks to my daughter Jess for reading my first drafts and letting me talk endlessly about my stories. Thanks, honey.

And most of all, I want to thank you, the reader, for buying my books and for spending time with me in Harmony Harbor (and Christmas, Colorado). For your kindness in sharing my stories with your friends and family, for your lovely e-mails, Facebook posts, tweets, and reviews, I hope you know how truly grateful I am.

Sugarplum Way

Chapter One

♥

With each frantic beat of my heart, Adrian's name echoes in my mind. I have to reach him before he discovers my secret. As I race across the ice-crusted meadow, my breath forms small, frosted clouds in the frigid, moonlit night. My throat, my chest, my legs, everything aches, but I can't stop until I reach the white castle by the turquoise sea. Adrian is there, waiting for me. He needs to hear this from me and no one else. If he...

A loud buzzing sound pulled Julia Landon out of the scene she was writing and onto the hard chair behind her desk in her cramped, one-bedroom apartment. She gave her head a slight shake to free herself from the grip of her heroine's emotions and reached for the Santa timer that danced on top of her narrow desk.

Julia's timers had saved her butt in the past, and this was no exception. Although it didn't feel that way at the moment, because her secret crush still filled the pages of her book for all the world to see.

She turned off Santa, set him on the crowded shelf

above her desk, and replaced him with a turkey. Julia had forty-eight timers in her collection, and she had a sinking feeling she'd use each and every one of them before she sent off *Warrior's Touch* to her editor. Her manuscript was due tomorrow at nine a.m. sharp. And unless things had changed while she was running through a meadow on a moonlit night in the Emerald Isle, there were still just twenty-four hours in a day.

Which was where the trouble had all begun. She'd mistakenly assumed she'd be granted a three-day reprieve due to the Thanksgiving holiday, only to discover that New York editors rarely took time off.

Asking for an extension was out of the question. She'd blown through one deadline already. If she blew through another one, she was afraid her editor would write her off as an unprofessional one-hit wonder and cancel the contract, ruining Julia's chance of making her dream come true.

Back in June, she'd published the first book in the Warrior trilogy, *Warrior's Kiss,* on her own. It had taken off almost immediately, exceeding her wildest expectations. Reader support had been phenomenal, and the extra money had come in the nick of time. Sales were down at her bookstore—Books and Beans—and fulfilling her vow to her late fiancé, Josh Winters, was costly.

But as much as the digital success of *Warrior's Kiss* had been mind-boggling in the happiest of mind-boggling ways, Julia's dream was to see her books sitting on the same shelves as those of the authors she adored.

The added benefit, which was almost as important,

was the hope that the four alpha males in her life—her father and three older brothers—would believe that seeing her in bookstores across the land meant they no longer had to worry about her, that she had what it took to support herself.

Maybe then every phone call home wouldn't begin and end with her dad and brothers exhorting her to move back to Texas so they could look after her—folding her like a burrito in Bubble Wrap to ensure she wouldn't get hurt or have her heart broken again.

Honestly, it felt like she'd been trying to prove herself to them her entire grown-up life. If opening Books and Beans hadn't convinced them she could manage on her own, she didn't know why she thought being published would. No doubt her brothers would tell her it was her magical thinking at work again. To her mind, there was nothing magical or wrong with being hopeful.

If she hadn't held on to the hope that things would get better these past couple of years, she didn't know where she'd be. Maybe cast adrift on a turquoise sea. She wished she didn't care what everyone thought about her, but sometimes it felt like she'd been born with an extra people-pleasing gene.

Emmeline, Julia's mother, would have been over the moon for her. The former actress would have held Texas-sized celebrations the day Julia had finished her first book at eighteen, the day she'd received her first non-form rejection letter at twenty-eight, and the day *Warrior's Kiss* hit number sixteen on the *USA Today* bestseller list a week before Julia's thirty-second birthday.

Every step of the way, every small victory and minor defeat, her mother would have been there cheering her on. Even though Emmeline had died when Julia was twelve, she believed her mother held parties for her in heaven.

She paid tribute to her mother in each and every book she wrote. In the Warrior's trilogy, an urban fantasy set in Ireland, Emmeline was the inspiration for the White Witch. In a way, it was like bringing her mother back to life. The White Witch looked, acted, and dressed exactly like Emmeline once had.

Julia refocused on the computer screen. She'd been a finger press away from deleting the last three chapters when Santa shook his booty and brought her back to reality. Sometimes reality sucked. Because no matter how much she wanted to, there was no way she could kill off Adrian Greystone, the trilogy's hero. He was the book boyfriend that readers lusted after and the reason they were clamoring for more.

Including Julia's friend Olivia, who had finished *Warrior's Kiss* a few weeks before. But unlike Adrian Greystone's other fans, Olivia had told her that she was uncomfortable lusting after the fictional hero. And it had nothing to do with her friend being a married woman. Olivia said it was because Adrian reminded her of her brother-in-law Aidan Gallagher.

All too clearly, Julia recalled the knowing look Olivia had given her that morning in the bookstore. She'd brushed off Olivia's silent insinuation with a laugh before making an excuse to run up to her apartment above the bookstore. She'd taken the back stairs two at a time to check for herself.

The evidence was overwhelming, from his physical description to his badass demeanor to his name. Adrian alone may not have raised eyebrows, but then Julia had made the fatal mistake of using Greystone as his surname. Greystone Manor, the fairy-tale castle standing sentry over the town of Harmony Harbor, was the Gallagher family's home as well as a hotel.

Julia knew exactly where to lay the blame. It was because of that one kiss they shared under the mistletoe last Christmas at the manor. Given the length of time Aidan's mouth had been on hers, it probably wouldn't even qualify as a kiss—more like a peck. He hadn't known her, and she hadn't known him, and Kitty Gallagher had been standing right there with a twinkle in her eyes demanding they take advantage of the long-standing tradition or risk a lifetime of bad luck.

Since Julia had suffered enough bad luck at that point, she wasn't willing to take a chance she'd have to live through decades more. Besides that, Aidan was big and beautiful, and at that moment, she'd needed something big and beautiful to distract her.

She should have risked a lifetime of bad luck.

Because while the kiss was merely a brief touch of his firm lips upon hers, it had an earth-shattering effect on Julia. She'd felt like she'd been transported to another place and time, as if she were dancing among the stars. And when she looked into Aidan's extraordinary blue eyes, something inside her clicked into place. She'd known then that she'd found him. Her soul mate. Her one true love. In her head, she could almost hear her brothers groaning at the idea she'd discovered her true love after sharing only one kiss.

But they'd be happy to know that thoughts of tall, handsome princes and fairy-tale endings had vanished the second the Gallagher matriarch had introduced the two. Aidan Gallagher would never be the man of Julia's dreams. He couldn't be. Because if he ever found out why she'd taken on the job of the Gallaghers' fairy godmother, he'd have her thrown in jail and would instruct them to lose the key.

Oddly enough though, she'd begun writing *Warrior's Kiss* months before she met Aidan. But it wasn't until he kissed her under the mistletoe that the story took on a life of its own and her hero, Adrian Greystone, came fully alive.

As much as Julia knew a relationship between her and Aidan could never be, it didn't stop her from living vicariously through her heroine and embarking on a love affair to end all love affairs with Adrian Greystone.

Within hours of discovering that Olivia was right and that Julia had exposed her secret crush for all the world to see, she'd developed a debilitating case of writer's block. Every time she sat at her desk, her brain would freeze and her fingers would seize, and her first deadline flew by. And now here she was again, staring another deadline in the eyes.

As she saw it, she had three choices. One, get the manuscript to her editor on time and take the risk that someone other than Olivia—who'd been sworn to secrecy—discovered that Julia was author J. L. Winters. Two, kill off her hero and risk alienating both her readers and her new publisher. Three, ask for an extension and risk the possibility of being dropped by her editor.

She went with number three and brought up a new file on the screen. As she worked on a believable way to disguise Adrian's resemblance to Aidan, she noticed wisps of smoke floating past her. It always amazed her how quickly the real world faded away and she stepped into her imaginary one, but this was downright freaky. Never before had she...

The thought was abruptly cut off by the beeping of the smoke detector and a disembodied voice repeatedly saying *fire.*

Her head snapped up, and her gaze shot around her apartment, searching for the smoke's source. She made out the Christmas tree in the corner of her living room, its colorful miniature lights twinkling through the fog. If it wasn't the tree... *The bookstore!* She jumped from the chair.

And that's when the smell of burning cookies invaded her nostrils.

Her Santa timer hadn't gone off to remind her to get up and shake her booty; it was to remind her that her contribution to Thanksgiving dinner was ready to come out of the oven!

Frantically, she searched for her cell phone on her cluttered desk, around the boxes of Christmas decorations she'd yet to unpack on the floor, and the clothes on the couch that she'd forgotten to put away. Her cell phone was nowhere to be found.

And her overprotective father, who was more overprotective than most fathers of daughters because he was a sheriff, had ordered and installed a state-of-the-art alarm system the last time he'd visited. As soon as the smoke detector went off, Julia had four minutes to call the company and report a false alarm or the Harmony Harbor fire trucks would be on their way, sirens wailing.

Just like they had last month.

* * *

Julia walked down the narrow, smoke-filled stairway from her apartment to the bookstore with a fishbowl in her arms while apologizing for a second time to the fire chief. The sixty-something man with a full head of silver hair bore a striking resemblance to Paul Newman, right down to his blue eyes, which appeared to be glinting with amusement as he held open the door leading into her store.

"I really am sorry, Mr. Gallagher. From now on, I'll make sure I have my phone on me before I put anything in the oven."

He scratched his chin, obviously fighting back a grin. "Colin, remember? And if I'm not mistaken, last time you were making spaghetti sauce, and the time before that it was oatmeal. So let's make a deal. You don't use the stove or oven until you're fully awake, okay?"

She typically started her day at five a.m. to get in her word count before opening the store. But it wasn't like she could tell Mr. Gallagher she set things on fire because she disappeared into her make-believe world, so she'd told him she'd fallen back to sleep. She'd used the excuse so often that he probably thought she had narcolepsy.

"I think I'll give up cooking altogether," she said as she placed the fishbowl on a low table in the children's section. Her worry that Ariel and Eric had been affected by the smoke in her apartment was alleviated when they began swimming around. But while she could set aside her concern over her goldfish, she had another worry to contend with... "My dad didn't happen to have the alarm system wired so that he gets notified too, did he? Like a three-strikes kind of thing?"

"Not that I know of," Colin said, no longer holding back a grin. He was giving her a smile that she was unfortunately familiar with. It was the same smile people got on their faces just before they pinched her cheeks. She'd known a lot of cheek pinchers in her thirty-two years.

"He didn't tell you to call him if my alarm went off, did he?" She made a mental note to ask Paul Benson, the chief of police, the same question. She'd forgotten her passcode and set off the intruder alarm last Sunday when she came back from a walk. In her defense, it was a new password. She'd had to change it when... she forgot it the last time. She needed to think about using one password for everything.

"No, he didn't, but your oldest brother did." At her groan, Colin added, "Don't worry. I won't call unless it's for something other than a false alarm. You should be glad they worry about you like they do, honey. It shows how much they care."

Of course he'd side with the men in her family.

Just like her father and brothers were the to-serve-and-protect Landons, Colin and his sons were the to-serve-and-protect Gallaghers.

There was one big difference though. Her family got an extra Texas-size helping of alpha, which made them way more annoying than the Gallaghers. Thinking back to her interactions with Aidan Gallagher this past summer, she revised that thought. He was the *a* in *alpha* and *annoying*.

"I know they do, and I love them too. I just wish they'd remember I'm thirty-two and not fifteen."

Colin looked down at her feet, and his lips twitched. She followed his gaze. She had on a cozy red plaid onesie with fake fur lining the hood and reindeer slippers on her feet. She shrugged, smiling up at him. "What can I say? I love Christmas."

"No one would argue with you there. That's quite the plan you've come up with for decorating Main Street. I got a look at it yesterday."

"Do you think it's too much? I made sure there was enough room for the fire trucks to pass under the lights and garland." It was her first year as head of Harmony Harbor's Christmas committee, and she wanted to do a good job.

"It's ambitious, that's for sure."

"If you think I'm being ambitious, you should see what they're doing in Bridgeport. It's important that we keep up, you know? For the manor's sake." Bridgeport was the town adjacent to Harmony Harbor and was the home to Greystone Manor's biggest competitor.

Which was the reason Julia had volunteered to head

up the committee despite having a bookstore and coffee shop to run and a book to write. Now that she thought about it, it was no wonder she couldn't keep the code for her alarm straight. But it's not like she had a choice. Greystone played an important role in ensuring the Gallagher family's happiness.

"So my mother and the Widows Club keep reminding me," Colin responded to her keeping-up-with-the-Joneses comment, or in this case the town of Bridgeport. "Don't worry, I approved the plan. A few of the boys have volunteered to give you a hand on Sunday. I'll e-mail you their contact information."

She hoped his second oldest son wasn't one of them. "That's great, thank you. Now we just have to pray that Mrs. Bradford doesn't try and file another injunction against us."

The seventy-something woman's husband owned the local bank, and Mrs. Bradford had chaired the Christmas committee for the past twenty years. She wasn't happy that she'd been replaced by Julia, and she'd made her unhappiness known by taking the town to court for wrongful dismissal. The case had been thrown out, of course, but Mrs. Bradford still managed to put them two weeks behind in their decorating schedule.

"She won't try again. Not with the Widows Club threatening to close their accounts at the bank if she does." His radio crackled. "I better get going. Give your apartment an hour to air out before you go back up."

She nodded and followed him through the bookstore and the small coffee bar to the front door. "Thanks so much for coming so quickly. I'm just sorry it was for another false alarm." She wrinkled her nose. "Umm, not that I wanted it to be a real fire, just that...well, you know what I mean."

He laughed and patted her cheek. "You're welcome. Happy Thanksgiving, honey."

She held back a heartfelt sigh. Colin Gallagher was the nicest man, and so handsome too. After everything he'd lost, he deserved the happiest of happily-ever-afters. She was glad that she'd played a small role in helping him achieve it. "You have a happy Thanksgiving too. Say hi to Maggie for me and tell her two o'clock Sunday is fine."

Julia smiled at the thought that all her scheming and plotting to get Maggie and Colin together had finally paid off. She'd spent most of the fall maneuvering the couple into chance meetings all around town.

Her smile fell at the look that came over Colin's face. It was not the look of a man who'd just heard the name of the woman he loved. He looked like a man hearing the name of the woman he'd just dumped. Again.

He shifted on his booted feet. "The thing is, Maggie and I...Maybe you should just call and let her know the time."

The bell above the door tinkled as Colin said goodbye and closed it behind him. Through the frosted glass, she watched him get into the fire truck. She didn't understand it. The man was brave, heroic even. Every day he put himself in danger on the job, and he had been doing so for more than thirty-five years. But when it came to opening his heart to love again, he got cold feet. This was the second time he'd bailed on poor Maggie. As far as Julia was concerned it would be the last because, one way or another, she was getting the couple together for good.

The Gallaghers' happiness had been her priority, her mission, for eighty-four-plus weeks. And as much as she wanted Josh to rest in peace, she also wanted to hang up her fairy godmother wings and move on with her life. Being responsible for someone else's happiness—make that five someones'—was a heavy burden to bear.

She'd hoped that by helping the Gallaghers achieve theirs, she'd find her own. Weighed down as she was by guilt, true happiness had been an elusive thing these past few years. She was ready to change that. Her goal had been to hang up her wings on New Year's Eve. She'd been thrilled when it looked like she'd achieved her objective months before her self-imposed deadline. Now here she was strapping her wings back on with only five weeks until the ball dropped.

Disappointment and a small dose of self-pity caused her stomach to head for her toes as slowly as that big old ball in Times Square. But before she managed to sink even a foot into despair, Julia reminded herself of something her mother used to say: *Nothing is impossible; the word itself says* "I'm possible."

A few years ago, she'd discovered her mother had borrowed the line from Audrey Hepburn. Julia decided she'd borrow some of that positive thinking for herself today. The odds of accomplishing her goal by New Year's Eve weren't impossible or insurmountable. After all, she had only Colin left. And whether he'd admit it or not, he was in love with Maggie. Everyone in town knew it... Obviously he didn't, or at the very least, he was a pro at denying his feelings.

Another small flicker of doubt crept up on her at the thought that Colin's fear of loving again might be stronger than Julia's matchmaking skills. But like before, she brushed those pesky worries aside, this time with the reminder that she had four successes to her name. Colin's sons, Finn, Griffin, and Liam were all happily married, and Julia credited herself with playing a small role in helping them achieve their dreams.

Their brother Aidan's dream hadn't included a wife, for which Julia would be eternally grateful. And it had nothing to do with her secret crush on the man. Tall, dark, and dangerous had destroyed any tender feelings Julia might have had for him last summer. Up until then, she'd thought he was a prince among men. But he'd turned out to be a beast. In good conscience, she couldn't match him with any of her friends.

So yes, she'd been relieved to learn that what Aidan wanted most was a job. The former DEA agent had moved home to Harmony Harbor in order to prove to a judge that he could provide a stable environment for his six-year-old daughter. But he'd needed a job to do that.

So, in true fairy godmother fashion, she'd managed to convince Paul, the chief of police, to hire Aidan at HHPD three weeks ago. She'd even been able to conclude her assignment without any direct contact with Aidan. Not an easy feat in Harmony Harbor. In her book, that made it a win all around.

As long as she didn't think about Paul, who apparently assumed that they were an item. Because while she didn't have to interact with Aidan to make his wish come true, she'd had to interact with his boss-to-be to get him the job. Interact as in date him. Three dates to be exact.

However, she didn't have time to worry about Paul now. If she planned to be fairy wing–free by New Year's Eve, she had work to do and no time to lose. She turned to look over her bookstore, and a plan began to formulate in her mind. One that would require a predawn visit to Maggie's house on Breakwater Way.

There was just one teensy problem with her plan. Detective Aidan Gallagher was staying in his childhood home across from Maggie's. But surely it was early enough that he was still in bed dreaming of sugarplums. She snorted at the thought of something sweet entering Aidan Gallagher's dreams. He'd probably shoot it if it did.

Chapter Two

♥

Aidan Gallagher woke up to a golden retriever licking his face and wondered what had become of his life. The question had nothing to do with the family dog kissing him awake instead of a hot blonde. It was because, at the age of thirty-seven, he hadn't expected to be waking up in a too-small bed in a room decorated with superheroes.

Now, if it was a temporary thing, that would have been a different story. But he'd been living with his dad at the family home on Breakwater Way for more than three months.

Figuring out why things had gone wrong wasn't especially difficult—he'd let emotions cloud his judgment. And every single time he let that unreliable organ called a heart overrule his brain, he suffered the consequences. But this time the fallout didn't only affect him.

Eight years ago today, he married a woman he'd been casually dating for two months. His family told him it was a mistake. But he was desperate to ease the pain of losing his mother and sister and went ahead with the wedding only six weeks after the accident. Then one morning, after years of trying to make his marriage work, he looked into his four-year-old daughter's wary eyes and realized he was doing her more harm than good and pulled the plug. The woman he married became hard and bitter, and she took him to the cleaners. He didn't fight her, because he let emotions mess with his head once again, and he felt guilty that he no longer loved her and wasn't sure that he ever had. But the one thing he never doubted was that he wanted to be a good father to his daughter.

A close call on his last assignment with the DEA and then a threat from Harper, his ex, had shown Aidan the light. If he wanted to be there for Ella Rose the way his dad had always been there for him, he needed to make a change. So he quit the job that he loved and moved back to the small town he'd done his best to avoid for the past eight years.

By then Harper had changed the rules of the game. As a psychiatrist, she knew how to play the system. And the system liked her a whole lot more than it liked him. For Ella Rose's sake, Aidan couldn't allow his ex to continue using their daughter as a pawn. He'd been up half the night trying to figure out a way to stop her.

Following up a chin-to-ear lick with an insistent bark, the family dog effectively put an end to Aidan's internal battle with his *feelings*. He lifted his hand to wipe Miller's doggy drool from his beard and glanced out the window across the room. "I don't know what your problem is, but I am not taking you out until the sun comes up. So just—"

The retriever latched on to the blanket that Aidan was thinking about pulling over his head, dragging it off the bed.

"Seriously, I'm not doing this right now. Go back to bed."

Somehow Miller interpreted that to mean *let's play* and began racing from one side of the room to the other. Aidan bowed his head. These days no one listened to him, so he didn't know why he expected Miller to.

"All right, you win. Cut it out before you scratch the floors." And Aidan got tagged to refinish them.

He threw back the sheet and grabbed his jeans from the end of the bed, barely managing to get them on before Miller was head-butting him out the door. Something was up with the dog. His behavior wasn't normal. Aidan corrected himself—unless Miller saw Maggie, who lived across the street.

The dog galloped down the short flight of stairs and raced to the bay window facing onto the street. His nose pressed to the glass, Miller whined.

The dog had been in a funk since Aidan's dad stopped dating Maggie. "You gotta get over her, buddy. Find a girl of your own," Aidan said as he walked across the living room to stand at the dog's side.

While Miller was disappointed the couple were no longer an item, Aidan wasn't. Maggie was a nice lady, but everyone knew there was only room in his father's heart for Aidan's mother. It was better that his dad ended it before Maggie got hurt.

"Come on, buddy. Maggie doesn't get up until nine on a workday, and today's a holiday. She'll probably sleep till... What the hell?" He pressed his face to the glass to get a better look at the shadow moving across Maggie's front lawn. There was only one reason for someone to be creeping around her house at this time of the morning.

"Good dog," Aidan said, and sprinted to the entry-way. Miller was getting an extra doggy treat today.

Shoving his feet into his boots while shrugging into his leather jacket, Aidan contemplated getting his Glock from the safe but decided he didn't have time to waste. He didn't want the dirtbag to step one foot in the home of a sleeping woman. From what he could make out of the shadow, the guy was short and slight. At six three and two-twenty, Aidan would have no problem taking him down.

He'd barely gotten the door open when Miller darted past him. Aidan's stomach lurched at the thought the perp might have a weapon. If anything happened to the dog on his watch... "Miller, get back here!" Aidan yelled, now more concerned about the dog than catching the intruder unaware.

Barking, Miller charged across Maggie's lawn to the side of the house where the man had been looking in a window. Aidan raced after Miller, registering that the perp was a woman just before the retriever leaped into the air and took her down. By the time Aidan reached the side yard, Miller was giving the woman's face a bath.

It was a woman Aidan recognized. The sweetheart of Harmony Harbor.

At least that's how he thought of her. A thought that was filled with a heavy dose of sarcasm. You couldn't mention Julia Landon's name in town without being subjected to a litany of accolades. Any time he'd voiced his legitimate concerns about her to his family, they shot him down with talk about how kind and sweet she was.

Aidan didn't buy it. He was good at his job for a reason. He could spot a liar and a con from a mile away. In Julia Landon's case, also a stalker with a couple screws loose.

He wondered what his family would think if he shared the news that she'd given Old Lady Rosenbloom ten grand to secure the house on Primrose Lane for Olivia back in June. Scratch that. He knew exactly what they'd think, and that's why he'd decided to keep the information to himself until he dug a little deeper.

Because while they'd no doubt credit the gift to one more example of Julia's largesse, he knew better. She couldn't afford to dole out thousands of dollars to his family like she had been over the past year. The woman was up to her pretty violet eyes in debt. He frowned at the thought, wondering why he was thinking about her eyes.

Then he realized he was standing over her and looking into her big eyes, and he couldn't deny that they were pretty. They were also shadowed by an emotion he didn't like. Fear.

She was looking at him the same way she had the day he'd hauled her to the station to interrogate her about Olivia's disappearance. Considering how aggressive and confrontational he'd been with Julia that morning, he couldn't say he blamed her for being nervous.

In his defense, he'd been desperate to find his sister-in-law, and Julia had a weird obsession with his family. On top of that, none of her excuses rang true.

There was no gray in his world. You were either innocent or guilty. And Julia Landon was guilty of something. He just hadn't figured out what yet.

"Miller, get off her," he said, trubled by the gruffness in his command. The only explanation he could come up with was that the way Julia was biting down on her cherry-red lips reminded him of the time he'd kissed her sweet mouth. For some reason, the memory of that brief moment with her under the mistletoe had stuck around for nearly a year. Even now he felt a flicker of interest, of heat. It didn't make sense. She wasn't his type. He liked his women tall, blond, and edgy. A woman who could hold her own against him.

Even last Christmas it had been obvious that Julia, with her midnight-black hair and big purple eyes, didn't have any edges. She was sweet and soft and smelled like candy canes.

For a fraction of a second while he'd stood under the mistletoe with his mouth on hers, he'd wondered if blond and edgy were overrated. Until fifteen minutes later when Julia gifted his niece with the cottage she'd just won in the manor's Christmas raffle. A cottage that was worth at least two hundred grand.

Yeah, something definitely didn't add up with her.

He thrust out a hand. "Give me one good reason why I shouldn't arrest you."

She blinked up at him, and then her eyes skittered away like a frightened deer. "Um, you need a legitimate reason to arrest me? I don't think stopping by to drop off an invitation at a friend's will cut it with the chief," she murmured, ignoring Aidan and his outstretched hand to gently push at Miller's chest. "I'm happy to see you too, boy, but I have to get up."

Aidan's teeth clenched at the mention of his boss. Benson had let it be known he wasn't a fan of Aidan's tactics or his record with the DEA when he'd grudgingly hired him last month. But everyone at the station knew he was a fan of the woman trying to get out from under Aidan's dog.

"Maybe you can explain to your boyfriend why you were pulling your Peeping Tom act." He lifted his chin at the side window she'd been looking into and then scooped up Miller, who looked as happy with Aidan as the woman attempting to push herself to her feet, her red fur snow boots sliding on a frozen puddle left by the drainage pipe.

"I'm a woman. I can't be a Peeping Tom. But even if I could be, I wasn't, peeping, I mean. I was just checking to see if Maggie was awake."

"Sure you were, Peeping Tomette." He put Miller down and turned to help Julia up. It didn't escape his notice that she didn't deny Benson was her boyfriend. Nor did it escape his notice that the muscle in his own jaw was flexing at the thought of her with his boss. Aidan assured himself that his reaction had nothing to do with an interest in Julia. It was because Benson was at least twenty-five years her senior.

Instead of offering her his hand this time, because she'd no doubt ignore it, Aidan grabbed hold of her puffy black jacket and pulled her upright. Her left boot slid across the frozen puddle and out from under her. She grabbed him at the same time he yanked her toward him, ensuring she ended up plastered against his chest. The feel of her small, curvy body against his reminded him of another time he'd been this close to her.

Only then it had been a hot summer day and he'd been sprawled on top of her naked body while she lay facedown in the sand. The memory was so clear and so real that he jerked back as if he'd been burned. She must have been having a flashback of her own because she sucked in a breath, scrambled backward, and held up both hands.

They stood staring at each other, panting as if they'd been in a race, their breath glistening in the frosted air. The porch light went on, dissipating the heat that had been simmering between them.

The front door opened to reveal Maggie. The fifty-something woman wore a bright, floral-print housecoat, her shoulder-length red hair showing signs she'd just woken up. "Julia, Aidan, what's—" She didn't get a chance to finish. Miller bounded up the stairs to shower the love of his life with doggy kisses.

"Oh, I miss you too, my handsome boy," she murmured, and gave Miller a rubdown.

Maggie's voice and smile wavered, and Aidan realized he'd been wrong earlier. His father hadn't broken up with Maggie soon enough. The typically vivacious artist was heartbroken. Still, it was better now than later. If she and Miller were this bad off after only a week...

"You're welcome to take him anytime, Maggie,"

Aidan offered. Just because he had a reputation as a hardass didn't mean he couldn't feel sorry for both the dog and the woman.

After gathering her hat, scarf, and bag from the ground, Julia straightened and smiled at him. She had one of those infectious grins that made people smile in return. Most people. Not him. And it wasn't only because he didn't smile a lot or have a lot to smile about these days. It was because the smile she gave him was the kind you offered someone with a shared interest. And other than books, this particular woman's interest was his family's love life.

He crossed his arms and narrowed his eyes at her, hoping that was not what she was up to here.

She lifted a shoulder as though his lack of a smile and suspicious look were par for the course and stuck a Books and Beans bag between her knees. Using both hands, she wrapped the furry red scarf around her neck and then jammed a green knitted tree hat decorated with red glitter balls on her head.

He gave his own a slight shake at her getup and then turned back to Maggie.

His dad's ex looked from him to Julia. "Is something wrong?"

"Miller and I saw Julia skulking about your place and thought she was trying to break in." He jerked his thumb at the two streetlamps that had burned out before the sun came up. "I'll put in a call to have them fixed."

"I wasn't *skulking*, Maggie. I wanted to drop off a Thanksgiving invite to Hazel's and, um…" She glanced at Aidan as though waiting for him to leave.

He raised an eyebrow and cocked his head. No way was he going anywhere until he learned what she was up to.

She looked like she intended to wait him out, but when Maggie wrapped her arms around herself, Julia dug in her bag and hurried up the stairs. Miller scooted past Maggie and into the blue Victorian.

Julia pulled out a book, cast a furtive look Aidan's way, and then lowered her voice. "I found this by the window. It looks like you have a secret admirer, Maggie. I must have scared him off. I saw a man"—she shot another glance at Aidan as he came up the stairs and finished quickly—"a tall man with silver hair fast-walking in that direction."

She shoved the book, *A Thousand Mornings* by Mary Oliver, in Maggie's hands when Aidan joined them on the porch.

"Brr, it's freezing," Julia said, giving what Aidan suspected was a fake shiver. "Get inside before you catch cold, Maggie. I hope you can make it to Hazel's for Thanksgiving dinner. I'll talk to you later." She reached for the doorknob.

Aidan leaned his shoulder against the doorjamb and looked down at Julia while saying to Maggie, "I should probably take a look at that. You can't be too careful with these secret admirer types. Could be a stalker."

"A stalker? Don't be silly." Julia tried to nudge him out of the way to pull the door closed. "Poor Maggie's freezing. Let her get inside."

Maggie nervously handed him the book. "Have you had a problem with this kind of thing in town?"

"Now and again." He flipped through the poetry book. A piece of paper fluttered to the ground. Julia lunged for it, but he was faster. "What do we have here? I can probably get some prints off this."

"And waste taxpayer dollars? Don't be silly," Julia said, trying to take the paper from his hand.

He held it out of her reach and scanned the over-wrought lines comparing Maggie's hair to a burning bush in autumn and her eyes to newly budded leaves in spring. Aidan worked to keep a straight face. "I'll bring it to the station and let the boys have a look, but my guess is your secret admirer's a woman, Maggie."

Noting the disappointment on the older woman's face, Aidan felt bad for being the one to burst her bubble. Which might have been why he let Julia take the poem from him.

"Let me see that." She tugged the paper from his hand. With an intent look on her face, as though giving careful consideration to the lines, she said, "Don't listen to him, Maggie. This was definitely written by a man. Someone who obviously knows you well." She took the book from Aidan, holding it up as evidence before giving it back to Maggie. "You were telling me just a few weeks ago how much you enjoyed Mary Oliver's book *Upstream*, remember?"

Maggie nodded and clutched the book to her chest, a hopeful light shining in her eyes. "I remember. It was the day Colin and I stopped in to try your pumpkin spice lattes."

Pressing a hand dramatically to her chest and making her big eyes even bigger, Julia gasped. "Oh my goodness, I forgot Mr. Gallagher was with you. I wonder if... That line about your hair and the *burning* bush—"

Aidan took Julia by the arm and leaned in to close the door. "You can talk to Maggie later. She's freezing." He looked at the older woman, who now appeared to be glowing with hopefulness thanks to Julia. "Do you want to keep Miller for a while or—"

"Of course she does. Your dad can pick him up when he gets off work. Dinner's at four, but don't worry if you're a little late, Maggie. We'll wait. Unless you and Mr. Gallagher—"

Aidan tightened his grip on Julia's arm and propelled her toward the stairs. "I'll pick up Miller in a couple of hours, Maggie."

Julia waved goodbye to his father's ex. "I can manage on my own, thank you very much," she said, tugging her arm free.

"My dad can take care of himself, too, so butt out of his love life. You're wasting your time, and it's not fair to get Maggie's hopes up."

Julia stopped in the middle of the driveway to stare at him. "You. You're the reason he broke up with Maggie, aren't you?"

"What? No." But her accusation made him wonder if he might have said or done something that his old man misconstrued as disapproval.

"I knew it," she muttered, and began walking down the road talking to herself. He thought he heard her say something about five weeks. Her shoulders rose on what sounded like a heavy sigh, and she turned to walk back to him. "Okay, so if you aren't the reason your dad broke up with Maggie, maybe you can help me get them back together?"

He hadn't gotten anywhere with Julia when he interrogated her at the station last summer, so he decided to try a new tactic. "Maybe. But before I decide whether I'll help you or not, you have to tell me why you're obsessed with my family."

"An obsession is a persistent, disturbing preoccupation with an idea or feeling." Her head tilted as if she was thinking that over.

He crossed his arms. "Yeah..."

She sighed and then closed her eyes, taking a long moment before answering. "It's not as if I spend every waking minute of every day thinking about your family. I think about a lot of people in town. I like people, and if I can do something to make someone happy, I will. Maggie's my friend, and she deserves to be happy. So does your dad." She lifted her hand to play with her earring.

It was pretty much the same spiel she'd given him at the station. And while he could tell by the way she'd closed her eyes, the length of her pause, and the way she twisted her earring that she was lying, he'd been back in town long enough to see her in action. There was a reason everyone in Harmony Harbor loved the woman.

Every day she went out of her way to put a smile on someone's face. Whether it was the kids she entertained at her bookstore or the transients she left blankets and food for at the park or the stray cats she fed at the waterfront, it was obvious she truly enjoyed making others happy. It came naturally to her. But there was nothing natural about her need to make the Gallagher family happy. He could almost feel the desperation coming off her.

"You're not going to help me, are you?"

"Look, if I thought being with Maggie would make my dad happy, I'd talk to him about it. But it won't. So no more secret admirer crap. You're just setting Maggie up for more disappointment."

Slowly moving her head from side to side, Julia said, "Okay, fine. Have a happy Thanksgiving."

She'd just lied to him again. And for some reason that made him want to laugh. Probably because it was hard to take a woman wearing a Christmas-tree hat seriously. Besides, he had more important things to worry about. Like how to explain to his family that his daughter didn't want to spend Thanksgiving with him. At least that's what his ex had told him when she refused to abide by their visitation schedule for the holiday.

Standing in the middle of the street, he watched as Julia fake-skated her way to the red car parked at the end of Breakwater Way. The woman had a way of making even something as simple as walking look like fun. He probably should have asked her how to make his daughter's visits with him more fun. Maybe then Ella Rose would want to come. He turned to walk back to the brick two-story. If he was thinking about asking the Gallagher family's stalker for advice, he needed more sleep.

Chapter Three

♥

He stood over me like a marauding pirate with his heavy, dark beard and thick, overlong hair curling below the collar of his brown leather jacket. "Give me one good reason why I shouldn't arrest you."

There was a rough edge to his deep voice that made me shiver. Or maybe it was the way his eyes moved over me that caused the tiny ripple up my spine. Trapped by the heat in his cobalt gaze, I didn't notice him pick anything up. At the clink of metal, I drew my eyes from his to see a pair of handcuffs dangling from his forefinger. With more gentleness than I imagined him capable of, he lifted my hand and placed it against the wooden spindle of the headboard. His thumb stroked the fluttering pulse on my wrist, and lips that rarely smiled curved as he expertly snapped the...

"Careful, dear, you'll burn the gravy."

Hazel's voice jerked Julia out of her captor's bed. Before she came fully back into her body, which was standing by the stove in the mayor's stark, white kitchen, a cry of frustration bubbled up Julia's throat and out of her mouth.

She grimaced, racking her lust-fogged brain for a way to cover up what she now realized sounded more like a genuine sob of utter despair than simple frustration. It wasn't like she could tell Hazel that she'd made the noise because she'd yanked Julia out of her daydream just before sexy times with Aidan got under way.

Tell Hazel? Julia didn't even want to think about it herself. But she did, and was more than a little relieved when she came to the conclusion that her anguish had nothing at all to do with missing out on Aidan having his big, experienced hands or his firm, beautiful mouth on her. Her sob of utter despair was because he'd hijacked her internal plotting session.

Her stories played out in her mind like a movie, and while she'd been stirring the gravy, she'd taken the opportunity to rethink the first half of *Warrior's Touch* in order to ward off any comparisons of her hero to Aidan. She'd come up with the idea that Adrian Greystone was simply a persona her hero had taken on to outwit his enemies in book one. He'd no longer be a member of the Garda—Irish police force—but a modern-day pirate loosely based on Robin Hood.

However, thanks to her early-morning run-in with the marauding pirate himself, Aidan had messed with her head just like he'd messed with her plan this morning to get Maggie and Colin back together.

Giving Maggie the book of poetry with a note from her secret admirer had been an inspired idea. Or so Julia had thought until Aidan cast both a scary and creepy light on the gesture. There was a word for what he was doing. It wasn't one Julia would use, even in her head. She'd replace it with something like *roosterblock*.

With the help from a bar of soap, her mother had broken Julia of the cursing habit she'd acquired from her three older brothers. Emmeline had washed Julia's mouth out so often she swore she'd blown bubbles in her sleep for a year. Now, if her temper got the best of her, she fake-cursed.

But fake-cursing Aidan in her head wasn't a good idea. She had to get him out of there once and for all. Which admittedly wasn't easy, given that she'd yet to shake off the fantasy that involved him, her, and a pair of handcuffs.

"Julia, dear, are you all right?" asked the woman who'd taken on the role of Julia's mother-in-law despite her son's death six months prior to the wedding. A concerned frown was visible beneath Hazel's teased cinnamon-brown bangs.

Afraid that the heat thrumming through her body would show on her face, Julia leaned over the pot of bubbling, golden gravy and sniffed its nutty fragrance. Once she'd spent enough time with her face stuck in the steam to cover what she imagined had been her flushed cheeks, she straightened and smiled at Hazel. "I'm wonderful, and I think the gravy is too. It smells as delicious as always. The whole kitchen does." The aroma of turkey, stuffing, green beans, and potatoes permeated the warm air, reminding Julia how much she loved the holiday.

Her smile fell at the sight of three black dots rolling around in the gravy. She attempted to mash them with the wooden spoon while sliding the pot to the back burner.

"Don't try and hide it from me, dear."

Beneath the wrap dress made of purple merino wool, Julia's shoulders rose on a sigh. It seemed she couldn't do anything right today. She should have known Hazel would notice the burnt specks. There wasn't much that got past the older woman, which had made for a stressful eight months leading up to and after Josh's death. But it was just a little over two years now and Hazel rarely brought up his...how he died. Julia ignored the mental hiccup, about to confess that she'd burned the gravy and apologize.

Before she got a chance, Hazel continued. "I know how hard the past week has been on you. It's been difficult for me too, of course. But we should be celebrating. Do you know it's five years today that Josh brought you home to meet me?"

"I was just thinking about that this morning. It's crazy how fast time goes."

Sometimes it didn't go fast enough. They should be celebrating though. Julia felt lucky to have met and kept Hazel in her life. But she'd be less than honest if she didn't admit there were times over the past few years when she'd envisioned what life would have been like if she'd stayed in Texas instead of moving to the East Coast after graduation. She'd grown up listening to her mother's stories about New York City and thought of it as a place where dreams come true. Sometimes she wondered if she'd mixed up her mother's dream with her own.

Julia had met Josh while performing in a play that was so far off Broadway she didn't think there were enough offs to qualify just how far off it had been. She hadn't cared. It wasn't like she'd thought she was destined to be a star or even wanted to be. She'd been lonely when she'd first moved to New York and accepted a job in advertising. She'd quickly discovered she wasn't as passionate as her colleagues about branding or writing copy for the next big thing.

As low man on the totem pole, she spent her days inputting product survey results, and she needed a creative outlet that had the added benefit of getting her out of her closet-sized apartment. She found that and more in a hole-in-the-wall theater in Midtown Manhattan.

Josh was the playwright and director. Of average height with curly auburn hair, he had the soul of a poet and the face of an angel. They hit it off almost immediately. He helped her get into character for her very minor role, and she liked to think that she helped him sharpen the play's dialogue and plot.

"I have just the thing to help us celebrate. We had it for our first Thanksgiving toast," Hazel said, and walked to the refrigerator. She wore her regular uniform of a jacket over a sleeveless black dress. Today's jacket was decorated with colorful fall leaves. The intricately tied silk scarf at her neck was the same shade of fire-engine red as her lipstick and shoes. Her chin-length hair was teased and sprayed to resemble what Julia thought of as Texas hair—kind of big and kind of square.

Hazel was a short, solid woman with a pleasant face

who gave an inordinate amount of time and attention to what she looked like and what people thought of her. Julia had wondered if it was because of her job. Hazel had been mayor of Harmony Harbor for more than a decade. She was up for reelection again next year.

But Josh had thought his mother's preoccupation with her looks and popularity had more to do with his father having an affair than Hazel's position as mayor. Julia often wondered if things would have turned out differently had Hazel not been in the public eye. So much of what had happened could be traced back to Hazel running for reelection that fall. So many lives devastated by one phone call. If only…

Julia pushed the thought aside. Playing the "if only" and "what if" game was fine when she was writing a book. It wasn't the same in real life. Right or wrong, she'd made her decision two years ago. There was nothing she could do about it now. She blanked her mind to the horrors of that bitterly cold November night.

Despite years of practice locking the image away, it took some extra effort to do so today. It was because she was here in the house on Mulberry Lane. The cedar writer's shed Hazel had built for Josh had sat in a grove of trees at the back of the property, far enough away that no one recalled seeing Julia that night. Hazel had the shed torn down as soon as the HHPD gave her the okay. But even with the structure gone, it was difficult to be here. Julia did her best to avoid the house on Mulberry Lane.

She turned the burner to low, distracting herself by digging for the burnt bits with the wooden spoon.

The refrigerator door closed. "Look, it's even the same brand."

Julia glanced over her shoulder. Hazel held up a bottle of pink Moët and Chandon and went to retrieve two champagne glasses from the brushed-silver coffee bar, a recent addition to the otherwise utilitarian kitchen.

"We should probably join the guests. They'll be wondering where we are," Julia said as she stealthily tapped the burnt specks onto the spoon holder beside the stove.

She'd fled the living room with the excuse she had gravy to make. Like Hazel did every year, she'd invited her staff and heads of departments who didn't have family in the area to celebrate Thanksgiving with her. For many of the guests here today, it had become a long-standing tradition. Paul Benson was one of those guests. He was also the reason Julia needed an escape.

She liked Paul, and that was part of the problem. She didn't *like* him like him, and he was acting like he liked her a lot. There was no denying the man was handsome. He reminded her of Tom Selleck. Emmeline had never missed *Magnum, P.I.* when she was alive, something Julia had just remembered, and it only added to the creepy factor of her dating a man twenty-three years her senior. He was old enough to be her father. He was also a very nice man, and she didn't want to hurt his feelings.

Maybe it was unfair, but she blamed Aidan for everything that had gone wrong in her life these past six months. He was indirectly responsible for the conundrum she now found herself in with Paul. And no matter how much Aidan denied it, she had no doubt he'd stuck his nose in his father's love life and was the reason Julia hadn't already hung up her fairy wings. He was also the reason she was behind on her deadline. Of course, that was unintentional on his part, but still...

There was something else though, something far more troublesome and threatening. She'd felt it when she was lying on Maggie's front lawn with Aidan towering over her, his broad shoulders blocking out any light. She'd felt the same something again when his big body crowded her on Maggie's front porch and when his hand closed around her arm. And that something was an undeniable sizzle of attraction.

It was like her nerve endings had pulled tight, heat pooling...where it wasn't supposed to be pooling. And there'd been a lot of heat and lustful thoughts where he was concerned. Way more than was safe given her involvement in the cover-up.

He was a threat, a danger to her freedom. And to Hazel, she reminded herself. Hazel was the real reason Julia had done what she had that night. She'd been protecting the woman who'd welcomed Julia into her small family of two within minutes of meeting her. The mother figure Julia had been missing since the day she'd lost her own. And if the truth ever came out...

Hazel handed her a glass. "Don't worry about them. They have plenty of appetizers and drinks." At the sound of laughter, she rolled her eyes and added, "Entertainment too."

Julia recognized the voice. It was Dr. Bishop. She hoped his story had nothing to do with Kitty Gallagher and her archrival Rosa DiRossi. They'd been fighting over Dr. Bishop since last summer. The rivalry between Aidan's grandmother Kitty and Kitty's childhood best friend had gotten so bad that Paul had threatened to throw them in jail.

Julia prayed Kitty and Rosa were over Dr. Bishop, or she would be forced to date Paul again to keep Aidan's grandmother out of trouble. And like it sometimes did if Julia wasn't careful, a small flicker of anger at Josh flared to life inside her. In the past, she'd dealt with it by reminding herself how badly he'd suffered for what in the end had been a horrible mistake.

Hazel pulled Julia from her thoughts before she had a chance to remind herself of all that Josh had been through, and the anger inside her grew unchecked. But a watery smile from his mother as she clinked her glass against Julia's took care of the dark and troubling emotions.

"You know, I can still hear Josh's voice when he called to tell me he was bringing you home like it was yesterday. I knew right then that you were special. He'd never brought anyone with him before. Hadn't even bothered making the effort to come home two years running, so him bringing you here was a big deal that year."

He hadn't come home for Thanksgiving because he couldn't live with what he'd done. But Julia hadn't known that then. She hadn't found out until the night in the writer's shed.

"Hazel, everyone's wondering… Sorry, I didn't mean to interrupt," said Delaney Davis, Hazel's chief of communication and constituents.

Two years older than Julia, Delaney was her exact opposite. At five foot four, Julia was short. At five foot ten, Delaney was tall. Julia had dark hair, and Delaney had blond. Delaney was head-turning gorgeous with blade-sharp cheekbones and a willowy figure. Julia fell more in the cute category with pinchable round cheeks and a body that was more curvy than thin.

But the biggest difference was that Delaney Davis would walk over anyone and everyone to get what she wanted. The woman was ambitious, and right now her ambitions were tied to Hazel. Delaney would do anything to ensure her boss won another term. Which Julia assumed was the reason she was on the receiving end of Delaney's aggravated stare. She wanted Hazel out there mingling instead of in here with her.

"Well, they can wait. Julia and I—" Hazel began.

Julia cut her off. Obviously Hazel didn't notice that her assistant's cheeks had flushed with anger. That was another big difference between them, Delaney had a temper and Julia didn't have much of one to speak of.

"Delaney's right. You should get out there and enjoy your company, Hazel. Dinner's almost ready to be served. We'll have lots of time to talk after everyone leaves."

"Actually, Hazel and I have things to discuss after dinner."

Julia forced a smile to cover her disappointment. It wasn't like she wanted to continue the conversation about Josh, but she and Hazel always watched a movie after everyone left. "Oh, okay. I'll just—"

Her lips pressed in a firm line, Hazel silenced Julia

with a raised, manicured finger. "Whatever you want to discuss will have to wait, Delaney. Thanksgiving movie night is a tradition for me and Julia, and one I hold dear. Just like Julia is dear to me," she said, a chiding tone in her voice.

Huh, so maybe Julia had been right all along and Delaney didn't like her. The underlying message in Hazel's comment seemed to confirm Julia's suspicions.

"I didn't realize. Not about you being close to Julia of course, but that you had a movie-night tradition."

Which was undoubtedly true. Delaney wasn't from Harmony Harbor. She'd moved to town to take the job when Hazel's former chief of communications left in January.

Delaney continued. "Perhaps we can take a few minutes in your study during dessert, then. We really do need to firm up details for the Ladies Auxiliary Christmas lunch."

"Oh, don't worry about that. Julia will handle it for me, won't you, dear?"

Julia glanced from Delaney's tight face to Hazel's smiling, expectant one. She really didn't want to be caught in the middle, especially since Delaney didn't seem to be the forgive-and-forget type.

Before Julia could come up with an excuse, Hazel answered for her. "I don't know why I even bothered to ask. Of course you will. We're a team. Do you remember how hard we worked to convince Josh to move back home? You should have seen us in action, Delaney. You'd have thought we'd known each other for years."

Delaney might not be able to roll her eyes in front of her employer, but the action was evident in her voice. "I can imagine."

Hazel's remark probably sounded like hyperbole, but it was actually the truth. They'd had an almost instant connection and a common goal. The moment Josh had turned off the highway and into the charming coastal town of Harmony Harbor, Julia could see herself living there. The feeling had grown even more pronounced during a walk after Thanksgiving dinner.

She'd been enchanted by the copper-domed clock tower, the twisty, narrow streets that were lined with the Colonials, Cape Cods, and Victorians that had once been owned by sea captains and merchants. The family-owned boutiques, art shops, pubs, and gift shops that were housed in quaint ocean-blue and sea-foam-green clapboards, had her skipping along Main Street in joyous wonder. And as though carried on the brisk ocean breeze, an idea came to her that day. She knew exactly what she wanted to do with her future. New York wasn't the place where her dreams would come true; Harmony Harbor was.

Hazel had been over the moon at the thought of her only son moving back from New York and had quickly become Julia's staunchest supporter. It had taken more than a year for them to finally get Josh on board. Little did Julia know then that the decision would ultimately lead to her fiancé taking his own life.

Chapter Four

♥

Paul stuck his head in the kitchen, saving Julia from going down the "if only" path again. "Sorry to interrupt, ladies." He gave her a warm smile.

As she did each and every time, she made note of his exceptionally white teeth. He had great teeth—kind of like a mouthful of Chiclets. *The better to eat you with, my dear*. She swallowed a laugh at the inappropriate thought.

"Maggie just arrived," he told her.

"Okay, great, thanks." Julia didn't have to work on swallowing her laughter now. It dried up with the knowledge nothing had changed between Maggie and Colin.

As though Paul picked up on something from her smile, he looked at her more closely and sauntered to her side. He was a tall man—though not as tall or as powerfully built as Aidan—and had an easy way about him, unlike Aidan, who'd yet to shed the persona he'd assumed while working undercover investigating a motorcycle gang for the DEA months before.

The first two words that came to mind when she thought about Aidan were *dangerous* and *badass.* Well, maybe not the first two exactly, *hot* and... *What are you even doing?* she asked herself. In her head, of course. She had to stop thinking about the man.

"Hazel, why don't you and Delaney start bringing out the food while I help Julia with the gravy? I'll carve the turkey while I'm at it."

Julia stifled a groan. Somehow Paul knew she'd burned the gravy.

As most people did when he made a suggestion in his smooth, low-pitched voice, Hazel and Delaney did as they were told. But not before the mayor's narrowed gaze moved from Paul to Julia. And that suspicious glance had nothing to do with Hazel expecting Julia to be true to her son's memory and stay single for the rest of her life. No, the woman who would have been her mother-in-law was on the hunt to find Julia a man.

Hazel wanted her married and living in Harmony Harbor for the rest of her life. Even though it could be a tad annoying, the reason behind Hazel's matchmaking was endearing and a little sad. She was afraid Julia's brothers and father would eventually convince her to move back to Texas. Julia was the only family Hazel had.

From the look the older woman was giving Paul, he wasn't in the running for Julia's hand in marriage. No doubt she'd hear about it before the night was over. Probably when they were watching *While You Were Sleeping*, their favorite Thanksgiving-night movie.

"How did you know I burned the gravy?" Julia asked

Paul when Hazel and Delaney carried the vegetable dishes and warming trays out to the dining room table. With twenty-four guests, they had gone with a buffet instead of a sit-down dinner.

Paul's thick mustache twitched as he pointed at the black pieces rolling around in the pot.

"How did they get there? I could have sworn I got them all." That settled it. She had to go on a gravy hunt. Thanksgiving dinner wouldn't be the same without it. She reached back to untie her apron. "I'll go to the manor. I'm sure they have gravy to spare."

"No need. I've got this." He rested his big hands on her shoulders, turning her so he could retie her apron. She tensed at the feel of his fingers grazing her butt, a little surprised because he'd always been the perfect gentleman. But the more she thought about it, the more she was convinced it wasn't intentional. Between where the apron strings fell, the size of his hand, and her good-sized behind, it had to have been an accidental finger brush.

"Can't have you messing up your dress," he said, tying the apron strings into a perfect bow.

Knowing what he was alluding to, heat rose to her cheeks. They'd gone out for a spaghetti dinner on their third date. She hadn't quite mastered the fork and spoon roll and splattered sauce all over the front of her blouse. Paul had fashioned a bib out of her linen napkin.

He smiled, a warm gleam in his brown eyes. "Did I tell you how pretty you look today?"

"Yes. Yes, you did." Several times. It's why she'd escaped to the kitchen. "You look pretty too. I mean handsome."

He did. He wore a camel-colored crewneck sweater that showed off his well-toned upper body. An image of Aidan at the beach wearing nothing but board shorts tiptoed across her mind. *Really?* She had to stop thinking about the man and comparing the two. It wasn't like she was dating either one. Her brain sabotaged the not-thinking part of her plan by flashing a memory of Aidan's bulging biceps, ripped pecs, and six-pack.

Thanksgiving, guests, dinner, she silently repeated in her head in an effort to keep her mind where it should be instead of where it shouldn't. "So, how are we going to save the gravy?"

Obviously, they weren't. Paul dumped the entire contents into the sink. She grimaced upon seeing the blackened bottom of the pot. She must have been daydreaming for way longer than she'd thought. As Aidan and a pair of handcuffs flirted with her brain, she picked up the champagne glass from the counter and tossed back its contents.

While Paul moved the turkey pan with the leftover drippings onto the front burner, Julia walked to the coffee bar to pour herself another glass of champagne. "Can I get you something to drink, Paul?"

"No, I'm good, darlin'. Now get over here so I can show you how this is done."

Julia inwardly cringed. Like the whole rolling spaghetti with a fork and a spoon, Paul's teaching sessions never ended well. She'd almost destroyed her exhaust system when he'd given her parking pointers.

"I'll just say a quick hi to Maggie." Before Paul came up with a reason for her to stay, Julia grabbed a pickle tray with her free hand and fast-walked toward the dining room.

In contrast to the stark kitchen, the living and dining rooms were elegant and inviting. The walls were painted a calming slate gray with white wainscoting and dark hardwood floors, a perfect complement to the old Victorian house and its antique furniture.

Hazel wasn't big on food preparation, but she loved to entertain. At that moment, she and Delaney were standing by the Queen Anne table they'd moved against the wall in the dining room talking to a handsome, golden-haired man and his equally attractive sister.

Byron and Poppy Harte were good friends of Julia's. They published the *Harmony Harbor Gazette* and usually spent Thanksgiving with their grandmother, who'd left last week to spend the winter in Florida.

Julia wondered if Poppy and Byron were second-guessing their decision to join them today. Delaney was trying to convince them that dedicating a full page to Hazel and her plans for Harmony Harbor was just the thing to boost weekly readership.

"We wouldn't have to worry about declining numbers if I could find Colleen Gallagher's memoir," Byron said, turning his head at Julia's gasp.

Panic made her stumble. She'd wrongly assumed Byron had given up hunting for Aidan's great-grandmother's book, *The Secret Keeper of Harmony Harbor*. A hundred and four when she passed away last November, the Gallagher matriarch had known a lot of secrets, including Julia's. Rumor had it that Collen had recorded everything she knew about everyone in town in her book. Julia figured there was a fifty-fifty chance that Colleen had written about her.

Byron reached out to steady her. "Careful, love." He took the pickle tray and placed it on the table.

"Thanks. I hope I didn't splash anyone. I must have caught my heel on the rug." She made a production of checking the bottom of her shoe, spotting Maggie in the living room as she did.

Even in the crowded room the attractive redhead was hard to miss. She stood in a corner beside the baby grand piano wearing a pumpkin-colored silk shirt with matching wide-leg pants, her gold and copper bangles jangling as she raised her hand to her mouth.

Assuming Maggie's concern was meant for her, Julia smiled and finger-waved. "I'm okay."

Maggie's gaze flitted to her, and she offered Julia a small smile. So she hadn't been looking at her after all. Byron, Julia decided. The tense expression on Maggie's face didn't have anything to do with Julia and everything to do with the book. Maybe they should start a club. Because Julia knew for a fact that she and Maggie weren't the only ones worried about the book being found.

But it wasn't like there was much they could do about it. Colleen's memoir had been missing since she'd died. Julia prayed it stayed that way. She imagined Maggie did too. Though she had no idea what the other woman's secrets were. She didn't know a lot about Maggie. She'd opened her art gallery in town a little more than a year after Julia opened Books and Beans.

She waved Maggie over and then went up on her toes to kiss Bryon's sun-bronzed cheek and Poppy's pale one hello. Julia hadn't figured out if Byron used bronzer or had a tanning bed in his home. "I'm so glad you both decided to come."

Delaney pursed her lips at Julia, probably ticked that she'd interrupted her pitch to the Hartes. It was Thanksgiving for goodness' sake. She'd assumed Delaney would give her campaigning a rest in deference to the holiday. Then again, the statuesque blonde lived and breathed her job. For that matter, so did Hazel.

"I'll give Paul a hand," Delaney said with a flick of her stylishly cut blond hair. Julia studied how the light from the chandelier caught in the warm and cool shades that swung across the back of Delaney's little black dress. It would be the perfect style for Julia's heroine from *Warrior's Touch*, Gillian Connolly. Hmm, maybe Julia shouldn't be casting workaholic aspersions Delaney and Hazel's way after all.

Byron winked at her. "Always happy to spend time with you, love."

Julia rolled her eyes. She no longer took Byron's flirtations seriously. He wasn't interested in her. However, Hazel, who hadn't seen him in action, was looking at him in a whole new light.

Julia was just about to take care of that by mentioning Byron's girlfriend, Lexi, when Maggie joined them and asked, "How are you? No bruises or scrapes from your fall?"

"What fall?" Byron and Hazel asked at almost the same time with the same level of concern. Which earned the reporter another considering look from Hazel. *Gah.*

"It was nothing. Just—" Julia began, only to be cut off by Maggie.

"Miller and Aidan thought Julia was a burglar and—"

"Are you kidding me? Aidan Gallagher took you down... again?"

Julia really wished Poppy hadn't said that. Last summer she'd convinced the Hartes to keep the incident at the beach out of the paper and hadn't mentioned it to Hazel. "Of course he didn't. Miller was just happy to see me."

Hazel frowned. "Wait, what do you mean *again*, Poppy?"

Julia opened her mouth, about to suggest they get the rest of the food on the table, when Poppy decided to reveal photographic evidence of the *incident*. Scrolling through her phone, Poppy found what she was looking for and held it up for Hazel. Maggie leaned in to have a look too. Both women's eyes went wide, and they gasped.

Really? Could her day get any worse?

As if in answer, a smooth, low-pitched voice asked from behind her, "What are you all looking at?"

Julia whipped around. "Nothing. Nothing at all. Here, let me help you with that." She went to take the platter of turkey from Paul.

A hand pressed to her chest, a distraught Hazel said, "I don't understand. Why would Aidan rip off your mermaid costume and leave you stark naked for everyone to see, Julia?"

"It was an accident. Aidan thought I was a shark." She'd been trying out her costume, swimming under water to get into character for her performance later that day. Like Julia once had, Millie the Mermaid, the character she'd created, didn't feel like she fit in at home or at her school for fishes. Millie was very popular with the children in town, who undoubtedly felt the same at one time or ... *Wait a second.*

"Poppy, please tell me you don't have naked pictures of me on your phone," Julia said, horrified. She'd been wearing a Lady Godiva wig that day and had been positive it had covered all her bits. Sweet Caroline, she hoped it had.

"As if. You can't see anything. But it's obvious you are. Aidan's holding up your bikini bottom and your costume."

A grim-faced Paul placed the turkey platter on the table and then gestured for Poppy's phone. Which she immediately handed over.

"You know, Julia, if Aidan's harassing you again, all you have to do is tell the chief." Poppy looked at Paul. "He thought she was a burglar and took her down at Maggie's this morning."

If Julia hadn't already been thinking Poppy had an ax to grind against Aidan, she would be now. Her friend had thrown him under the bus and then drove over him for good measure.

"What are you talking about, Poppy? He didn't *take me down*. He didn't do anything wrong. He was just being a good neighbor and looking out for Maggie." She could tell by the expressions on Paul's and Poppy's faces that they didn't believe her.

The distraught sob of twenty minutes ago was back and warbling in her throat, and Aidan was once again the culprit. There was no help for it—she was going to have to go on another date with Paul.

* * *

As Aidan leaned against the bar at Greystone Manor, he took in the morose expressions on his brothers' faces. He'd worried needlessly about getting grief over Ella Rose not showing for Thanksgiving. His brothers felt sorry for him.

It was his own fault, he supposed. He shouldn't have told his sisters-in-law how much he'd been looking forward to having his little girl for the long weekend. But it was hard to hold out against them. They got their jollies ganging up on him and trying to get him to talk about his *feelings*.

"Knock it off with the long faces. You'll upset Grams and your wives, and I don't want to have to deal with the four of them. Five of them," he corrected himself. Half the time, Lexi, the ex-wife of his oldest brother, Griffin, was a bigger pain than his three sisters-in-law and grandmother combined.

"You don't have to pretend with us. We know how tough this is on you. We're here for you, bro. Let it out."

He stared at his dark-haired, blue-eyed baby brother. A firefighter like their dad, Liam was married to Sophie, who managed the manor. They had an eight-year-old daughter, Mia, and a newborn baby boy. Ronan Jr.

was five weeks old. Maybe lack of sleep was having an adverse effect on his brother.

But before Aidan had a chance to ask Liam what he meant by *let it out*, and he sure as hell hoped it didn't mean what he thought it did, his second youngest brother, Finn, a family physician, who also had dark hair and blue eyes, gave Aidan's shoulder a comforting squeeze. "I feel for you, brother. In your place, I don't know what I'd do. All I can say is you're handling it better than I would." Finn looked away, cleared his throat, and then took a swig of his beer.

Aidan narrowed his eyes. Did Finn just... tear up? What was he smoking? Of course he didn't. Then again, his brother had nearly lost his wife, Olivia, a couple of months ago, so Aidan supposed he might be more emotional than usual. And he was a new, adoptive father to seven-year-old George and had a baby on the way. Still...

"Yeah, man, Finn and Liam are right," Griffin said, brushing his light brown hair from his blue eyes. A former Navy SEAL, Aidan's oldest brother was now with the Coast Guard. At least Aidan didn't have to worry about Griffin getting emotional. He was tough as they come. He'd endured a lot over the years. But he was now happily remarried to Ava and saw Gabriel, his baby boy with Lexi, every day.

Ah hell, Aidan thought, when it looked like Griffin might be tearing up too. "Okay, you know what? You guys are ticking me off. What did you do with my brothers?"

Griffin frowned. "What are you talking about?"

"You're all so…emotional. Next thing I know, you'll be telling me I'll feel better if I get in touch with my feelings and have a good cry."

"You don't have to pull your tough-guy act with us. We know that under that grumpy, snarly exterior is a guy who's missing his little girl. We get it, bro. We're on your side. If you need us to have a come-to-Jesus moment with Harper, we're there," Liam said.

"Yeah, just give us the word. Whatever you need from us, you've got," Finn said, clinking his beer first to Aidan's and then to his other brothers' bottles.

That was more like it. These were the brothers he knew and loved. "Appreciate it. But for now I'm staying the course. I'm not giving in to Harper's demands."

"What demands?" Griffin asked. "You never said anything about demands, just that she reneged on the original agreement."

"Well, she did. Unless I agree to supervised visitation, as in Harper has to be with us at all times, and that means her spending Thanksgiving with me and Ella Rose, I can't see my daughter. It's a ploy. She wants to get back together, and she's using Ella Rose as a pawn."

"I totally called it at GG's funeral. It was obvious Harper was still hung up on you back then. I told her I saw through her act. Mike did too. You should talk to him," Liam said. Their cousin Mike had been an assistant district attorney before becoming an FBI agent.

"I did. And both Mike and my lawyer say the same thing. It's hard to fight her because she has a solid reputation as a psychiatrist. She's well known and has connections in family court." Aidan gave them the short version of what Mike and his lawyer had said. The long version was even more infuriating and depressing.

"She's not the only one with connections. Say the word and I'll get Liv involved," Finn offered.

A wealthy Boston socialite, Finn's wife, Olivia, had plenty of clout. "I appreciate the offer. I'm hoping Harper will relent once she realizes she can't manipulate me by using our daughter. She loves Ella Rose, so I've gotta believe she'll eventually come around." What he didn't tell his brothers was that he was worried Ella Rose didn't care whether she saw him or not. Their relationship had changed after his last undercover assignment. It was like she didn't know or love him anymore.

"You should just ask…Maybe it's Harper," Liam said when Aidan's cell phone rang.

He was thinking the same thing. Hoping she'd finally seen the light. He dug in his jeans pocket for his cell phone.

Finn grinned and held up his phone. "It's Julia Landon. She just texted me for his number. Didn't think you'd mind."

"What does she want?" Aidan muttered, disappointment a heavy weight in his chest.

Liam waggled his eyebrows. "Julia Landon, eh?"

"You been holding out on us, bro?" Griffin asked.

"You might want to keep it down. If Grams finds out he's talking to Julia…" Finn trailed off, chuckling as he brought the beer bottle to his mouth.

Aidan gave them a one-finger salute as he walked across the slate floor and took the call. "Gallagher."

"Is that how you always answer your phone? It's a little off-putting, you know."

He would have recognized her voice even if Finn hadn't told him who it was—sweet and clear with a subtle hint of her Texan roots. "Sorry. What can I do for you?"

"And that was so much better," she murmured and then said, "I, um, just wanted to warn you not to pick up your phone if the chief calls."

Aidan bowed his head and pulled in a frustrated breath through his nostrils. "Great. Thanks for the warning. But here's the thing. It wouldn't have been necessary if you didn't go running to your boyfriend to tell on me."

This day was getting better by the minute. He should have stayed in bed. An icy wind swirled around him as he reached the massive stone fireplace. He looked toward the stairs leading to the entryway, surprised to find the heavy doors shut. He moved closer to the crackling fire to warm up.

"*I* didn't, but he's, um, not only upset about this morning. It's about the mermaid incident. At the beach last August?"

As if he could forget. He no longer needed the fire to keep him warm. The memory of Julia that day was heating him up just fine. He moved to the brown leather wingback chair and took a seat.

Something *yowl*ed.

"Jesus!" He jumped up and looked back. He'd sat on Simon, a black cat who'd arrived at the manor just before Aidan's great-grandmother Colleen had died. "Sorry, buddy. No hard feelings."

"That's okay. I knew it wasn't intentional. I tried to explain to Paul, but he was—"

Aidan pinched the bridge of his nose between his thumb and forefinger. "I wasn't talking to you. I was talking to Simon."

"Oh, I see. Okay then. I'll let you go. I just wanted to give you a heads-up. I'm sure Paul will cool down by tomorrow..." Her voice trailed off at the sound of raised voices in the background, and then she continued. "For sure by next week. Sorry I interrupted your Thanksgiving. Enjoy your day with your daughter."

"My ex didn't let me have her," he said without thinking. Then winced when he realized what he'd done. "Anyway, thanks for the—"

"Wait! What do you mean she won't let you have your daughter? You have an agreement. You were supposed to have her all weekend."

His Spidey sense went off. This was exactly what he kept talking about to his family. She shouldn't know or be interested in this kind of stuff. "How do you know that?"

"Olivia, of course. It's not some big secret, is it?"

"No, but... It doesn't matter. Enjoy your—"

"No, that's not true. It matters very much. To you and to your daughter."

"You're right, it does matter to me. A lot. But according to my ex, it doesn't matter to my little girl. She doesn't want to see me unless her mother's there. She makes it sound like Ella Rose is afraid of me." He heard her breathing over the line. "Whatever you want to say, just say it."

"Well, from what Olivia told me, your last assignment kept you away from your daughter for months. And it sounded like your split from your ex was contentious..."

"So..."

"Don't let your feelings toward Harper keep you away from your little girl, Aidan. You need to spend time with her so she's comfortable with you again. Who knows what she thinks or what her mother tells her when you don't visit. And when you're not with her, call her. Call her every day and let her know just how much you love her."

He'd never thought of calling Ella Rose. He supposed because he still thought of her as a baby. "Thanks, that's a good idea. I'll do that. I'll call her."

"And spend Thanksgiving with her?"

"I don't want to give Harper the wrong idea. Today's our anniversary. She wants to get back together. She's using my daughter to get to me."

"So, let her. At least you'll be able to spend time with your little girl. Just be open and honest with your daughter. Bring her flowers. Jasper has a beautiful Thanksgiving arrangement on the pedestal table in the entrance. And take some of the s'more cupcakes Theo made yesterday," she said, making a humming sound in her throat.

The soft, sexy sound was turning him on, and he shifted uncomfortably on his feet.

"They're to die for," she continued, adding, "Oh, oh, and make sure to take some of the carrot cupcakes with caramel and cream cheese frosting too. Give one to your ex. She'll forgive you for everything."

Her enthusiasm made him want to laugh. He didn't, but it was there, just below the surface. Quite the feat considering how he'd been feeling only moments before. And he realized Julia had done what no one else had been able to. She'd shown him another way to look at the situation. "Okay, I'll give it a shot."

"Yay!" she cheered as if she'd just won the lottery. At the sound of someone calling her name, she whispered, "I have to go. Have a wonderful Thanksgiving with your little girl."

Her over-the-top reaction gave him pause. She was acting like she had a vested interest in this. Or maybe his brothers were right and he had major trust issues. Not everyone had an agenda. "Thanks, Julia. You enjoy yours too."

With his boss, who would probably fire him tomorrow.

Chapter Five

♥

Aidan turned in to the gravel drive of the home he'd once shared with his wife and daughter in Newton, Massachusetts, a white Colonial that he was still making payments on. Harper didn't want Ella Rose uprooted, and neither did he. But something had to give. Between paying the mortgage and child support, it wouldn't be easy to find a nice place in Harmony Harbor that he could afford. If he had only himself to worry about, he'd settle for a bachelor apartment or a shack in the woods. He wasn't fussy.

But he wanted Ella Rose to have a room of her own and a backyard to play in. Then again, the way things were going, he might grow old in his childhood home on Breakwater Way. Just him, his dad, and Miller. Great. He was already nervous, and now he was depressing himself.

He released his seat belt and reached for the cupcakes and the flowers Jasper had wrapped up for him. The old guy had been as happy as the rest of the family that Aidan was spending Thanksgiving with Ella Rose.

Which made sense since the old man had been around so long that Aidan and his brothers thought of him as family, something of an honorary great-uncle.

In reality, he'd been their great-grandmother's right-hand man and confidant. And just like GG, Jasper hadn't exactly been a Harper fan. A week before he'd gotten married, the old man had warned Aidan that he was making a mistake. Aidan thought he was making another one today. Only this time Jasper and the rest of the family hadn't warned him to stay away.

Enough with the stalling, he told himself. If he sat there much longer, Harper would call the cops. She wouldn't recognize his wheels. He'd traded in his Dodge Ram for a secondhand four-door black sedan. He missed the Ram, but not as much as he missed his daughter. Harper had given him grief for taking Ella Rose in the truck. It didn't seem like he could do anything right in his ex's eyes or his daughter's.

At the sound of an incoming text, he pulled out his phone and gave his head a slight shake as he read. *Hey there! Julia here! Just checking to see how it's going with your little girl* 🙂 *Did she *heart* the flowers and cupcakes??*

So, she was as excitable in her text messages as on the phone. Now he had to figure out if she was like that with everyone or just with him. If it was only him, he had a problem. Because it meant that he was now in the crosshairs of his family's stalker. For a brief moment, he considered not responding.

Not engaging was the first thing he'd recommend

to anyone dealing with a stalker. The only problem with that was she'd made him feel better for a few minutes back at the manor. Maybe she could calm the anxious churning in his gut. Because ever since he'd called Harper to tell her he was coming, he'd had a feeling today was a turning point, a do-or-die moment.

Just got here, so not sure if Ella Rose will *heart* the cupcakes and flowers or not.

Ur being sarcastic, aren't u?

What gave me away?

Okay, sorry for bugging u. I won't bother u again.

He blew out an aggravated breath and leaned back against the headrest. He was overreacting, seeing a threat where none existed. It'd gotten worse since his last undercover assignment. He knew why. One of the *benefits* of being married to a shrink was the ability to self-diagnose his issues.

A light in the window of the master bedroom pooled on the sugar maple below. The four-bedroom house sat on a cul-de-sac in the exclusive bedroom community seven minutes west of downtown Boston. It'd been valued at over a million bucks. A bitter resentment rose up inside him at the reminder. Maybe his last assignment wasn't solely to blame for his negative emotions after all.

He looked down at his phone and typed. *You're not bugging me. Ella Rose will *heart* the cupcakes. No sarcasm intended.*

Where are u?

Sitting in my car.

Why? Are u nervous?

No. I'm "talking" to you.

He was watching the screen, waiting for her to respond when his cell phone rang. He rolled his eyes and answered. "I'm not nervous."

"I don't believe you. You have performance anxiety," she whispered.

"Ah, no I don't," he said, offended. "Besides, she's my ex-wife. It's not like we'll be—"

"That's not the kind of performance I was talking about. Honestly, all you men have a one-track mind. Look—"

He cut her off. "Who's harassing you?"

"What? Where did that even come from?"

"You just said..." Okay, so maybe he'd misread the situation and was once again overreacting. It wasn't as if he could accuse his boss of anything untoward anyway. "Where are you, and why are you whispering?"

"Um, the usual reason someone whispers? I don't want anyone to hear me. I'm in the pantry at Hazel's."

Right, he knew she had close ties to the mayor. She'd been engaged to Hazel's son, Josh. He'd been a few years behind Aidan at school, so he hadn't known Josh all that well. He remembered him as a nice kid, kind of shy. Maybe a little different. He'd been surprised when he'd heard Josh had accidently overdosed on prescription drugs. Though Aidan had a hard time buying the *accidental* part. Most likely due to his experience with the DEA.

"The chief still after my head for upsetting his girlfriend?" Even to his own ears the question sounded loaded with censure. Julia dating his boss really didn't sit well with him, did it?

"I'm not his girlfriend."

At the feel of his mouth lifting at the corner, he frowned at himself in the rearview mirror. Despite knowing he shouldn't care one way or another, he said, "Good to hear. He's too old for you."

"Oh, I... Well, anyway, he didn't say much after he threatened to demote you to bicycle patrol—"

No, no way could Aidan afford a demotion. Not with his payments. "You tell him for me that I'll take him to—"

"Don't worry. I'll talk to him once everyone leaves. It'll be fine. I promise." He heard a door open and the sound of her muffled voice talking to someone before she came back on the line. "I have to go. And you have nothing to be nervous about. Just act like you always did with your daughter. Do exactly what you did when you came home from work before you and your wife divorced. Don't think about the past visits. You have cupcakes." She said, as if they were a magic cure-all and then whispered, "Bye."

Before she disconnected, he heard her say in that over-the-top excited voice of hers, "Just my dad. He misses me. No, it's—"

"Happy Thanksgiving, Sheriff Landon. Chief Benson here. You might not remember me, but we met last time you were in town."

Aidan was about to disconnect, but the chief would probably think the call had dropped and hit redial.

Thanks to Julia, Aidan was damned if he did and damned if he didn't. If he lost his job because of her...

He made a noncommittal sound into the phone.

The chief seemed to buy it. "I just want you to know that you don't have to worry about your little girl. I'm taking really good care of her."

Okay, how does Benson not get weirded out talking to a guy who is probably just a couple years older than him about his daughter? Aidan frowned. *Wait a minute.* Julia distinctly told him she wasn't the chief's girlfriend. So what was going on here? Maybe Benson didn't get that *no* meant *no*.

Aidan cleared his throat, deepened his voice, and added what he thought of as Texan swagger. "Don't you worry none about my daughter. She's a bit of a thing and young, but she can take care of herself. She doesn't need another daddy."

The chief didn't respond. Aidan heard him talking to Julia, but their voices were muffled. And then they were unmuffled, and he clearly heard the chief say, "What do you mean it's Aidan Gallagher and not your father?"

He groaned. He was going to kill her.

"Gallagher, is that you?" the chief gritted out.

Aidan pressed his forehead against the steering wheel, and the horn blasted, drowning out his *yes*.

"My office tomorrow morning. Nine sharp."

He didn't get a chance to respond. The line went dead. Seconds later, his phone came alive. *I'll fix it. I promise.*

She was lucky she didn't add a happy face.

A red door with a cornucopia wreath hanging at its

center opened. His ex looked out at him. She wore a gold and black plaid skirt with a bow at the front and a black sweater. Her hair was honey brown, her eyes golden. At forty, she was even more beautiful than when they first met.

Ella Rose joined her. She had on the same outfit as her mother, looking older than the last time he'd seen her. Maybe because in a week she'd be seven. Or maybe it was because she wore her chestnut-brown hair in a bun on the top of her head. Her blue eyes were big in her delicate face. She looked like his sister. Riley had been close to the same age as Ella Rose when she'd been killed in a car accident. Frozen in time and in his mind.

He pushed away the depressing weight that always accompanied memories of his sister and got out of the car. Even though he was angry at Julia, he followed her recommendation. Forgetting the last couple of visits to focus on how it used to be when he came home, he smiled at his little girl. "Hey, pumpkin. You and your mommy are looking beautiful today."

And there it was, a hint of the smile he hadn't seen for a while. She glanced up at her mother as though looking for a reaction. Ella Rose twisted her foot at the ankle, something she did when she was anxious, and then she brought her gaze back to him and said, "Happy Thanksgiving, Daddy."

Her smile had disappeared, and it wasn't the welcome he'd been hoping for, but it was an improvement over the past few months. "Happy Thanksgiving to you too, pumpkin," he said as he crouched in front of her.

"Grandpa Colin and your uncles and aunts all say hi. Great-Grandma Kitty and Jasper too. They sent you cupcakes." Once again, she glanced at her mother.

Harper gave him a tight smile. "That's very nice, but we're cutting back on sweets. I'm sure our guests will enjoy them though. And you, of course."

He stiffened, worried that he knew the reason for the no-sweets rule. In Harper's eyes, you could never be too thin or too rich. Just two of the many reasons they were no longer together. And why it was so important for him to spend more time with his daughter. Time that he wouldn't get if he had it out with Harper like he wanted to right now. So he kept his smile in place and stood up.

"Thanks for having me," he said, and handed her the bouquet.

The tightness left her face. She looked genuinely pleased and smiled. "How lovely. Thank you." As she drew back the paper, her smile widened, and her face softened further. "Look, darling, Daddy bought Mommy a bouquet of flowers almost identical to this when he asked her to marry him."

He cursed roundly in his head. No one escaped his anger, not Julia, not Jasper or himself. But then Ella Rose looked up at him and smiled like she used to, like he was her hero, and she reached for his hand. Just like that, his anger vanished, and he thought that maybe, just maybe, it would all work out.

Harper tucked her arm through his. "This will be nice. Our neighbors are here. Mother and Father too. It'll be just like old times."

* * *

Harper hadn't been wrong. Last night's dinner at her place had felt exactly like old times. And not in a good way. Julia's advice had backfired. Thanks to the flowers and his attitude adjustment, Harper apparently believed he'd come around to her way of thinking and they'd be back together in no time at all. Her parents hated him as much as they always had but were too highbrow to be obvious about it. He was counting on them to convince their daughter that her life was better without Aidan in it.

The only bright spot had been Ella Rose. She hadn't ignored him or made him feel unwelcome. He'd even managed to convince Harper to let Ella Rose have a quarter of a cupcake. The actual dinner of course had been great. It always was. Harper didn't do anything halfway. The woman was a perfectionist and exceled at whatever she tried her hand at. Still, he'd needed four antacids before he got to sleep last night.

As he headed toward the dining room at the manor, he had a feeling tonight wouldn't be much better. Mr. Wilcox, the Gallagher family's attorney, had insisted they meet at Greystone.

Instead of giving the old guy a heads-up, Aidan should have paid an unexpected visit to his law office on Main Street. But after the meeting with his boss this morning, the last thing Aidan needed was to be caught leaving work early or coming back late from lunch. He was already on thin ice. The chief was looking for any excuse to get rid of him. As it was, Aidan was on desk duty until further notice.

So whether his family liked it or not—who was he trying to kid, they'd hate it—he wanted to know exactly what his options were in regard to his great-grandmother's will. GG had left the manor and the five-thousand-acre estate to her great-grandchildren. The only way they could sell out was if they all agreed. Supposedly there was an offer on the table from a mystery corporation who wanted to build high-end condos. A local Realtor, Paige Townsend, had been handling the deal before GG died. Rumor had it that, if they sold out, Aidan and his cousins would each walk away with well over a million bucks after taxes.

The problem was that his brothers and his cousin Mike were already members of Team Greystone. Easy for them. Aidan was in a precarious position at work, and he wanted custody of his daughter. Especially after the cupcake thing. He was meeting with Wilcox tonight to see if he could put his share in the estate up for sale. He hoped the attorney would keep it quiet, or someone might take it upon themselves to poison Aidan's food.

As he walked toward the dark wooden staircase that led into the dining room, Aidan caught a glimpse of the harbor lights through the large back windows that faced onto Kismet Cove.

A cute brunette in red caught his attention. He stopped short at the top of the stairs. For about a minute, he considered canceling his meeting with Wilcox. Then Aidan reminded himself that if anyone should feel awkward about being here, it was Julia. She was the reason he was even having the meeting. Along with his boss, who just then got up to talk to Doc Bishop at the table three over from them. Did Julia really expect him to buy that she wasn't dating Benson? They wouldn't be out for a romantic dinner at the manor if they weren't seeing each other. She'd lied to him before; he didn't know why he was surprised she'd done so again. Or why it bothered him.

"Hi, Erin," he said to the blond waitress filling out a seating chart.

"Oh, hi, Aidan, I didn't expect to see you tonight. Can I get you a table?"

"You mind if I take that one?" He gestured to a table for four near the French doors that led onto the patio. The shrubbery and trees were lit up with miniature white lights. He'd picked the table for a reason. He had a clear view of Julia, who was still sitting alone on the opposite side of the octagon-shaped room. The dining room was situated in one of the towers and richly decorated to reflect the maritime history of Harmony Harbor.

"Sure. Will anyone be joining you?" Erin asked, picking up a menu.

"Yeah, one other person." He decided to keep his guest's identity a secret. It'd give him time to talk to Wilcox before word got out. Though he wouldn't be surprised if the attorney had already given the family a heads-up, despite Aidan warning him not to.

He ordered a beer and kicked back in the chair to study Julia. Her raven's-wing-black hair was piled on her head in a messy knot, she wore a red cowl-neck sweater—he leaned to the right—black leggings, and red fur boots. She hadn't noticed him yet. Probably because she'd closed her eyes. She appeared lost in thought, her head moving slowly back and forth like maybe she was having an internal conversation with herself. Which wouldn't surprise him in the least.

He glanced at his boss, who hadn't noticed him either, and then went back to looking at Julia. As though she sensed his attention, her eyes blinked open. She glanced around at the other diners. Her expression was almost comical when her gaze landed on him. Her mouth dropped open, and then she grimaced. She glanced over her shoulder to where Benson was deep in conversation with Doc Bishop before returning her gaze to Aidan.

He crossed his arms.

I'm sorry, she mouthed, forcing him to focus on her plump lips.

Pulling out his cell phone, he typed: *Thought you said you weren't his girlfriend.* He'd pressed Send before he realized what she might make of that. There was a lot more he could have said or asked.

I'm not. We're just having dinner together.

He waited for her tell. Sure enough, she began playing with her earring.

I'm going to talk to him. Make things right. She lifted her gaze to meet his, and he saw the regret in her eyes. Still, she had a lot to answer for.

Don't bother. You've helped enough.

Ur being sarcastic again, aren't u?

He raised an eyebrow.

She took another quick glance over her shoulder before typing. *How did it go with ur little girl?*

Even though he was mad at Julia, he wouldn't have

spent Thanksgiving with Ella Rose without her pushing him. *Pretty good, actually. Thanks for the advice.* He looked up to see a wide smile spread across her face. She was cute, but when she smiled... *Stop smiling at me and stop texting. Your boyfriend is on his way back to the table. Thanks to you, I'm already on desk duty for the next month. There's only so many cold cases to keep me busy, I don't want to be grounded for two months.*

He frowned, confused as to why all the color had drained from her face.

Chapter Six

♥

Colleen Gallagher hovered—or perhaps *floated* best described what she did—on the stairs leading into the dining room at Greystone Manor. One thing she knew for certain she wasn't doing was walking down the dark wooden steps like she'd done a million times in the past. Though that might sound like a load of malarkey, it wasn't. She'd lived to the ripe old age of a hundred and four and had walked these very stairs every day since she'd arrived at the manor more than eighty-six years before.

On November 1, she'd celebrated her first anniversary as a ghost. Just saying the word in her mind caused her to grimace. She knew it to be true, but still…A ghost? She felt as alive as ever. Even better because she no longer felt pain. She knew the reality of it though. More than a year had passed since she'd missed the magic carpet ride to heaven.

She had yet to figure out the why or how of it. Perhaps dying on All Saints' Day had something to do with her spiritual state of affairs. Though she was hardly a saint. Something everyone in Harmony Harbor could, and would, no doubt attest to.

However, she realized in short order that it was a good thing she'd missed her appointment with her Maker that day. There were things she had to make amends for before she reached the pearly gates. Most important, she had to protect the Gallagher family's legacy. And the best way she knew how to do that was to match her great-grandchildren with their true loves. Otherwise, they'd sell out to the muckety-mucks who wanted to buy up their land and tear down the manor.

She'd been feeling more confident about her chances for success these past few weeks. Probably because three of her great-grandsons were now happily married to their true loves.

"Yes, we have much to be thankful for, Simon," she said to the black cat who followed her into the dining room. He was the only one who could both see and hear her. "In case I haven't told you, I'm thankful for you, my friend. Without your help, Olivia might not be with us today." She shuddered at the memory of what Finn's wife had been through last summer.

Colleen glanced at Simon, who did a full-body shiver and shake. It had been a terrifying time for all of them. "Don't you worry. Getting Aidan and Julia together shouldn't be too difficult."

As long as Julia's secret didn't come to light. Colleen couldn't make herself utter the words aloud. It was as though by not speaking them, she protected Julia and all those involved. Sometimes the truth did not set you free.

Meow.

Colleen frowned. If she wasn't mistaken, that was a mocking meow. She followed Simon's gaze to where Aidan sat at a table on his own with a serious expression on his handsome face. Her great-grandson was looking across the dining room at Julia.

"Maybe my hearing's going or I don't interpret cat-speak as well as I used to, but there's no call for ridicule if you're seeing what I am, Simon. Aidan can't take his eyes off Julia."

She chuckled. Oh, but her great-grandson had met his match in the owner of Books and Beans. Julia was exactly what the boy needed. She would bring light and laughter to his life. And Colleen couldn't wait to watch their romance play out, especially at her favorite time of year. "A Christmas Eve wedding like Liam and Sophie's would be just the thing, wouldn't it, Simon?"

Meow.

There was a wealth of meaning and emotion behind that *meow.* It was as though Simon had just asked if she'd lost her marbles at the same time telling her it would be a cold day in hell before that came to pass.

"All right, so perhaps a wedding might be pushing it. But mark my words, those two are meant to be together. I have a gift, Simon. I know these things. And the one thing I know for certain is..." She trailed off as she turned her attention to Julia. The rest of what she was about to say was interrupted by the shocking development happening right before her very eyes. Paul Benson joined Julia at the romantic table for two and reached for her hand, bringing it to his lips.

"For the love of all that is holy, what does the chief think he's doing? Julia is young enough to be his daughter." That was the problem with being tied to the manor: For the most part, Colleen had no idea what was going on outside her little world or how to impact it. She shot a look at Aidan, who'd gone from frowning to scowling, and smiled. "There it is, Simon. Right there is proof that I'm right. Though he'd best get off his tuchus and intervene."

Colleen's body practically vibrated as someone walked through her. It was a stout, bald man with a briefcase in hand. He headed straight for Aidan's table.

"What's Harper up to now?" Colleen wondered aloud as she recognized the Gallagher family attorney. She'd known from the very beginning it would never work out between Aidan and his ex. Her great-grandson had made the mistake of marrying too soon after the death of his mother and sister. The loss of Mary and Riley had changed him, as had his marriage. He wasn't the same sweet boy Colleen remembered. He'd become hard and cynical. His mother would be sad to see the changes in her son.

Colleen made her way to the table, assuming her old friend and attorney must have taken it upon himself to advise Aidan on his custody battle with Harper. Thankfully, Aidan's sisters-in-law had daily meetings at the manor and the topic of their single brother-in-law came up often so Colleen had some idea what was going on.

After Erin had taken their order, Wilcox reached in his briefcase and took out a copy of her will. He handed it to Aidan. "As you can see, your great-grandmother gave a lot of thought to this. The Gallagher legacy was important to her, Aidan. She hoped that you and your cousins, given time, would come to feel as she did. It's why the sale of shares to an outside party is prohibited prior to a unanimous decision being reached by you and your cousins."

Colleen watched Aidan as he read the document, panic tightening her chest. Her great-grandson was smart, too smart. If anyone could find a way around the clause, it would be Aidan.

He lowered the paper to look at George. "I'll sell my share to one of my cousins, then."

Aidan's brothers and their cousin Michael had signed up for the Save Greystone Team, but the rest of her great-grandchildren were wildcards. They could go either way. She had to stop this now.

Her gaze shot around the dining room, looking for someone to intercede. Rosa DiRossi had just walked into the dining room. With her dark, shoulder-length hair and exotic features, the seventy-something woman still managed to turn heads in her black dress and black leather knee-high boots—including that of the man who stood up to greet her. Dr. Bishop. He kissed Rosa's cheek and then held out her chair.

Colleen's night had gone from bad to worse. Or it would if her daughter-in-law Kitty happened to walk by the dining room and spy the couple together. Kitty and Rosa had been feuding over Kyle Bishop since last summer. It wasn't the first time the women had been involved in a love triangle. And knowing how badly it had ended the last time...

"I have a good mind to dump Kyle Bishop's wine on his head. What is he thinking meeting Rosa here?" Colleen muttered to Simon as she looked from Aidan back to Rosa and Kyle, trying to decide which situation was most urgent.

Simon meowed. Like the rest of the diners, Colleen turned as an elegant woman with white-blond hair and blue eyes entered the dining room. It was Kitty.

"Simon, find Jasper!" Colleen said, hurrying to Dr. Bishop's table in hopes of staving off a battle royale. She hadn't completely mastered the art of haunting, but at times she could move things and make her presence known. All she had to do was scare the bejaysus out of the three of them so they would leave before making a scene.

Out of the corner of her eye, she noted a tall, lean fellow wearing a black suit shoo Simon from the dining room. It was Jasper. She saw the moment he realized why Simon had been trying to gain his attention.

He wouldn't make it in time to avert the disaster. Kitty was almost at the table. It was up to Colleen to stop the drama that was about to unfold, although she was surprised the fight hadn't already broken out. Colleen's hand passed through Kyle as she reached for the glass of water on the table.

"Kitty, my dear, you look as beautiful as always." Like he'd done with Rosa, Kyle kissed Kitty's cheek and held out a chair for her.

Jasper slowed his approach, looking as confused as Colleen felt. What the bejaysus was going on?

"Thank you." Kitty took her seat, giving her once childhood best friend a regal nod. "Rosa."

Rosa unfolded her napkin and then greeted Kitty. Her dark eyes moved to where Jasper now unobtrusively stood with his hands behind his back at the window, overseeing the dining room, and she pursed her lips. She wasn't Jasper's biggest fan. Little did Rosa know how much she owed the man or the price he'd pay if word got out about what he'd done to protect her.

"I'm honored you both agreed to join me. At our ages, we can't afford to hold grudges. And I certainly don't want you fighting over me," Kyle said. Yet his smug tone indicated he was more than flattered by the attention. "I was also hoping to continue our *friendships*, if you know what I mean?"

Colleen was afraid that she did. Behind her, she could practically feel Jasper's blood boiling.

Rosa's eyes narrowed. "With me or Kitty?"

"With both of you, of course. I thought we could agree upon some sort of schedule. One week with you, Rosa, and one week with you, Kitty. Unless you're interested in—"

Both Rosa and Kitty picked up their water goblets at the same time and leaned over to dump them on Kyle's head.

Colleen grinned, happy the two women weren't so desperate for love and affection that they'd let themselves be treated that way. Jasper instantly appeared at the table to defuse the situation. Just because Kitty and Rosa were calm at the moment didn't mean they'd stay that way. Especially Rosa.

"Dr. Bishop, if you'll come with me, I'll have your car brought around to the front. Ladies, Erin will set you up at another table," Jasper said.

"Why? We'll stay here. He's wet. The table isn't," Rosa told Jasper.

That moment earlier when Colleen had felt her heart was about to explode from her chest was almost worth it to see Kitty smile and agree with Rosa. They'd stay and have dinner together, the feud forgotten once more.

Colleen didn't have time to enjoy the moment though. If Jasper hadn't shooed off Simon and the darn cat obeyed, Colleen would have had him draw Kitty and Rosa's attention to Aidan and his dinner companion at the other side of the room. Both women were intent on saving the manor and keeping the estate in the Gallagher family. Somehow, Colleen had to clue in Kitty to what was going on. She'd need her help to stop Aidan from selling out.

As Colleen hurried to her great-grandson's table, she noticed Julia looking Aidan's way. She should have thought of that from the very start. This was a job for the Gallaghers' fairy godmother. And Aidan had just given Colleen the perfect opportunity to set it in play. Frowning at his grandmother's table, Aidan said something to the attorney and got up to check on Kitty. The older man followed him, leaving the paper on the table unattended.

Colleen got eye level with the table and blew with all her might, pleased when the paper fluttered to the floor. Going down on her hands and knees, she blew it all the way across the room to the side of Julia's chair. The girl didn't give it a passing glance. Colleen tugged on the linen napkin on Julia's lap. It took several tries before the white cloth fell onto the floor.

"Thank the good Lord," she said when Julia finally leaned over and picked up both. The girl frowned at the sheet of paper and then her eyes went wide. "Paul, I have to use the restroom and return a call. I won't be long. If Erin comes before I'm back, just order me a Caesar salad with chicken, please."

"Julia, is everything all right?" the chief asked.

"Fine. Perfectly fine," she responded, intent on her phone, speed typing as she walked toward the stairs.

Colleen turned to see Aidan standing at his grandmother's table. He pulled out his phone, frowned and looked around, and then typed something before excusing himself. As soon as Aidan walked off, Wilcox filled in Kitty and Rosa. It wasn't as though he was breaking his oath as a lawyer. All Aidan had wanted to know was his rights in regard to her will.

Relieved that her daughter-in-law was now aware of the situation, Colleen followed her great-grandson.

Aidan scanned the lobby as he walked toward the atrium. There were two people at the bar and a couple checking in at the reception desk. "Julia, where are you?" Aidan said, turning in a circle.

A red-wool-encased arm shot out, dragging him behind the artificial Christmas tree at the atrium's entrance.

"Keep your voice down," Julia ordered Aidan.

He looked down at her and crossed his arms. "Why? Because you don't want your boyfriend to know you're arranging secret rendezvous with other men?"

"You're not *other men*, and he's not my boyfriend."

"Ah, last time I checked I was definitely a man and—"

"Believe me, I know you're a man. What I meant was you're not *another* man, like someone I'm seeing secretly on the side."

"Was that supposed to make sense?"

"Yes, and it did. I—" She made a small frustrated sound in her throat. "I don't have time to play word games with you. What's this?" She held up the paper.

"None of your business." He frowned, taking the document from her. "Did you take this off my table?"

Colleen had seen that expression on her great-grandson's face before, and it didn't bode well for Julia or the conversation.

"No, I wouldn't do something like that. I dropped my napkin and it was there, on the floor."

"I'll take you at your word, this time. Just don't let it happen again."

"I told you... You know what, never mind. I'm not fighting about this when we have more important things to discuss, like the manor and keeping it in the Gallagher family." She crossed her arms, mimicking Aidan's stance. "You're on the Save Greystone Team, aren't you?"

"No, I'm on Team Aidan and Ella Rose. I can't afford to be sentimental about this, Julia. My job isn't exactly a sure thing, and I have a daughter to think about."

"You don't have to worry about your job. I was just getting around to explaining everything to Paul. He wasn't in the mood to listen last night, so I thought I'd bring him here for a nice dinner and smooth things over. I promise, Aidan, I am going to make this right. You don't have to worry about being shut in an office going through cold case files for the rest of your life."

By all that is holy, how did that happen? The last thing they needed was for Aidan to look into the deaths of his mother and sister. The members of HHPD were good at their job, but Aidan was better. Nothing got past him. And they couldn't afford for the truth to come out.

Two weeks after Josh died, Colleen had been at church for a private confession. It'd been late, and she'd heard someone crying in one of the pews. It turned out to be Julia. She'd told Colleen everything that night.

It had been Colleen's decision to keep the truth from the family. She didn't see what good it would do. It wasn't like it would bring Mary and Riley back. After so many years had passed, the family had slowly begun to heal. However, she'd had another reason for covering up the truth. And it wasn't only because she could use a hand bringing her family together again. The day after Josh had died, someone else had shared their secret with Colleen.

Too many people would be hurt if both truths came out. She wished she could help Julia, but the poor lamb was on her own. *And up against the Big Bad Wolf,* Colleen thought, looking at her great-grandson's cross face.

"Are you telling me you asked Benson out for dinner so you could plead my case?"

"Uh, no?"

Colleen didn't blame Julia for not knowing whether

she should lie or tell the truth. Aidan had no idea how intimidating he could be. Even so, Colleen thought his reaction to Julia having dinner with his boss might be a sign that their relationship was heading in the right direction after all.

"Okay, yes, that's the main reason I'm here," Julia amended. "So please, can you hold off selling your shares? This isn't about only your family. It's about the town, Aid—"

"Julia..." Chief Benson began as he rounded the Christmas tree. His features tightened when he spotted Aidan. "I thought I told you to stay away from her, Gallagher."

Chapter Seven

♥

Julia had been trying to ignore her sore throat all morning, along with the sneezing that had accompanied it. Though that annoying symptom seemed to have cleared up, she thought with a sniff. Too bad she hadn't been able to stop sneezing while writing today's love scene. She hadn't exactly been in a hot and steamy mood and had a feeling that when she went over her pages later that night, they'd need major revisions.

She blamed her cold on stress. In less than two days, she'd gone from having only one Gallagher to worry about to having two plus the manor... Oh, and Paul. She couldn't forget about him.

Until she'd ensured he wouldn't fire Aidan, she had to continue dating the older man. Given his comments after discovering her with Aidan behind the Christmas tree, she was off the market for the foreseeable future. No biggie, really. *Who has time to date anyway?* she thought, digging in the white apron she wore over the ankle-length blue dress. She found the zinc lozenge in her pocket and popped it in her mouth.

At least last night's dinner at the manor hadn't been a total disaster. Before her assignation with Aidan, she'd managed to convince Paul that, with all the Christmas festivities going on in town, they needed a strong police presence on the streets. She hoped that was enough to guarantee Aidan would be on patrol and not locked in a room with cold case files.

Though after her near panic attack upon reading his text, she'd had time to think more rationally. It had been more than eight years since the accident on the bridge. Knowing the Gallaghers like she'd come to, if there'd been anything to find, they'd have found it by now. But if she had any hope of convincing Paul that Aidan was exactly the kind of officer he wanted working for HHPD, she needed Aidan out and about and not behind a desk at the station.

Just the thought of all she had to do made her want to curl up under the Christmas tree. Between playing the Gallaghers' fairy godmother, heading up the town's Christmas committee, running her business at the busiest time of year, and erasing any sign of Aidan from her book, Julia would be lucky if she found time to sleep.

"Thanks so much, Aidan Gallagher," she muttered, hanging a miniature book cover on the eight-foot pre-lit tree, its branches heavy with fake snow and ornaments. Along with covers of the children's classics, she'd bought figurines and ornaments that depicted scenes and characters from the books.

They'd cost a small fortune, and she wasn't looking forward to opening her credit card bill next month. But seeing them on the tree made her happy and excited for the upcoming holidays. The feeling never lasted for long, not like it had years before. Now it seemed like she spent the entire month of December trying to recapture the magic with a new tradition, a new event, something that would fill her up with that remembered joy.

"How about it, Mrs. Potts? Do you have any words of wisdom for me?" she asked the teapot as she hung it on the branch beside Mrs. Potts's son, Chip, the teacup.

From behind her she heard a familiar little girl's voice say, "You should talk to Livy instead of the teapot. She doesn't think you should be dating the police chief."

"George!" An elegant blonde wearing a silver-gray padded jacket and matching suede winter boots cringed as she rushed to the side of the little girl with the curly dark hair and big blue eyes. "I'm so sorry, Julia. George joined us at our meeting at the manor yesterday morning, and I guess she overheard us talking... All right, that sounds just as bad and so does my comment about Chief Benson. But it's not exactly what I—"

"She said he's too old for you."

"George," Olivia groaned, and crouched at the little girl's side.

Julia looked around the store. There were several people browsing in the mystery and new releases sections. Far enough away that they hadn't heard George, whose voice tended to carry.

"Sweetheart, you can't repeat private conversations." Her cheeks pink, Olivia looked up at Julia. "It all started with me suggesting that we ask you to help with the Snow Ball on Christmas Eve. We thought it would be even more special if we added some entertainment, and I mentioned what you were doing for the Festival of Lights and how it would fit perfectly with our theme. We're taking George to Kenya to spend the holidays with her mom, so I won't be here…Anyway, that got us talking about how much we all love you and want to see you happy."

It didn't bother Julia that her friends were talking about her. She knew they were coming from a good place. Still, she had to work to keep the panic from showing on her face. She didn't have the time or energy to play the dating game, and she didn't know how to say no if Olivia asked her to take over the Snow Ball and organize a performance from *The Nutcracker*.

"Aunt Sophie wants you to go on a date with Cousin Michael. He's an FBI man, but I think you should have a date with Uncle Aidan. So does Grandma Kitty."

Olivia gave a nervous laugh. "I don't think Uncle Aidan is a good match for Julia, sweetheart."

"How come?" George asked.

Before the conversation got any more depressing, because of course Julia knew she wasn't a match for Aidan, she tried to think of a way to change the subject. She'd both seen and heard all about his ex-wife. Dr. Harper Granger was a stunning blonde who was not only a renowned psychiatrist but a contributor to the *New York Times* bestseller *Where Evil Lurks*.

Julia forced a bright smile as the front door's chime kept chiming and the store suddenly filled up. "I have to check and see how the girls are doing at the coffee bar. Why don't you come with me, George? You can pick out what kind of cookies we serve during story hour."

"What can I do to help, Julia? You look like you're swamped," Olivia said, removing her jacket to reveal a winter-white sweater that hugged her willowy figure, her baby bump barely noticeable.

"Just sit and…Oh, shoot, would you mind making up the gift basket?" She nodded to where a package of sugar cookies, jelly beans, a book, and a small stuffed Belle and Beast sat on the low table beside a basket. Once a month Julia held a draw for the members of the storytime club, in part to attract new members while at the same time introducing a child to a book they might not have picked on their own.

Twenty minutes later, the stresses of earlier fell away as Julia sat in the oversized red velvet chair with her hair held back with a big blue bow that matched her dress. This was one of her favorite bookstore activities. Her eager audience sat on the red, yellow, and blue foam squares, leaning forward expectantly when Julia lowered her voice. She loved acting out the stories, changing her voice and expressions to play the different characters, using whatever she had at hand to engage the children. Right then, as Julia made the low groan of a castle door creaking open, the children looked afraid for Belle.

To their left, what sounded like a shelf of books crashing to the floor was followed by a deep male voice growling a frustrated oath.

"It's the beast! It's the beast! Hide!"

"It's not a beast. It's my uncle Aidan," George said.

Julia looked to where George was pointing. Aidan slowly stood up from behind a shelf with several books in his hand and a guilty expression on his face. "Sorry about that—" As though just noticing her, he stopped and stared and then cleared his throat. "Julia."

"She's Belle, Beast," a little boy said, holding up a toy sword. "And I'm Gaston."

Two little girls gasped. "He's the man who tried to kill Millie the Mermaid!"

As though to calm their fears, Aidan came around the bookcase wearing a weather-beaten brown leather jacket, jeans, and boots. With his overly long dark hair and his heavy beard, he looked badass and dangerous.

Unlike Julia and several of the other mothers enjoying storytime, the little girls were probably more into good boys than bad ones. A taste for bad boys was something that women seemed to acquire later in life, and it caused no end of trouble. Aidan was definitely trouble, and Julia didn't need those tiny, heated zings of desire to tell her so.

He crouched beside Julia's chair. "I'm not the Beast, honest. I'm George's uncle." He nodded at the little girl grinning at him from the front row. The other children didn't look like they believed him. A couple of boys positioned themselves as though ready to pounce.

"You could vouch for me, you know," Aidan said out of the side of his mouth.

She could, but at that moment she was afraid something inappropriate—like *you are so hot I want to jump your bones*—might slip out. Because not only did he look like every bad-boy fantasy she'd ever had come to life, but she'd never been able to totally banish the feeling from last Christmas that he truly was her soul mate.

He raised a dark eyebrow.

"Sorry," she said. "Boys and girls, this is Mr. Gallagher. He's one of the good guys. He's a detective with the Harmony Harbor Police Department."

"Do you have a gun?" one of the boys asked.

"Yeah, I—"

"Get him," yelled the boy playing Gaston, and three other boys and two girls threw themselves at Aidan, laying him flat on his back. The commotion drew the attention of several curious shoppers as well as coffee shop patrons, one of whom just happened to be Poppy with her trusty camera in hand.

The last thing Julia wanted was for Aidan to end up on the front page of the *Harmony Harbor Gazette*. Before Poppy could get a clear shot, Julia jumped from the chair. Positioning herself in front of the hill of children, she leaned over to hit the sound system's On button. She'd planned to end storytime with *A Tale as Old as Time*, but they needed a distraction now.

Olivia, along with another mother, scooted around Julia to pull off the children beating on Aidan. No doubt afraid he might hurt one of his attackers, he lay perfectly still on the floor with his arms over his face.

"Come on, kids. Let's dance to our favorite song. Whoever participates wins an extra chance for the gift basket raffle." Encouraged by their parents, the children quickly paired off.

Just as Julia had hoped, the shoppers and Poppy were entranced by the pint-size dancers, drawing their attention from Aidan, who accepted a hand up from Olivia.

"Uncle Aidan, you be the Beast and dance with Belle," said George. Noting the mischievous twinkle in the little girl's eyes, Julia decided George had been spending too much time with the matchmaking Widows Club. She knew that was definitely the case when George took matters into her own hands and dragged Aidan to stand in front of Julia. "If you want to turn into a prince, you have to dance with her, Uncle Aidan."

Since George's voice carried, half the store heard her. A couple of older women, who'd obviously known Aidan since he was young, voiced their encouragement. Then the good-boy-loving little girls got in on the act, pleading with Aidan to listen to George so he could turn into a prince.

"Dance with her, Beast," the mini Gaston ordered, plastic sword pointed.

Most likely afraid to be attacked again, Aidan took Julia's hand and placed his other one at her waist. He drew her closer. "Your store is a dangerous place."

Today it most definitely was. Everywhere he touched her heated. If he held her any closer she was in danger of melting at his feet in a mindless puddle of lust.

He cocked his head, looking down at her as though wondering why she hadn't responded to his remark.

"Not usually," she said, impressed that her voice didn't come out breathy and give her away. Maybe being annoyed that his touch affected her so deeply helped. Even Josh, whom she'd once loved, had never made her feel this way. She gave herself a moment to mentally prepare herself before lifting her gaze. She met his shocking blue eyes, and her heart fluttered like a butterfly in love. She hoped he didn't feel it and guess the cause.

Though maybe, like her, he'd believe her racing pulse was due to nerves. The first few times it happened, she'd attributed it to the memory of how frightened she'd been when he'd dragged her to the police station. Similar to how terrified Belle must have been when she'd first encountered the Beast.

But Julia wasn't afraid of Aidan. Growing up with three older brothers and a taciturn father, she had a wealth of experience with growly men. Still, as with any contact with Aidan, it took a moment for her to settle. Once she did, she tried to think of him as one of her brothers' friends, ignoring the off-the-charts attraction as best she could.

She smiled. "So, what brings you here today?"

"Ella Rose. It's her birthday on Wednesday. She'll be seven."

This was it, the perfect opportunity to make things right between Aidan and his daughter. If Julia could do that, her fairy godmother list wouldn't seem quite so daunting. "I can totally help you with that. Story hour is almost over, and then I'm all yours." She winced, worried he'd take her remark the wrong way. Maybe because as soon as the words were out of her mouth her body seemed to shout *hooray*. "Strictly in a shopkeeper-shopper kind of way."

He raised a sardonic eyebrow as if to say *You can't be serious?*

It would take much more than a dance to turn him into a prince, Julia thought.

* * *

The first time Aidan had met Julia she'd been dressed as an elf and playing Santa's helper at the manor. And yeah, he'd kissed her, but only because his grandmother had insisted. The second time had been last summer at the beach when Julia had been dressed as a mermaid. And yeah, an image of her that day would be forever burned in his brain, but he hadn't intentionally stripped her down to her birthday suit. He'd thought she was a shark circling her prey in the shallow end at the beach. He'd seen danger where none existed and overreacted once again.

And here she was today, dressed as another character from a book, and he'd just danced with her, so he could do without his sister-in-law Olivia looking at him like he really was a beast.

He walked to where his brother's wife stood beside the bookshelf he'd nearly knocked over. "Okay, what did I do now?" he asked her.

"It's not what you did that has me worried. It's what you're going to do." She looked to where Julia knelt with the kids on the primary-colored squares holding a Santa hat upside down.

They were choosing the winner of the basket. The announcement had drawn cheers a couple of minutes ago.

"You have a problem with Julia helping me pick out a gift for Ella Rose?" It wasn't like he couldn't ask his sisters-in-law or his nieces for help, but it was because of Julia's advice at Thanksgiving that he finally felt like he'd made progress with his daughter. He didn't want to mess with a good thing.

"No," Olivia said slowly, but it was obvious she did. She took a deep breath. "What are your intentions toward Julia?"

He blinked. "What? How did we go from me asking for birthday advice to asking Julia out?" Several pairs of eyes turned his way, and if he wasn't mistaken, one pair were big and purple. *Great.* He'd raised his voice. "Thanks a lot."

"I'm sorry, but Julia's a good friend, and I'd hate to see her hurt."

"I think I'm offended." And he kind of was, because somehow everyone in Harmony Harbor, including the members of his own family, seemed to think he was a jerk. "If it makes you feel better, I have no interest in Julia—or any other woman, for that matter. All I want is to fix my relationship with my daughter and get my life back on track. That's it."

Olivia made an apologetic face. "I'm sorry. I shouldn't have said anything. I know these past few months have been difficult for you. If I can do anything to help, let me know."

"Appreciate it." There was something about the way Olivia was looking at him that suggested she had more to say but didn't know how to. Since no one had mentioned his meeting with the family attorney, Aidan had a feeling they were trying to figure out a way to get him to change his mind about selling out. Which meant it was probably best if he left before Olivia worked up the nerve to confront him.

He looked around the store. A line had formed at the cash register, and the coffee shop was packed. "You know what, I think I'll just get going. Tell Julia I'll stop by on my lunch hour next week."

"Wait." Olivia stopped him with a hand on his arm. "This probably isn't my place or the time to bring it up, but Kitty mentioned you were interested in selling your shares—"

"Okay, are you ready to do some birthday shopping?" Julia looked from him to Olivia. "Did I interrupt something?"

Aidan looked at her, positive that she knew exactly what she'd interrupted and had done so on purpose.

"No, nothing at all. Come on, George, we have to get going," Olivia said, picking up their jackets.

"You're busy, Julia. I should probably get going too. I can come back Monday when it's quieter," he said, helping Olivia with her jacket.

"I don't have extra staff on during the week. So, unless you have something pressing, I can give you a hand now."

"You should let Julia help. She knows what kids like," George informed him.

"George is right. You should stay, Aidan." Olivia looked at Julia and pressed her palms together. "Please tell me you're okay to take over the Snow Ball. I can help up until the twentieth. I'll have everything organized, so there won't be a lot to do. I even have a list of people willing to take on roles in *The Nutcracker*. Everyone's really excited about it. Ticket sales are going really well too."

Julia twisted her earring. "Sure, of course I will."

Aidan waited until they'd said their goodbyes and the storytime kids had taken off before asking, "Why didn't you just tell Olivia you don't have time to help out?"

"Because she's my friend. Besides, it'll be fun." She made a face and took something from her pocket and popped it in her mouth.

"I believe you as much I believe that you didn't know what you were interrupting with Olivia."

She wrinkled her nose. "Okay, I know it's none of my business, but it's not a decision to make lightly, Aidan. Greystone is as much your daughter's legacy as your own. I get that things are difficult right now, but it doesn't mean they always will be," she said, and began tidying up the children's section, stopping to help a grandmother who was searching for a Christmas gift for her grandchildren.

Aidan took over the cleanup, watching Julia with the older woman as he did. It was obvious she was as knowledgeable as she was passionate about books and her business. Her face was animated as she talked to the woman, her enthusiasm contagious. By the time Julia was finished, Grandma had filled her basket. Julia walked her to the cash register, talking to several other customers along the way.

"You didn't have to do that," she said when she finally made her way back to him.

"I didn't mind." He returned the children's book he'd been flipping through to the shelf. "You sure you have time though?"

"Absolutely. I'm looking forward to it." She glanced at him from under her lashes. "So, did you give any thought to holding off before making a decision on selling your shares?"

"The thing is, I don't know how long I can hold off." He didn't know why, maybe because he'd opened up to her about Ella Rose, but he ended up confessing how tight things really were.

She stared at him as she lowered herself onto the big, red velvet chair. "That's lovely and honorable, but you can't keep it up, Aidan. I know it's none of my business, but shouldn't Harper be paying her share? She's a psychiatrist. Surely she can afford to."

"If she were working, she could. But other than consulting here and there to keep her foot in the door, she's devoted herself entirely to Ella Rose since we split up."

"Don't get me wrong. I think it's amazing that your ex puts your little girl first. But Ella Rose is seven and in school full-time. It doesn't seem fair that you're carrying the entire financial burden when Harper could be working part-time. You should sell the house."

"I can't uproot Ella Rose. It was hard enough on her when Harper and I split."

"You were the one who wanted the divorce, weren't you?"

"Yeah." He knew what she was getting at, and

she'd be right. He did feel guilty. No doubt Harper knew it too and played on it. She was awfully fond of quoting statistics to demonstrate how detrimental divorce was to children. Aidan thought it was just as bad, probably worse, for a child to be raised in a home where all their parents did was fight. "So, do you have any idea what I should give Ella Rose for her birthday?"

Julia gave him a sweet smile and didn't press him further, for which he was grateful. "I have an idea, but if you don't like it, you have to be honest."

"Sure. Shoot."

"Okay, I thought we could do a gift basket for her. My storytime kids love them, and I have lots of fun things to put inside. You just give me a budget, and we'll go from there. Don't worry. It doesn't have to be a big one. We can wrap small things in different size boxes too. She'll love having lots to open."

"Other than the *we* wrapping things, it sounds great."

"Hey, you never know. You might enjoy wrapping things up."

"Trust me, I'm an expert at unwrapping…" Which of course she knew from the time he'd *unwrapped* her at the beach. He cleared his throat. "Okay, that was awkward. I did apologize about that, didn't I?"

"Grudgingly, but yes, you did," she said, her eyes sparkling with amusement.

Julia's features lacked the symmetry that most people associated with a beautiful face. Her eyes were a little too big, her cheeks round, there was a tiny bump on the bridge of her small, upturned nose, and her mouth was wide and full. But at that moment, she looked pretty perfect to him. "So, do you want to change out of your costume before we get started?"

"Um, I'm not sure what you mean by that. Are we still talking about you being an expert unwrapper?"

Chapter Eight

♥

Good morning, Mr. O'Malley!" Julia called out to the diminutive older man putting up a wreath on the door of the hardware store.

"We missed you at church this morning, pet. Everything okay?"

Across the road, she jogged on the spot to keep warm. "Everything's good. Just slept in."

Thanks to her sore throat and stuffed nose, she'd barely slept a wink. On the bright side, no sleep meant she had plenty of time to daydream some new scenes for her book. She probably had Aidan to thank for inspiring the dance scene she'd added this morning to *Warrior's Touch*. Although their dance at the bookstore was much tamer than Adrian and Gillian's. "All set for the big day?" Julia asked Mr. O'Malley.

"Yep, me and John are putting up the last of the Christmas lights today. He'll give you a hand this afternoon."

"Awesome!" She waved. "I have a meeting at Jolly Rogers." More like a fairy godmother plan to put into action. The time for pussyfooting around was over.

"Order the Irish omelet. It'll fill you up for the rest of the day. Knowing you, you'll be running around and forget to eat."

He was just the sweetest. She loved her girlfriends who owned businesses on Main Street, but she had a soft spot for the old-timers. She could talk with them for hours. One day, when she found the time, she planned to write their stories.

"Will do. I'll tell Caleb you're recommending it to everyone. See if I can't get you a discount for next time you're in."

At the top of the hill leading down Main Street to the harbor, the bright morning sunlight danced on the copper-domed clock tower, drawing her attention to the time. Yikes, it was twenty to ten. She had to hurry if she wanted to be at the diner before Colin and Maggie arrived. She'd arranged it so they wouldn't show up at the same time.

When she finally reached the diner, her breath was sawing in and out of her lungs, her throat was on fire, and her eyes watered due to the cold. Still, if she got Colin and Maggie to sit at the same table and exchange a few words, she'd consider it worth the discomfort.

She'd been doing a little digging and found out the couple hadn't been within a hundred yards of each other in more than two weeks. Though she supposed the proximity of their houses qualified as...Didn't matter. All she knew was she'd fallen down on her fairy godmother job.

A brisk wind off the Atlantic whistled through the bare branches of the trees behind the diner and Julia huddled deeper in her jacket. She reached for the door and tugged. It wouldn't open. As she knew from past experience, it wasn't exactly a light door to begin with, and the gale-force winds obviously weren't helping matters.

Digging the heels of her red boots into the snow-dusted sidewalk, she grabbed the handle with both of her mittened hands and pulled. It didn't budge. She tried again and got the same result. She pressed her nose against the glass and looked inside. The diner was definitely open. She knocked, trying to get the attention of the cashier and waitress.

She was just about to give it another go when an arm reached around her. *Duckety duck, duck, duck.* She recognized the weathered brown leather and his big, beautiful hand.

She slowly turned and looked up at Aidan. A glint of what looked to be amusement creased the corners of his eyes.

"Hey there. The door's stuck." Wow, she sounded incredibly calm given that her heart was racing. Emmeline must have passed on some of her acting genes to Julia after all. She patted Aidan's chest. Whoa, it was really broad and hard. She resisted the urge to rub it and said, "Big guy like you must be starving. Why don't you head over to Ship Ahoy? I hear they serve a great brunch."

"You wouldn't be trying to get rid of me, would you?"

She pointed to herself. "Who? Me? Gosh no, it's just

that... *whoomph*." The breath was knocked out of her when the door suddenly opened, glancing off her back and sending her straight into Aidan's arms.

"Oh, Julia, dear, I'm so sorry. I didn't see you there," Aidan's grandmother said.

Taking advantage of the situation, Julia rested her head against Aidan's chest for a minute and sniffed, disappointed when she didn't get even a whiff of his alluring scent. She'd forgotten her nose was stuffed.

She glanced up. He was looking down at her, his brow furrowed. "You okay?" he asked, gently rubbing her back.

She was about to say *no*, because even though there wasn't a chance for her and Aidan, she liked the feel of his hands on her. Still, she had no time to lose. She had to get rid of him before his father and Maggie showed up.

"I'm fine, thanks," she said, and stepped back, turning to Kitty. Rosa was standing beside her on the sidewalk. Both women were dressed in their Sunday best. "It was my fault, Kitty. I shouldn't have been standing there."

"Tell the truth. You were enraptured by my grandson, weren't you? He has a mesmerizing effect on women just like his father and brothers."

Aidan groaned. "Grams—"

Since she *was* a tad enraptured by Kitty's grandson, Julia thought it best to change the subject and hurry the three of them along. She cut off Aidan. "So, what are you two doing here? Don't you usually have Sunday brunch at the manor?"

"Yes, but Rosa and I have decided to broaden our horizons."

"*Sì*, we dumped Dr. Bishop, and now we're looking for a new man. Men," she quickly corrected herself.

Now that they'd confirmed what Julia had suspected had been behind the water dumping incident at the manor, she felt like doing a happy dance. No more feuding over Dr. Bishop meant she wouldn't have to intercede on Kitty's behalf by dating Paul.

But just to be on the safe side and ensure they didn't go after the same man again, she said, "Oh my gosh, that is so awesome. You have to let me help. I've got some great matchmaking books in stock. Stop by tomorrow, and we'll get started."

"You know, we're quite the matchmakers ourselves, dear. Rumor has it a certain couple I've set my sights on were seen dancing together yesterday afternoon. Anything you two want to share?"

"Grams."

"Oh now, don't get all growly. I just want you to know you have my blessing."

For one teensy-tiny second, Julia allowed herself to be immersed in the fantasy. She was standing with Aidan on their way to brunch, and his grandmother had just given them her blessing. They smiled at each other, and then Aidan got down on bended knee, right here on the sidewalk...

He killed the fantasy with the next words out of his mouth. "It's not happening, Grams. Not now, not ever, so put that idea out of your head." He moved around Julia to reach for the door.

She positioned herself in front of it. "You know, I nearly fell on black ice earlier, so you should probably walk Kitty and Rosa to their car. Just to be safe, you know."

He gave her a look when his grandmother and Rosa each latched on to an arm.

"I left the car parked at the church and Rosa walked," Kitty told her grandson.

"How perfect is that. Ship Ahoy is just a few doors down from the church. Enjoy your breakfast, Aidan. See you tomorrow, ladies."

A man walked out of the diner, and Julia quickly slipped inside before the door closed. Owner Caleb Malone stood behind the stainless-steel counter. He'd taken over from his grandfather a few years before. Rumor had it the elder Malone wouldn't step foot in the restaurant since Caleb had renovated, going with a sleek sixties diner look instead of the inside of a pirate ship. The old look had appealed to Julia more, but the food was so much better she doubted Caleb had many complaints.

"Reserved the back booth like you asked, babe. You want the usual?"

Then again, the lack of complaints were probably due to the fact that Caleb was a total hottie. The man with the dark blond hair and inked muscular arms had fueled several of Julia's bad-boy fantasies before Aidan moved to town.

"Nope, Mr. O'Malley recommended your Irish omelet. I'll just have coffee until my party arrives." She dug in her messenger bag for her wallet and pulled out a few dollars. "Put this toward his breakfast the next time he's in."

Caleb laughed and shook his head. "You're a soft touch, you know. The old man probably has more money than we do. His generation always cries broke."

"That's okay. He's a sweet old guy." She left the money on the counter. "Did you get your Christmas lights up?"

"Yes, ma'am. I'll be turning them on at six thirty sharp just like you ordered." He looked over the crowded diner. "I should be able to get away for a couple hours this afternoon to give you a hand."

They talked about the holiday events that were scheduled over the next few weeks until Caleb was called back to the kitchen. Julia said hello to several people she knew as she walked to the far end of the diner.

Never gets old, she thought, smiling to herself as she settled in the red pleather booth. She loved knowing so many people and feeling like part of the community. It was why, even though she was burning the candle at both ends, she didn't resent heading up the Christmas committee.

She sat where she could see the customers entering the diner. That way she could tuck Maggie in the corner—she was supposed to arrive first—and Colin wouldn't know until he got back here that Maggie was with her. He was too polite to do anything other than join them.

"Thanks." She smiled at the waitress who brought her a coffee and took a grateful sip.

She hadn't had time to grab one this morning. She'd been writing, and her Rudolph timer hadn't gone off to give her a forty-five-minute warning. She sat back, enjoying being able to chill for even a few minutes. She looked at the mural of Harmony Harbor that covered the entire wall and wondered if it was Maggie's work. It looked like she could ask the older woman herself, At that moment Maggie walked into the diner wearing a winter-white cape that set off her flaming red hair and pretty face.

Julia raised a hand to wave her over. She frowned, wondering why Maggie wasn't smiling. She always smiled. Something must be wrong. As soon as Maggie started walking toward the booth, Julia spotted the problem. Colin had just walked in the diner . . . with Aidan.

Duckety duck, duck, duck.

Julia could swear, okay, fake-swear, all she liked, but that wouldn't cut it. She had to come up with something fast. Her body was overheating, her forehead damp. She wondered if it was caused by a fever or nerves and then realized she'd yet to take off her jacket. Good. She was just hot. No nerves involved. She wasn't nervous about dealing with a ticked-off Aidan. Nope, not all.

She'd go all Gillian Connelly on him. She'd invented the heroine from the Warrior's trilogy, so it stood to reason that deep down inside Julia there was a kick-butt woman dying to come out.

As Julia undid the zipper on her jacket, she forced a wide, confident smile for Maggie. She stood up to hug the other woman. "I'm so glad you made it. Come, sit down."

"Colin's here," Maggie whispered.

"I know. Isn't that great? You scoot in the booth." Julia turned with a wide and welcoming smile for Colin…and Aidan. Well, him she tried to ignore. But it was a little hard because his eyes felt like laser beams, and she couldn't look away. "Colin! So glad you made it. Oh, Aidan, hi. I didn't know you were coming."

"I'm sure you didn't. So, what's going on here?"

"Just a meeting of the Christmas committee, you know. Really boring stuff. It looks like there's a spot for you at the counter."

"Nah, there's lots of room here. I'll join you guys. You scoot in over there, Julia, Maggie." He held Julia's gaze, letting her know by repeating what she'd said to Maggie that he knew exactly what she was up to. By the time Aidan had the table organized, Colin sat across from Maggie.

"It's a little warm in here, isn't it?" Julia said, finding the silence oppressive. "Do you mind?" She raised her eyebrows at Aidan as she tried to shrug out of her jacket. He was sitting too close. Instead of sliding down, he helped her out of her jacket.

His gaze moved over her, and he murmured, "That explains a lot."

"What explains…?" She trailed off when she noticed Maggie and Colin were looking at her too.

She didn't understand what was going on until Maggie said, "I didn't know you were a writer, Julia."

She looked down at herself. In her hurry to get out of the apartment, she'd pulled her jeans over her sleep shorts but hadn't thought to change her long-sleeve pur-

ple T-shirt, which read I'M A WRITER. WHICH MEANS
I LIVE IN A MAKE BELIEVE WORLD AND HAVE HIGH EX-
PECTATIONS. THANK YOU FOR UNDERSTANDING.

"I dabble," she said, hoping that would be enough.

"What are you working on now?" Maggie asked.

Of course Maggie would be interested. She was a
creative person. It also got her off the hook from talking
to Colin.

"A children's book," Julia said, because she had
played with the idea. And then to give Aidan a jab, she
added, "It's about a mermaid. Her name's Millie." She
looked at him and smiled. "You remember Millie, don't
you?"

"Yeah, sure do. I won't be forgetting about her anytime soon. So, Julia, what's the meeting about? Dad
said it was important."

She should have known better than to poke the beast.
"It is. It really, really is. But we should probably order
first. In case you want a recommendation, Mr.
O'Malley says to go with the Irish omelet." She smiled
at the waitress who'd just walked over. "That's what I'll
have, thank you."

"Cal's got something special in mind for you," the
waitress said with a wink.

"Really? That's so awesome. I'm excited."

Aidan crossed his arms and angled his head. "You're
not stepping out on your boyfriend with Caleb Malone,
are you?"

"Caleb and I are just friends. And either you're hard
of hearing or you tune me out, but I've repeatedly told
you that I don't have a boyfriend."

"You might want to tell that to Benson."

Colin looked from Julia to Aidan. "I had no idea you two knew each other so well."

Aidan gave her a look before saying to his dad, "We don't."

At almost the same time as Julia said, "We've gotten to know each other pretty well."

"Is that right?" Colin said with a smile for her and a pointed look at his son. "I'm really glad to hear that, Julia. My son could use a friend."

Aidan shook his head and rubbed his hands over his face. Julia thought she heard him say "You have got to be shitting me" before he lowered his hands and gave the waitress his order.

"All right, so I guess you're probably wondering why I asked you to meet with me, Maggie and Colin."

Sharing a nervous glance, the couple missed Aidan leaning in to her and whispering, "Nope, I know exactly what you're up to, and you better cut it out."

She ignored him, waiting for Maggie and Colin to look her way before continuing. "I had this vision come to me yesterday, and it was so cool. I just knew I had to somehow incorporate it into the plan for Main Street. And—"

"How does that work exactly? The vision thing?" Aidan asked, pretending to be interested, but she could tell he was silently laughing at her.

"We don't have a lot of time, so I'll explain it to you later," she told him, moving her foot to gently step on his.

"Ow, jeez, that hurt." He bent down to rub his foot, his head under the table.

"What's wrong? You all right, son?"

"I'm sure he's fine," Julie said. Ducking her head under the table, she whispered, "You're a big faker. I barely touched you. And it was an accident. Maybe if you weren't sitting nearly on top of me, it wouldn't have happened."

"You only have yourself to blame. Next time think twice before you go up against me."

"This is not about you. All I'm trying—" She broke off at the sound of someone clearing their throat. She glared at Aidan, pasted a smile on her face, and peeked her head above the table. "It's okay...Paul, wow, what a surprise."

Aidan's body shook with laughter, and she stepped on his foot, harder this time.

"Okay, that did hurt," he muttered. Obviously forgetting he was under the table, he bumped his head as he came up from under it. Rubbing the back of his head, he scowled at her before giving the man standing at the end of the table a chin lift. "Chief."

"You're welcome to join us, Paul," Maggie said, glancing at Julia as though checking to see if she wanted her to shift over and let Paul sit beside her. Which, under the circumstances, would probably be smart. But Julia didn't trust Aidan and gave a subtle shake of her head.

Aidan snorted and then moved his foot before she could step on it.

"Yes, please join us, Paul. I'd like your opinion too." Julia smiled at the older man, whose eyes had narrowed at Aidan.

"On?" Paul asked, as he slid in beside Maggie and turned his attention to Julia without his usual wide smile.

"Yes, Julia, tell us about your vision," Aidan said just as the waitress returned with their orders.

"I'll take a coffee, thanks," Paul said, looking at the platter the waitress placed in front of Julia, a beautiful golden omelet filled with corned beef hash and caramelized onions, and topped with Swiss cheese and hollandaise sauce. As a special treat, Caleb had added a slab of Canadian bacon and hash browns too. "On second thought, bring an extra plate. Julia will never be able to eat all of that. Will you, darlin'?"

"No, of course I won't," she said, wondering if anyone noticed the whimper in her voice.

It didn't seem to matter that her throat was sore; she was starving and everything looked so good that she really didn't want to share. She twisted her Sugar Plum Fairy earring while trying to figure out a way not to give Paul her bacon and hash browns. The omelet was big so she didn't mind giving him half...maybe a quarter.

"I don't know about that. I've seen you put away more than me. You should probably just order your own, Chief."

Julia stared at Aidan. She couldn't believe he'd just said that. He had no idea how badly he was messing things up—for him and for her. And if that wasn't bad enough, either Paul's flat stare or hers seemed to egg him on, and Aidan put his arm around her.

"Now, don't be embarrassed. There's nothing wrong with having a healthy appetite, sugarplum." He rocked her against him with a grin, then made an *oomph* sound, and his leg jerked.

This time it wasn't her who stepped on his foot. It appeared to be his father, who then did his best to draw Paul's attention away from Aidan. Maggie got with the program, too, and Julia knew why. She'd seen the brief glance the couple had exchanged. They were joining forces to protect Colin's idiot of a son. It was a beautiful thing, and Aidan seemed oblivious to the fact he was responsible for bringing the couple back together. Okay, so maybe that was overly optimistic, but they were in a much better place than they had been a few days before. Julia at least had something to work with now.

Still, it ended up being the most excruciating hour she'd ever endured. She sagged against the bench after Paul and Maggie left. Colin was talking to Caleb at the counter, waiting for his son, who'd hung back, no doubt to give her grief.

"Stop pretending I'm not here. I'm not leaving until I know we're on the same page."

"Why can't you see it? They're perfect together," she said, standing up to put on her jacket.

He took it from her hand and held it open for her. "If they were, they wouldn't have broken up."

"Oh, please. People break up all the time and get back together," she said, frustrated by the knowledge that, for every step the couple moved toward each other, Aidan was going to make sure they took two steps back. She didn't have time to waste if she planned to be wing-free by the New Year.

"Look, Maggie's a nice lady. I don't want to see her

hurt. If you want to set her up with someone, set her up with Benson. At least they're closer in age."

Fix Maggie up with Paul...Julia stared at Aidan. He'd come up with the perfect solution to her problem. If she got Maggie and Paul together, she'd no longer have to date Paul and Maggie would protect Aidan's job. And then Colin would get jealous and finally clue in to how much he loved Maggie and get the lead out and fight for her.

All right, so it wasn't completely perfect because poor Paul would be left in a lurch in the end. But she could deal with that then. Maybe Hazel's right-hand woman, Delaney, liked older men. She had been hanging around Paul a lot at Thanksgiving.

"Julia?"

"Huh?" She'd gotten so caught up in the idea that she'd forgotten where she was. Over the moon at the thought of no longer having to date Paul while at the same time protecting his feelings, she turned and grabbed Aidan by his leather jacket, giving him a grateful shake. "It's a brilliant idea. Thank you," she said, and went up on her toes and kissed his cheek.

"Yes, indeed, it's nice to know that my son has a *friend*," Colin said from behind her.

Aidan bowed his head.

Julia had a feeling he was saying a silent *Duckety duck, duck, duck.*

Chapter Nine

♥

Aidan walked over to where his father and brothers stood by the fire truck, blocking the upper end of Main Street along with a police car on either side. Volunteers were out in full force decorating the old-fashioned lampposts with evergreen wreaths and wrapping the trees lining the sidewalks in white lights. The Christmas carols being pumped through a sound system into the street competed with Julia calling out directions to the men suspending the garland across the intersection. She had on a Santa hat and was sucking on a candy cane when she wasn't bossing around the workers and calling out hey to everyone she knew.

"Does someone want to explain to me why they didn't do this in the middle of the night instead of on a Sunday afternoon when the stores are open for business?" Aidan asked.

"Your girlfriend's the head of the Christmas committee. Ask her." Liam grinned, nudging Finn with his elbow.

It was Aidan's own fault. He should have kept his

mouth closed at the diner this morning. Actually, there were any number of things he could have done differently to avoid his father getting the wrong idea. His first mistake had been sitting beside Julia. He shouldn't have put his arm around her or called her *sugarplum* either, but it bugged him when Benson started acting all proprietary toward her—calling her *darlin'* and treating her like she didn't have a mind of her own. She had to learn to stand up for herself.

"Don't listen to Dad. He's making a big deal out of nothing. Julia kissed me on the cheek because..." Probably best not to mention his suggestion that she set Maggie up with Paul. "Who knows why she did. It doesn't take much to get the woman excited." Aidan narrowed his eyes at his father, who was silently laughing as he took a drink of what smelled like hot chocolate from his thermos.

"Hey, Dad, you're holding out on us. You didn't mention that Julia kissed him," Liam said.

As a cop, Aidan knew better than to overshare. He'd just indicted himself.

"You're not going to ask why Liam got it into his head that you and Julia are dating?" Finn said, the corner of his mouth twitching as though he held back a laugh.

"No, I'm not. So can we—"

"Okay, I'll tell you then. We heard all about your romantic dance with Julia yesterday, Beast."

Finn might have been trying not to laugh, but Liam wasn't holding back. "Beast," his brother guffawed. "Good one."

"I didn't come up with it. That's what the kids called him. I thought I told you that," Finn said.

"Nope." Liam gestured to Aidan's face. "Maybe now you'll listen to us and get a haircut and lose the beard, you hairy beast."

Finn wasn't finished and talked over Liam, who was still chuckling at his own joke. "Something else our baby brother doesn't know is that you asked Julia to help you pick out Ella Rose's birthday present."

"Now he does. Thanks for that, pal," Aidan said to Finn.

"I was joking with you before, but this is starting to sound serious, big brother. Are you sure you're ready for a relationship? Harper did a number on—"

Aidan cut Liam off. "I'm only going to say this once, so listen up. I'm not dating Julia, nor am I interested in dating her. We're not even friends, more like acquaintances."

His father, who'd been drinking and grinning while his brothers razzed him, lowered his thermos. "That's not how it looked at Jolly Rogers this morning, son. You seemed to know quite a lot about her. She's a sweet girl. I wouldn't want to see her hurt. So maybe you should stop sending out mixed signals. What's she supposed to think when you put your arm around her, play footsie under the table, and act like you're jealous of Paul?"

Jealous of Benson? How did his dad come to that conclusion? It didn't matter one way or another; his father had done it now. Aidan could tell by the expressions on his brothers' faces that he could declare his innocence and non-feelings all he wanted, and they wouldn't believe a single word he said.

If they weren't married, that wouldn't worry him much, but they were. And they told their wives everything, and their wives talked too much, and soon everyone at the manor would know, including his matchmaking grandmother.

"Hate to tell you, but it looks like the chief is making time with your girl, bro."

If he knew what was good for him, he'd ignore Liam. But curiosity got the better of him, and Aidan looked to where he'd last seen Julia. Benson had his arm around her and appeared to be educating her on the finer details of megaphone use. His boss was a condescending jerk. It's a wonder Julia didn't...

"Maggie Stewart, paging Maggie Stewart," Julia yelled into the megaphone that was positioned a couple of inches from Benson's ear.

Aidan laughed when the man reared back.

His brothers stared at him, and his father smiled. "It's good to hear you laugh, son. It's been a while. Take it from your old man. You find a woman who can make you laugh, you hang on to her."

There was nothing he could say to that. He'd seen the truth of it with his own eyes. He'd grown up in a home filled with love and laughter. His marital home hadn't been remotely close to the same. Maybe because he and Harper were both serious, type-A personalities. Well, he didn't have any worries on that count with Santa's little helper. Julia was as far from...*What the hell?* He scrubbed his hands over his face. They were sucking him into their fantasy.

"What's wrong, Dad?" Liam asked.

Aidan lowered his hands to see what warranted the question.

"Nothing. Nothing's wrong," his father said, his brow furrowed. "It's just that Maggie's afraid of heights, and Julia has her climbing the ladder to put lights on the tree."

"She'll be fine. The chief has her covered," Finn said, obviously referring to Benson's hands hovering over her butt and thighs.

"Did I miss something? Are Maggie and the chief dating? I thought you said Aidan was..." Liam trailed off as their father expelled a heavy breath. His brother glanced at him and Finn and made an *I just stepped into that one, didn't I?* face.

This morning at the diner, Aidan had briefly wondered why Julia had acquiesced to his suggestion that she set up Maggie with Paul. It looked like he had his answer. And if he hadn't already guessed what she was up to, Julia turned to look his way just then and gave him a *cat that ate the canary* grin that would have clued him in. The woman was trouble, and he didn't need the laughter rumbling in his chest to tell him so. Or for her to be walking his way with her cheerful stride and sparkling eyes.

"Hello, Gallagher men. We need some extra muscle to get Santa and his sleigh and eight overfed reindeer up on the roof of the town hall. Any volunteers?" she asked as she approached.

"Hey, Julia, we were just talking—"

"About giving you a hand," Aidan interjected before Liam gave Julia the wrong idea.

"The boys will go with you. I have to stay with the

truck. I'll get Marco to bring the ladder engine around
to the back of the town hall. Make sure you all wear
safety gear," his father said before a couple's laughter
sharply drew his attention back to Maggie and Paul.

Aidan grimaced. They were both on the ladder now,
and Maggie had somehow managed to get tangled up in
the string of lights.

"Don't worry. I'll make sure they're careful, Mr.
Gallagher," Julia said, despite the numerous times his
father told her to call him Colin. Her lips pursed in such
a way that not only drew attention to her lush mouth but
indicated that she felt sorry for his old man.

Before she had a chance to put his dad out of his mis-
ery, Aidan began walking up the road. "If you want us
to get Santa on the roof by six, we better get moving."
At six thirty they were lighting up Main Street and all
the shops to kick off the holiday season.

There'd been a time when Aidan had enjoyed the
trappings of Christmas as much as the next guy. But that
had ended the night his mother and sister died.

In his mind's eye, the day played out as if it were
yesterday. Riley with her long chestnut-brown hair and
bright blue eyes tugging on their hands, trying to convince them to get off the couch and go with them to
Boston. Aidan and his brothers had come home for the
weekend to celebrate their dad's birthday. Back then,
not much kept them away from their family and Harmony Harbor.

But nothing their little sister or mom did or said
could motivate them to leave the house that day to go
early Christmas shopping. It was a decision that they'd

all lived to regret. Even after eight years, the pain and guilt were still there. He'd dreamed of them every night for more than a year after the accident. It had always been the same dream.

At the last minute, he'd change his mind and run to the car. He was the one behind the wheel. The one to notice the way the car coming up behind them weaved from one side of the road to the other, the headlights blinding as it barreled up behind them. Trained in tactical driving, Aidan wouldn't have panicked, wouldn't have steered to the right as the other car forced them off the road and over the bridge.

They'd never talked about it, but he imagined his brothers had a similar dream. In theirs, Griffin would have gotten them out of the car within seconds of them hitting the water. Liam and Finn would have saved them when they reached the shore.

Aidan never allowed himself to imagine what his dad's dream would be like. He couldn't let his mind go there. Couldn't let himself contemplate how his father had felt when the call came in and he'd arrived at the scene. How he'd dealt with losing the wife he adored and the little girl he'd called their miracle. After four boys, they'd given up on having a girl. And then Riley arrived late in life. The family's shining star. They'd doted on her, each and every one of them.

That was it, the one thing he hated about being here, being home, especially at this time of year. He locked them down, the thoughts, the feelings, the guilt, and the anger. Shut them off like a tap. He was good at it. He was trained to be. It's how he survived months-long undercover ops. Especially the last one.

He felt someone looking at him and blinked Julia back into focus. Julia with her innocent eyes and sweet smile. She radiated happiness and optimism, and there was a part of him that longed to take her in his arms and hold her, hold her until her joy spread through him and took away the darkness and the pain.

Jesus. He breathed in a lungful of cold, salty sea air to clear his head.

"Don't worry. If you have somewhere else to be, we should be good," she said, nodding to where his brothers had joined a couple of men on the sidewalk in front of the town hall.

"No, it's fine."

"Are you okay? You seem more quiet than usual. Not that you ever talk a lot but, well, you know what I mean."

"Sorry. I've got things on my mind."

"It's your job, isn't it? I know I promised to fix things with Paul, and I've come up with what I think is the perfect solution. I just haven't had a chance to put my plan into action yet."

Good. This was exactly what he needed. A reminder that the woman walking beside him held an odd and unexplained obsession with his family and the last thing he should be feeling is this incomprehensible attraction to her. "No. No trying to fix things for me, okay?"

"Gosh, you say that like you're nervous. Are you forgetting how well my idea for Thanksgiving with your daughter worked?"

"No, and I appreciated your help with her birthday present too. But I'm okay, Julia. And you have more than enough on your plate."

"I know." She groaned, and then shrugged with a wry smile. "I'm getting close to scratching off a couple things on my list. Life will be much less stressful once I do." She gave him a look that made him twitchy. "So...are your daughter and ex coming to the Festival of Lights?"

"Yeah, why?" He had to work on Ella Rose's birthday, so he'd organized a family party for her at the manor. Everyone would join them for dinner and cake, and they'd all go to the festival together. Of course, Harper had only agreed if she came along. He was hoping she'd bow out. She wasn't exactly a fan of the holiday.

Harper had her own philosophical reasons for skipping Christmas, and Aidan had been more than happy to go along with her. It wasn't until Ella Rose was three that they started celebrating the holiday. Following Harper's lead, they went Santa-free. It was just one of the many reasons they never spent Christmas in Harmony Harbor.

Julia was giving him an odd look. He cleared his throat. "Sorry, did you say something?"

"Yes, I said, 'you're a little intense.' I was just going to suggest that you stake out a spot in front of Books and Beans if they're coming. It'll be less crowded, and not only will you have a great view of the harbor, but I'm serving hot chocolate and cookies. And my window is fantabulous, if I do say so myself. Total Christmas magic." She did a little shimmy that was cute and kind of sexy too. "I can't wait to see the kids' faces when I hit the lights. Your nieces and nephews will be there. So, what do you say? Want me to save a spot for you?"

His Spidey sense went off. His answer seemed important to her. Too important. But what was he supposed to do? His whole family would be there. "Yeah, sounds like a plan."

* * *

"How much time do I have?" Julia asked Poppy and Byron, who'd agreed to help her out tonight. She'd given her staff the night off to enjoy the evening.

Poppy lifted the blackout fabric Julia had hung in front of the coffee shop window while Byron peeked under the one over the door. "Depends on how fast Delaney drives down Main Street and how well Hazel's wand is working," Byron said, a touch of sarcasm in his voice.

Delaney was driving down Main Street with Hazel sitting in the back of a convertible waving her wand. When she pointed the wand, the lights in the stores and in the section of the street would go on. At the bottom of the hill and Main Street, Delaney would stop the convertible, and Hazel would make a sweeping arc with the wand, and the boats that were decorated in the harbor would turn on their Christmas lights.

"I love the wand. I think it adds a touch of magic to the night," Julia said.

"Of course you do, sugarplum," Byron said,

tweaking one of her gossamer wings as she bent over to tie her ballet slippers. She'd added the wings to her plum-colored ballet costume so the children would know she was a fairy. She'd been pleasantly surprised to discover that her ballet costume still fit. Then again, her body hadn't changed all that much since she was in her teens.

Emmeline had insisted Julia take dance and singing lessons so she would be prepared to take either the American Ballet Theatre or Broadway by storm. Which, of course, hadn't happened. Julia didn't have the body type of a professional dancer or the voice and theatrical ability of a professional actor. But, if her performance of the Sugar Plum Fairy dance drew smiles from her audience tonight, she'd consider the years of ballet lessons worthwhile.

"I can't see much from here, but it shouldn't be long. You might as well get in the window," Poppy said.

Julia agreed and followed her friend out of the coffee shop to the picture window at the front of the bookstore. Julia had bought heavy, midnight-blue fabric and painted tiny stars with silver glitter to provide the backdrop. Mr. O'Malley had let her borrow two artificial white trees decorated with blue fairy lights to place on either side, and she'd hung snowflakes from the ceiling. Under each of the trees were presents wrapped in blue and silver foil with nutcrackers standing on top of them. She'd special ordered the Mouse King, Clara, Uncle Drosselmeyer, and the Cavalier figurines for the window, along with four times what she normally ordered of *The Nutcracker* book.

"I'll go out and take a few shots of Main Street," Poppy said with a hand on the pull cord.

Once Julia had taken her place, facing away from the window and posing in the fifth position, she heard the *swoosh* of the curtains opening.

"Remember, give the kids a couple of minutes to look at the window before you start to dance. I want to get some shots of their faces when they realize you're not a mannequin. Break a leg," Poppy said, and headed back to the coffee shop. "Byron, get off your phone and pay attention. I'll knock on the door at the exact moment you're supposed to hit the lights."

Julia heard Byron say something about bossy baby sisters and was about to comment herself, but the sound of Aidan's voice distracted her. It was so close that she was positive he was leaning against the window. A woman responded. His ex-wife, Julia assumed, and her heart gave a nervous flutter. For her plan to work, she had to get five minutes alone with Dr. Harper Granger. Julia thought her best chance of doing so was to have the woman sign the copies of *Where Evil Lurks* that she had in stock.

"Showtime, sugarplum," Byron called out a second before the exterior Christmas lights went on. Inside, the spotlights in the window illuminated the space where Julia stood. She'd changed the bulbs to soft purple and pink. Silently, she counted in her head to a hundred as Tchaikovsky's "Dance of the Sugar Plum" came through the store's speakers.

From outside came the sounds of *oohs* and *aahs* and clapping. She hoped it looked as magical as it had last night when she'd done a trial run. "Okay, sugarplum, you're on," she murmured to herself, smiling when the movements of the dance brought her face-to-face with her surprised audience. Her smile widened when the children pressed their faces to the glass. For one brief and shining moment, their wide eyes reflected the belief that magic was real. And that made all the long nights preparing for today worthwhile. Because to her, there was no greater gift to give a child than the belief in miracles and magic.

George pushed her way past the bigger children to the front and waved at Julia. Mia and a little girl with a heart-shaped face and long wavy hair and blue eyes joined her. If she had any doubt that this was Ella Rose, Aidan dispelled it.

When he'd talked about his daughter the other day, Julia had seen a hint of the man now standing on the other side of the glass looking down at his little girl like she was his sun and moon and stars. To see his love for his daughter shining from his eyes up close and personal nearly undid her. Underneath his grumpy, badass persona beat the heart of a warm and loving father. Now more than ever, Julia was determined to see her plan through.

Crouching beside Ella Rose, Aidan's gaze lifted to meet Julia's through the glass, a slow smile curving his lips. Maybe because he didn't smile often, it felt like a precious gift when he did, like you meant something to him, like you were special. The thought made her miss a step, but she quickly recovered and ended the dance by pirouetting off her tiny stage and out of the spotlight.

Her hands trembled when she reached for the warm hooded cape she planned to wear outside. She didn't want to miss the entire lighting ceremony, but she wasn't sure she could face Aidan. Last summer, she'd honestly thought he'd crushed any feelings she'd had for him. Some people would say, *What feelings? You shared a kiss. Big deal.* But they were the same people who didn't believe in soul mates and love at first sight. Over the past few days, as she'd gotten to know the man behind the fantasy, she'd sensed those feelings coming back to life.

Tonight had made it worse. Because where she'd once believed there wasn't the remotest possibility of Aidan ever returning her feelings, something about his smile made her think he wasn't completely immune to her.

She drew the cape around her and walked under the arch to the coffee shop. Behind the counter, Byron stopped filling small paper cups with hot chocolate to clap. "You're the star of the festival, sugarplum." He picked up his phone from the counter. "Poppy said to tell you she got some great shots."

"I couldn't have done it without you two. Come on, I don't want you to miss all the fun because of me." She picked up the tray of hot chocolate. "Can you grab the cookies, please?" Mackenzie, her friend who owned Truly Scrumptious, had made Clara and the Mouse King cookies. They tasted as scrumptious as they looked.

"Trade," Byron said, replacing her tray of hot chocolate with a tray of cookies. "You're more likely to get trampled than me."

As soon as she stepped out the door, Julia was greeted by cheers and clapping. She smiled and curtsied. "Thank you. Is everyone enjoying the Festival of Lights?" she asked, doing her best not to search the sea of people for Aidan. From the number of *yes*es though, it sounded like the event was a hit.

George hurried over with Aidan's daughter. Well, Ella Rose didn't so much hurry as she was dragged along by George. "This is our friend Julia. She owns the bookstore and coffee shop. Your dad got your present here. You should get him to bring you to storytime. It's fun," George said to Ella Rose.

"You're one of my favorite storytime kids, you know that," Julia said, giving George a hug. She smiled at the little girl looking at her shyly from beneath her bangs. "Happy early birthday, Ella Rose. Did you like your present your daddy bought you?"

She nodded, giving Julia a tentative smile.

"Can you say thanks to Julia, pumpkin? She helped me pick out your present."

Butterflies pirouetted in Julia's stomach. She should have known Aidan wouldn't let his little girl out of his sight. Her smile wobbled as she lifted her gaze to meet his. There was something about the way he looked at her tonight that was different from any time before. It felt like maybe he was seeing her for the first time.

Ella Rose glanced from Aidan to Julia. "Thank you. It was a really nice present."

"I'm glad you liked it. Your daddy said it had to be special because you're a very special little girl."

Ella Rose smiled up at Aidan.

"Would you guys like a cookie?" Julia offered.

George helped herself to three.

"George," Aidan said when she went for a fourth.

"They're for all the family, Uncle Aidan," the little girl said, not at all fazed by his growly voice.

He rolled his eyes, but the corner of his mouth twitched.

Noticing Ella Rose looking over her shoulder, Julia followed her gaze. Harper was speaking to a group of well-dressed older women. Julia couldn't help herself and groaned.

"What's wrong?" Aidan asked.

"Your ex-wife's talking to Mrs. Bradford and her friends."

"And...?"

"Since she took the town to court over me being named chair of the Christmas committee instead of her, I don't imagine she's here to do anything other than make trouble."

"You might be surprised. That was quite the performance, Julia. The whole night has been great."

She warmed at his praise. Especially since she had the feeling he wasn't exactly a fan of Christmas. "Oh gosh, you're going to miss the best part. Hurry. Get to the front so Ella Rose can see the harbor. You too, George."

Julia hung back, realizing her earlier plan to get Harper alone in the store wasn't going to work. It was already seven thirty, and Aidan's ex had at least a forty-five-minute drive ahead of her. It was now or never. Aidan towered over most people, and he had George in one arm and Ella Rose in the other, so it wasn't hard to see where he was. Julia offered the parade goers cookies and waved to her friends in the crowd as she inched her way toward Harper.

"There she is. That's her. The hussy, making a spectacle of herself. You should be ashamed of yourself, Julia Landon. I'm going to have you charged with public indecency." Mrs. Bradford practically shouted her charges as she held up her phone. "We have all the proof we need right here."

Julia's cheeks heated as people turned. She wouldn't let the older woman ruin everyone's memory of the night by causing a scene. "I'm sorry you were offended, Mrs. Bradford. That was never my intention." She moved to walk away, and the older woman grabbed her arm, causing the cookies to fall off the tray.

One minute there was no one in front of her and then Aidan was there, removing Mrs. Bradford's hand from her arm. "Don't touch her again. Are you okay?" he asked Julia.

"Assault! He assaulted me! Mavis, call Chief Benson. I think my wrist is broken."

Chapter Ten

♥

The front of Books and Beans was a crime scene. All they needed was the yellow tape. And for the Sugar Plum Fairy to act on the murderous intent Aidan saw in her purple eyes. Julia hugged herself, her gaze flicking to where one of his colleagues took Mrs. Bradford's statement.

"She ruined everything. Now all anyone will remember is this. They won't remember how magical the night was." Julia looked up at him, the Christmas lights glinting off the tiara she wore in her dark hair, which was gathered in a bun.

He thought she might be right, but he didn't want to make her feel worse than she already did. An unhappy and angry Julia was something he hadn't seen before. She usually sparkled with happiness and light—like she'd swallowed the sun. He imagined that's why people were drawn to her. Himself included, he thought as he remembered his reaction to her dance in the window. Like everything she did, Julia had put her heart and soul into tonight.

He glanced at the bitter old woman finishing up her statement, feeling a little murderous himself. "Most people won't even know it happened. The biggest crowds were at the town hall and down by the harbor. All any of us standing here will remember is you and your dance." He stroked her cheek, holding up his glitter-coated finger. "You sparkled. Don't let her ruin your night."

"If it was just me, I wouldn't. But it's not. It's you I'm worried about, Aidan. I've been working on an idea that would prove to Paul that you're an asset to HHPD, the best detective on the force. Nothing elaborate, just a couple of small things that would show him he's wrong about you. And now, thanks to Mrs. Bradford, I'm going to have to think of something really big." She sighed. "It was sweet of you to intervene, but I really wish you hadn't. I can take care of myself, you know."

He put his hands on her shoulders and ducked to look her in the eyes. "So can I. It's not your job to make things right for me, Julia. As much as you look like the Sugar Plum Fairy, you aren't her. You can't grant wishes and make everyone's dreams come true."

There was something behind the shimmer in her eyes, an emotion, a secret he couldn't read. He had the feeling though that he'd just caught a glimpse of the real Julia. The woman behind the many masks she wore.

She looked away and murmured, "The Sugar Plum Fairy doesn't grant wishes or make dreams come true. She rules the Kingdom of Sweets and plans the festivities."

"There you go. The perfect job for you. Now—"
He broke off at the sight of his boss pushing his way
through the crowd.

Julia followed his gaze, made an *eep* sound in her
throat, and wriggled out from under Aidan's hands.
Pretty sure he recognized the look that came into her
eyes, he said, "Do not..." She took off. He made a grab
for her, but couldn't get a hold of her cape. It was slip-
pery and so was she.

The muscle in Aidan's jaw flexed and his hands
balled into fists when she threw herself into Benson's
arms. Aidan told himself it was because he knew what
she was up to, not that she was being held by another
man, a man old enough to be her father.

"Oh, Paul, I was so scared. Sh-she threatened me
and called me horrible names. She ruined everything.
Mackenzie spent hours making special Nutcracker
cookies and look, look what Mrs. Bradford did. She
grabbed my arm and the cookies..." A sob broke in
Julia's voice as she gestured to the sidewalk. Unless she
was a better actress than Aidan had given her credit for,
she wasn't faking.

He speared the old woman being comforted by her
friends with a hard stare.

Mrs. Bradford gasped, calling to Aidan's colleague,
who'd been walking toward Benson, "Officer! He's
threatening me! He just threatened me again."

Benson glared at him, and Julia did the same before
returning her full attention to his boss, wrapping her
arms around Paul's waist to no doubt stop him from
confronting Aidan.

"Don't listen to a word she says, Paul. Aidan didn't do anything wrong but try and..." She hesitated before saying, "protect me. He knows how close you and I are, and he wanted to make sure nothing happened to me. And no matter what Mrs. Bradford says, he didn't so much as lay a finger on her. I heard him. He said in a very quiet and gentlemanly manner, 'Ma'am, will you kindly unhand Miss Julia.'"

Liam and his father joined Aidan on the sidewalk. Finn and Griffin had taken the women and younger kids home. George and Mia had stayed behind to keep Ella Rose company. They, along with Harper, were hanging out inside Books and Beans.

"So, were you channeling Rhett Butler or is Julia channeling Scarlett O'Hara?" Liam asked.

"What do you think?" he muttered.

Until that moment, he'd been more concerned about Julia than himself. He hadn't given much thought to how this looked to his ex and his daughter. He wondered if Harper would hold the incident against him and deny him access to Ella Rose or if he'd scared his little girl. If he lost his job, it might be a moot point. And, as he'd just realized, there was a good chance of that happening. The Bradford family were well known in town and held some influence.

If the tense expression on his father's face was any indication, Aidan was probably right, and his job actually was on the line. At least that's what he thought until he noticed Maggie moving to Benson's side. Looked like a small win for the Sugar Plum Fairy tonight. She'd succeeded in making his dad jealous

or, at the very least, aware he wasn't the only game
in town.

"It's all right. I think I get it, darlin'. You go inside
and get warm. You're shivering. You too, Maggie. I
won't be long."

Aidan frowned at Julia. She wasn't just shivering;
her teeth were chattering. Her cheeks were flushed
too. Probably because, in order to plead Aidan's case,
she'd worked herself into a state. And she looked like
she planned to keep pleading it. Aidan caught her
eye and jerked his thumb at the door, mouthing, *Go.
Now.*

She looked like she might object but then sighed and
moved toward the door.

"Chief. Chief Benson. If you value your job, you will
fire this man." Mrs. Bradford stabbed a finger in Aidan's direction and then at Julia. "I want her charged
with lewd behavior."

Julia turned, looking every inch the ticked-off fairy.
"That sounds like you're threatening the chief, Mrs.
Bradford. Is that what you're doing? Or is it a bribe in
disguise? Because from—"

Okay, if Benson wasn't going to put a stop to this, he
was. He cut off Julia. "Do me a favor and . . ." He didn't
think telling her to put a sock in it would help so he said,
"Check on Ella Rose and Harper."

"They're still here? In my store?"

The thread of excitement in her voice caused a nervous twitch in his left eye. Which got progressively
worse when he reluctantly nodded and she fast-walked
to the door.

He felt a little better when Liam said, "I'll go check on the girls."

"If you don't mind, keep an eye on Julia too."

His brother nodded and headed for the store.

Their father, who hadn't taken his eyes off Maggie, turned his attention to the chief when the door to Books and Beans closed behind her. "Paul, we've been friends a long time, and I've never interfered in you doing your job as you saw fit. But you should know, if I feel my son is being unfairly treated in any way, I will make a stink this town will never forget."

Whoa. Aidan wasn't expecting that. His typically mild-mannered father had just shocked the hell out of him. Too bad he hadn't videoed it. His brothers would never believe him. But while he appreciated his father standing up for him, Aidan preferred to fight his battles on his own. Besides, no matter that he wasn't a fan of his boss, his dad and Benson had been friends for more than thirty-five years.

"I'll treat your son as I would any of my officers, Colin. If you have a problem with that, take it up with the mayor."

"Take up what with me?" Hazel Winters asked as she walked toward them wearing a full-length fur coat with a matching hat on her head. It was the same color as her hair. She looked like a bear.

She was followed by her assistant, Delaney, a woman Aidan had gone out with for drinks a couple of times. Beautiful and ambitious, she was exactly the type of woman he was attracted to.

"Hey, stranger. It's been a while," Delaney said,

coming to stand beside him when Benson took the
mayor aside. The sky-high heels on Delaney's domina-
trix boots put her almost eye level with Aidan.

She was a strong woman who knew what she
wanted, and right now the look in her eyes seemed to
suggest she wanted him. A few months back, he would
have been more than happy to oblige. Not now though.
And he had an uncomfortable feeling he knew exactly
where to lay the blame for his lack of interest—a cute
fairy princess with big purple eyes.

His father glanced from him to Delaney, and then,
apparently assuming Aidan was distracted, sidled over
to speak with Mrs. Bradford and her cronies.

"Yeah, it has been. How are you doing?" he responded to Delaney while keeping an eye on his father.

"Ready to ring in the New Year if I make it until
then."

"Not a fan of Christmas, I take it?" Another point in
her favor.

"In moderation. You might not have noticed this, being a native, but no one does small in Harmony Harbor.
They take 'go big or go home' literally. Christmas is no
exception. Especially now that Julia has taken over."

Aidan stiffened at the faint curl of Delaney's lip.
"What's your problem with Julia?"

"Oh God, don't tell me. Someone else in this town
who thinks the woman walks on water. Forget I said
anything." She straightened when Hazel marched over
to Mrs. Bradford with Benson following behind, looking like he'd rather be anywhere else but there. Delaney
frowned. "What's going on?"

Aidan didn't have to give her the lowdown; Mrs. Bradford took care of that for him. Then the mayor went all mama bear on the older woman. No one talked smack about Julia around Hazel and got away with it. According to the mayor, Aidan was a hero for protecting Julia. Either that or Hazel was singing his praises in order to make it up to the Gallaghers for partnering with Paige Townsend last year.

"I could strangle Julia. All my work to get Hazel re-elected will be for nothing if Julia continues upsetting Mrs. Bradford and Hazel has to keep defending her."

"It wasn't Julia's fault. She—"

Delaney waved a dismissive hand. "Please, don't. I can't tell you how sick I am of hearing how wonderful Julia is. Trust me, no one is that sweet and kind. She has something to hide just like the rest of us."

Before he had a chance to ask Delaney what she was hiding, she pasted a fake smile on her face and walked over to the older women, no doubt in hopes of smoothing things over.

Benson gestured for his dad as he walked Aidan's way. "Before you get bent out of shape, Colin, this won't be on Aidan's record, nor will he lose pay. It's just to pacify the Bradfords, husband and wife. They have you on cell phone video, Aidan. You grabbed Mrs. Bradford's arm, and while you didn't leave a mark, the expression on your face... Well, let's just say it probably would play in her favor in court."

The last thing Aidan needed was for this to go before a judge.

Benson must have realized where his mind went.

"Keeping this out of court is the reason you'll be off for a week. I'd also like you to consider taking an anger management course."

"I don't need an anger management course." Benson and his father shared a glance. "You both know this is bullshit. But whatever, if I have to take a week off to make it go away, I don't care. What I do care about is what Mrs. Bradford pulled on Julia. She can't get away with it."

"Does that sound like she's getting away it?" Benson asked, nodding at the mayor.

From what Aidan could make of the conversation, Hazel was on the phone with Mr. Bradford, threatening to offer one of her empty buildings on Main Street to Bradford's major competitor if the man didn't control his wife. It didn't seem like Hazel was too worried about her reelection campaign. Delaney on the other hand...

Byron Harte, who Aidan had spotted hanging out in a dark corner near the older women, came out of his hiding place to saunter over. "Chiefs, Detective, anyone want to give a statement? Other than *no comment*?"

Ever since the mermaid incident the Hartes hadn't been a fan of Aidan's. After he'd brought Julia to the station to question her in Olivia's disappearance, he'd become public enemy number one. They took every opportunity they got to make him look bad. No doubt they were salivating over this story.

Still... "You wanna help Julia out, talk to Hazel. Get her to insist Mrs. Bradford take out a full-page ad praising Julia's job on the Festival of Lights. And when you guys run your coverage on tonight, make sure you use the word *magical*, a lot."

Byron gave him an appraising look. "I'll do that."

"Harte," Benson said, "if you could downplay the incident between my detective and Mrs. Bradford, I'd appreciate it."

"As would I," his father added.

Aidan doubted that saying anything would do any good and kept quiet. So he was more than a little surprised to hear Byron say, "What incident?" as he walked away.

For the first time since Aidan had moved back to Harmony Harbor, he wasn't feeling like every step he made was the wrong one. It was an odd feeling. And not entirely unwelcome.

Liam held open the door for Mia, George, Harper, and Ella Rose. "Everything good here?" his brother asked, taking George and Mia by the hands.

"Yeah, everything's fine," Aidan assured him.

"Good, good," he said, glancing to where Harper had stopped to put on Ella Rose's mittens.

Aidan's Spidey sense went off. "What did Julia do?"

"How did you...?" Liam looked down at the girls and then back at Harper, who began walking their way. "Looks like you're about to find out."

"I thought I told you to keep an eye on Julia."

"She's sneaky. It might be great though. Just, you know, be chill." Liam and the girls said goodbye to his dad and headed to where his brother had parked down the street.

The lights in Books and Beans went out, leaving

the store in complete darkness. The sound of dead bolts sliding across the door reverberated in the cold night air. The streetlights glinted off the crystals in Julia's tiara as she peeked from behind the glass. He made a gun with his fingers and aimed at the window in the front door, and the tiara disappeared. That told him everything he needed to know. Whatever she had done, he wasn't going to like it. He wasn't going to like it one little bit.

"I had a very interesting chat with Julia," Harper said.

"Is that right?" He leaned past her to lift Ella Rose into his arms. "You must be tired, pumpkin. Did you have fun?" She nodded and rubbed her eyes. "Say bye to Grandpa."

Colin kissed Ella Rose's cheek and gave her a hug. "It was good to see you, poppet." His father gave Aidan's ex a polite nod. "Thanks for bringing her, Harper. Don't be a stranger."

Harper looped her arm through Aidan's. "Actually, like I just mentioned to Aidan, I had an interesting conversation with Julia. She had an idea that might work for all of us."

His father raised his eyebrows at him. He shrugged, so his dad asked the question Aidan was afraid to, "Really, what is it?"

"Julia heard we had a home in Newton and has a friend who wants to buy there. She wondered if we'd be interested in selling. I was shocked to find out how much we could get for the house, Aidan. Anyway, Julia made a really good case for us moving here."

Aidan swallowed. "Here? You mean you and Ella Rose moving here... to Harmony Harbor?"

"Yes. Julia's read *Where Evil Lurks*. She actually has several copies in stock. She wondered if I had ever given any thought to writing fiction. She says there's a market for psychological thrillers and is positive that, given my talent and expertise, she can help me get published."

"Yeah, but you don't have to move here to write," Aidan said, positive that with Julia involved, there was something more going on, and he needed to get to the bottom of it. Because there's no way Harper would move from Newton unless she had a really good reason to.

Refusing to meet his gaze, Harper reached over to stroke Ella Rose's cheek and smiled. "I know, but I've been thinking about what you said, about how important it is for Ella Rose to spend time with you, and you're right, it is. This will make it easier for all of us to be..." She glanced at him and quickly changed the subject. "If Julia can help me get published, it will be the perfect way for me to feel productive again without taking time from Ella Rose."

His father was grinning from ear to ear. "If Julia said she can get you published, I have no doubt she can. She's quite the little miracle worker."

Harper laughed. "If she can pull off all she promised, it probably would qualify as a miracle. I'm not holding my breath though. But she has given me lots to think about."

And there it was, exactly what he'd been afraid of. Harper gave him a look that was frighteningly similar to the one Delaney had given him earlier. If Julia had planted an idea in his ex's head that moving to Harmony Harbor would lead to them getting back together, he might be the one strangling her instead of Delaney.

Harper continued. "To be honest, after speaking to Mrs. Bradford, I wasn't sure what to make of Julia... How did that turn out, by the way? I saw everything if you need me to talk to your boss."

"Thanks, but it's all good. Come on, we better get going. It's late." And he had someone he wanted to see before the night was over.

Chapter Eleven

♥

*A*idan *smiled that slow, sexy smile of his just before he lifted his gun and fired. The glass shattered, and the...*

A shrill beeping sound startled Julia, pulling her out of the story. Her initial thought was that she'd put on the teapot and had forgotten to turn off the burner. She blinked and opened her eyes. She'd been trying to get deeper into her character's point of view by typing with her eyes closed. It hadn't worked as well as she'd hoped. But it had ensured that she didn't see the smoke...*Smoke!* There was smoke filling her living room. Again.

Duckety duck, duck, duck.

The annoying voice on the smoke detector bleated *fire, fire.*

"Julia, open the damn door!"

Frantically searching under the papers littering her desk for her cell phone, she ignored the voice. Though she was impressed. It was amazing how real Adrian sounded. Like he was right outside...*Wait a minute.* He

was calling *her* name, not Gillian's. Crap, it was Aidan.
Double crap, she knew why he was here. She'd thought
she'd have until morning to face him.

"Hang on! I—" She heard a loud bang at the same
time she found her phone. "I'm coming!" she called,
running to the outside entry door as she punched in the
assigned number for the alarm company.

At the same time she realized there was no dial tone,
Aidan kicked in her door. It bounced off the wall and
the hulking shadow of a man filled the open doorway.
If she hadn't recognized his voice, she'd be terrified.
Given the intimidating expression on his face, she won-
dered if maybe she should still be afraid.

Fire, the smoke detector bleated again. Right, fire,
smoke. "Hurry, I need your phone!" She made grabby
motions with her fingers.

He looked at her like she'd lost her mind and strode
into the room. "Your alarm is connected to the station.
They'll be on their way. Where's the fire? Do you have
an extinguisher?"

"No, no, I don't need the fire department. I need your
phone." She rushed forward. He didn't seem to understand the urgency of the situation, and she began patting
him down.

He reached in his pocket, punching in a code before
handing her his phone. Of course his would be password protected.

"Thanks," she said to his back as he prowled around
her apartment, no doubt looking for the source of the
smoke. "I think my nachos are on fire."

She made a face at his muttered, "You have got to

be shitting me." And then went to look up the alarm company's number on her phone, only to realize she couldn't access it because her cell was dead. "Duck."

She raced to her desk and searched for the alarm company's business card while muttering to herself, "I need the number. Where would I put the number for the alarm company? Laptop. Of course." *Laptop, no!* It was on and open for Aidan to see. She slammed her laptop shut at the same time the oven door banged closed.

Aidan strode from the kitchen wearing her burned oven mitt and carrying a charbroiled tray of smoking ash. "It's usually on the unit," he said dryly before heading out the door.

Which went to prove that the man didn't miss a thing, even her half-whispered conversation with herself.

At the return of his heavy footsteps, she turned her back to her desk, attempting to use her body as a screen. Widening her stance and her arms, she wrapped her fingers around the edge of the desk and leaned back in hopes of concealing any evidence of her book from his all-seeing cop's eyes.

He glanced at her and then did a double take. She thought she heard a muttered "Jesus," before he retrieved his phone from her hand and continued across the living room, dodging a basket of laundry, a box of decorations she'd yet to put up on the tree, and a half-eaten bowl of cereal.

Wondering what was with the double take, she looked around. She didn't see anything out of the ordinary. Sure her place was a little messy, but he was a guy. He probably wouldn't even notice. She thought of something he might notice and looked down.

Yep, that was probably the reason for the look. It was obvious she was cold, and her body-hugging black T-shirt read SANTA'S FAVORITE HO with the jolly old elf *ho-ho-ho*ing, paired with black-and-white plaid flannel sleep pants.

When Aidan reached the other side of the living room, he placed the cell phone between his shoulder and ear and raised the window. "Yeah, it's Aidan Gallagher. The call from 232 Main Street is a false alarm. That's her. Five times, is that so? I'll tell her, thanks."

"It wasn't five false alarms. It was four," she said to his back before turning to bury a paperback copy of *Warrior's Kiss* and her contract for *Warrior's Touch* under some paper and turn her notepad upside down while doing a visual search for any other incriminating evidence.

"Doesn't matter. You still broke the record for false alarms in a six-week time frame. Dispatch says Mrs. Rosenbloom had three."

"Are they charging me?"

"No." He answered his ringing phone and then bowed his head. "Hello, Dad. Yes, she's fine. Is that right? Nachos. No, smoke's not too bad. Okay, I'll do that. Don't remind me," he grumbled, and then disconnected.

Whatever his dad said to Aidan didn't improve his already not-so-happy mood. Which was just one more reason to put off talking about the suggestion she'd made to Harper and why. Besides that, she wasn't exactly equipped to handle him tonight. She was tired, and her throat had passed sore an hour before.

"I really appreciate you dropping by, but it's late, and I have an early day." She forced a smile and moved to see him out...her broken door. She barely managed to stifle an anguished moan. She couldn't face the thought of repairing the door tonight.

He lifted his chin to the left of the kitchen. "Is that your bedroom?"

She ignored her inner hussy, who yelled *Who needs a bed* and suggested Julia throw herself on the floor at his feet. Her inner hussy was way more optimistic about their chances of getting lucky tonight.

"Yes, but I don't see... What do you think you're doing?" she asked as he walked over and opened her bedroom door. Umm, more like shoved it open. The clothes that had been hanging over her door this morning must have fallen off when she closed it.

"I'm not going anywhere until you tell me what you said to Harper. You're tired? Fine, you can talk to me from your bed while I fix your door." He looked around her bedroom. "If we can find your bed."

She grabbed a pink lace bra off the doorknob and held it behind her back. "I've been busy. I haven't had time to tidy up."

"What, like in a year?"

"Very funny. I'm sure your room isn't any better."

"Sugarplum, my bedroom didn't look this bad when I was a kid."

She kind of liked that he called her *sugarplum* but could do without the sarcasm. She scooted past him to scoop up her bras and panties and any other embarrassing items that were lying on the floor...and on the bed...and on her dresser. And half sticking out of her nightstand drawer! As breezily as she could, she moved to the front of the nightstand in hopes of blocking his view. "It's a little smoky in here. Maybe you should open that window too?"

She smiled. He sighed.

As soon as his back was turned, she thigh-checked the nightstand drawer closed. Only it didn't close. Instead it acted like a rocket launcher, and her fluorescent pink vibrator sailed through the air to land with a splash in the goldfish bowl sitting on the bench at the end of her bed. She slapped her hands over her mouth, releasing a muffled "I've killed Eric and Ariel!"

Aidan looked from the fishbowl to her and started to laugh, a deep rumbly sound that she would have enjoyed if it wasn't at her expense and if..."It's not funny! My fish are drowning. Save them!"

That made him laugh harder, and his shoulders started to shake. "Death by vibrator. Not a bad way to go."

"That's a horrible thing to say, Aidan Gallagher." She cautiously removed the vibrator from the water, her shoulders sagging in relief when Eric and Ariel swam to the surface. "And FYI, this is not a vibrator. It's a personal massager." She rubbed it against the nape of her neck, trying not to make a face when cool water trickled down her back. "See? You should try it."

He pressed his lips together and slowly shook his head, his eyes glinting with amusement. It took him a minute before he said, "Yeah, no. I'll just go fix your door, thanks. I've got a toolbox in my trunk. I'll be right back."

If she had more energy, she would have cheered. It appeared that he wasn't going to interrogate her about her conversation with his ex. At least not tonight. "Okay. Thank you. I appreciate it."

"FYI, I'm not going anywhere until I get some answers." He patted her arm when she groaned, and then he frowned. "You're hot."

Her inner hussy preened. "Why? Because I have a vibra...personal massager?"

"What? No. You're hot, as in you're burning up."

Well, that was embarrassing. But at least there was one benefit to feeling crappy. *Two,* she thought when he rested his palm on her forehead and slid it down to her cheek. He had wonderful hands. Big and strong and just a little bit rough, and she began thinking of what his wonderful man hands...

"Do you have any other symptoms?"

"I can barely swallow, and I'm tired, like really, really tired." She exaggerated a little in hopes he'd feel sorry for her and let the interrogation go for tonight. Though she really was tired.

"You're off the hook. For now. Come on, let's get you into bed." He swept everything off her mattress and onto the floor. "Okay, knock off the outraged look. It's not like you didn't already have a crapload of stuff on the floor. Don't worry, I'll pick everything up once you get into bed." He held back the comforter and sheets and, looking a little uncomfortable, said, "You should probably lose your pajama bottoms. They're flannel."

Once he'd covered her with only a sheet, he picked up a pillow that had fallen to the floor, fluffed it, and gently lifted her head to tuck it underneath. Then he crouched beside the bed and stroked her hair from her face. "You want something to drink—water or tea?"

"For a badass, you're pretty good at this," she said, doing her best to hide the fact that she was feeling a little choked up and incredibly touched. She blamed the emotional response on being so tired she couldn't think straight, but really, she knew better.

It had been a long time since someone had taken care of her like this. Oh, she knew all she had to do was pick up the phone and her family, Hazel, or any of her friends would come running. But as much as she liked to help others, she wasn't very good about asking or accepting help for herself.

The corner of his mouth lifted, and he straightened. "I'll get you some tea and ice water. And then I'm calling Finn."

"No, please don't bother him about this. It's just a sore throat."

"Better to be safe than sorry. Besides, what good is it having a doctor in the family if you can't use him?"

Julia must have dosed off because when she opened her eyes Aidan was placing a cup of tea and a glass of ice water on her nightstand. "Finn'll be here in twenty minutes. I couldn't find any ibuprofen. I checked the bathroom and kitchen. Anyplace else I should look?"

"No, I try to be careful with what I put in my body. I've been taking zinc and vitamin C. More natural, you know."

His lips twitched. "I've seen the inside of your cupboards and fridge, Julia. You have more junk food than a corner store." He leaned in to adjust her pillows behind her back before handing her the glass of water. "Drink up."

Brought down by kindness, she thought with a sigh. She took a couple sips of water before returning the glass to the nightstand. "Aidan, I'm sorry for butting into your business with your ex. I was just trying to help."

He sat on the edge of her bed, leaning over to pick up a book he'd swept to the floor. Placing his elbows on his knees, he turned the paperback in his hands and glanced at her. "That sounded a lot like *I'm sorry, but it was for your own good.*"

"Maybe. A little. You can't share custody if you live nearly an hour away from Harper, and you can't rebuild your relationship with Ella Rose if you don't spend more time with her. Not to mention your payments for that house could feed a small country."

"They're not that high."

"They're ridiculous. And why do they need a house with four bedrooms anyway? It's huge."

"Yeah, and that right there is the problem. How and why do you know anything about the house?"

"The how is easy. Google. And the why isn't as creepy-stalkerish as you're making it sound. You told me about your payments, and I wanted to see what kind of house would cost that much. I was curious, that's all."

"But you didn't stop there. You lied to Harper and told her you had an interested buyer."

"A lie means saying something with a deliberate intent to deceive, and what I did is more like embellish the truth."

"A lie by any other name is still a lie."

"How about an alternative fact? All right, all right," she said when he gave her a look. "I have a customer. She's one of the top relocation Realtors in Boston. I guarantee she'll sell your house for top dollar, and fast. I don't know if you realize this or not, but your house is in a much-sought-after neighborhood. It's like no one in Newton sells their home until they have a foot in the grave."

"Because it's a great place to live and bring up kids, Julia. Ella Rose's friends are there, and her school is..."

"Harmony Harbor is just as amazing as Newton. The schools here are fantastic, there's a ton of kids, and there's so much for them do. It's safe, clean, and gorgeous. Just an all-around great place to live. But you're forgetting the biggest selling feature of all, Aidan. It's you." She reached for the glass of water, worried she might have given herself away. She didn't need to be sold on Harmony Harbor but, if she did, Aidan living here would rank right up there in the top five.

But he didn't see his hometown the way she did. He saw it through the lens of loss. His mother and sister's accident had colored his view of Harmony Harbor in a negative light. And feeling somewhat responsible, no matter how indirectly, for everything he'd suffered and still did, she had a hard time keeping the emotion out of her voice.

She could feel him watching her and felt a little like she had the day he'd interrogated her at the police station. "This isn't just about you and Ella Rose though. Well, in a way it is, because if Harper is emotionally stable and happy, there's a better chance you'll be happy too."

"You think Harper is emotionally unstable?"

"Umm, you're the one paying her share of the mortgage because she hasn't worked since you separated. I mean, it's totally understandable and admirable that she wants to be home for your little girl, but that's a lot of pressure to put on Ella Rose. She's Harper's everything. This would be the best thing for all three of you. I've already found a house that I think Harper will love. It has lots of character and a view of the harbor, and I'm sure I can get her a really good price—"

"Okay, hold it right there. You make a good case for them moving here. But now it's time for you to stop talking and get some rest." He stood and moved to the door.

"Wait a minute. I can't tell if you're happy that I suggested to Harper that they move here or not? Are you? Happy, I mean."

"Am I thrilled that once again you've stuck your nose in my business? No."

"I was just trying to—"

"I get it, okay? And it's sweet that you're trying to

help. But here's the problem: You may have unknowingly given Harper the impression that we stand a better chance of getting back together if she moves here." His intent gaze roamed her face. "It would be unknowingly, wouldn't it? You didn't happen to tell her it would be a good opportunity for us to renew our relationship, did you?"

A few days ago, the idea of Aidan getting back with Harper would've been along the lines of hearing your movie star crush was getting married. It didn't devastate you, just left you in a mild funk for a day or two. Until you started fantasizing about their divorce . . . All right, she was getting off track.

Probably because she didn't want to think about Aidan with Harper, but sometimes you had to make a sacrifice for the greater good. "I may have embellished a little. Dangled you like a carrot, you know."

His hands balled on his hips. She shouldn't have been looking there, but she knew better than to look him in the eye.

"You what?" he said, his voice unnaturally calm and quiet.

She grimaced. "Don't worry, I'll fix it. I promise." She put her hand on her throat. "I probably should stop talking."

"Yeah, you should. If I'm lucky, you'll lose your voice for the next couple of months."

"I know ASL. Sign language." She demonstrated by signing *sorry*. He had no idea how sorry she was, for everything.

Chapter Twelve

♥

It was still dark when Julia woke up wrapped in damp sheets. She pressed her palm to her cool cheek and took a cautious swallow—better. The antibiotics Finn had prescribed must have packed a powerful punch to break her fever and soothe the pain in her throat within only a few hours.

She reached for the glass of water, noticing it had been refilled. A pill better suited for a horse than a human and an ibuprofen sat side by side on the nightstand. It seemed Aidan took his nursemaid duties seriously despite being angry at her. All things considered, she was probably lucky she'd been struck down by strep throat. A little bacterial infection was easier to deal with than being yelled at by Aidan. Actually, as she'd discovered, he didn't yell; he got scary quiet instead.

Except when Finn gave her grief for working when she should have been resting and for taking vitamins instead of ibuprofen. Her temperature had been 102, bordering on dangerous for an adult. Which is when

Aidan had added his two cents using stronger language than his brother. Maybe because at that point she was nearly delirious from fever—that was her excuse and she was sticking to it—she'd shown him another sign she knew. Though this time it was a universal sign. Finn had found it hilarious. Aidan, not so much.

It was kind of annoying that the man looked even hotter when he was ticked. Even more annoying was the fact she'd been practically on her deathbed and noticed.

"You're a head case," she told herself and brought the glass to her lips.

"Feeling better?" asked a deep voice in the dark.

She screamed, her arms jerked, and she banged the glass on her front teeth. Cold water flew into her face and onto her T-shirt.

"Sorry about that. I didn't mean to scare you." The voice came closer, and then Aidan was there, turning on the lamp beside her bed. "You okay?"

Eyes scrunched against the bright light, she fell back onto the pillows. "No. You scared the life out of me." She pressed her free hand to her saturated chest and her terrified heart. He pried the empty glass from her fingers. "What are you doing here? I thought you left after you brought me the prescription and ibuprofen." She was positive he'd been heading out after he'd made sure she took the pills. He'd fixed the door while Finn examined her.

Aidan lifted a shoulder in response to her question. He'd changed into a black, long-sleeved thermal Henley and faded blue jeans. "I didn't want to leave you alone. It's not a big deal," he said, most likely in response to the surprise he no doubt read in her expression.

Touched that he'd stayed with her, she said, "I think it is a big deal. You're a good man, Aidan. Thank you for hanging around. You should probably go home and get at least a few hours' sleep before you have to go to work though. My couch isn't the most comfortable place to sleep. What time is it anyway?"

"Eight."

"Really?" She sat up and stretched her neck to get a better look out the window. "It's pretty dark for eight. Is there a storm coming in? Storm, gosh, what am I thinking? I don't have time to shoot the breeze about the weather. I have to get ready for work." She threw back the covers.

"Hold on there. You're not going anywhere." He put his hands on her shoulders.

"I can't just take time off work. If I'm not there, my doors are closed, and I can't afford for my doors to be closed. So please, can you let me up now?"

"Okay." He gave her a hand. "Go grab a shower, change into a new pair of pj's, and I'll strip your bed and get you something to eat."

"Am I missing something? Or did I lose my voice and my hearing, and you can't lip read?"

"You lost twenty-two hours. It's eight o'clock Monday night, not Monday morning."

She slowly sank down on the bed. "That can't be. I—"

"Relax. It's all good. Your weekend staff were more than happy to fill in. Grams and Rosa stopped by, and they fixed them up with a couple of dating books. Receipts for the day are on your desk. Your staff said sales were better than a typical Monday."

"I don't understand. How did you—"

"Here." He handed her the pills. "Take these. We'll talk after your shower. Trust me, you'll feel better."

Aidan was right. She felt much better after her shower, albeit dazed at discovering how long she'd slept. Instead of putting eight hours in at work as she'd expected to, all she had to do was put on a fresh pair of pj's. It wasn't as easy as it sounded, and not because they were all in the laundry.

She had two types of pj's—cute and cozy or sexy. Cozy was out; she didn't want to get overheated. And she didn't want Aidan to get the wrong idea by going with sexy pajamas. Except she kind of did want him to get the wrong idea. She just didn't want him to think that she...Her feelings for the man were way too complicated to get her brain around tonight.

She pulled a cozy red hooded robe from the hook on the back of the bathroom door and slipped it on. Aidan was banging around in the kitchen as she walked to her bedroom, only to stop short in the doorway with shock.

He'd changed and remade her bed, going so far as to provide turndown service. On the nightstand, her water glass had been refilled, and there was a steaming cup of tea beside it as well as a pack of throat lozenges that hadn't been there before.

She got a lump in her throat. Aidan Gallagher was a big faker. He acted all dangerous and badass, but underneath he was all caring and kind. She'd seen a hint of

his sweetness with his daughter, and now she had proof.
The man was a marshmallow.

Something felt off about her room though, and she
looked around, wondering what...Her jaw dropped. It
was spotless—everything tidy and in its place. She felt
like she was having an out-of-body experience and took
a step back and into a wall of hard muscle.

She turned to stare up at him. "You cleaned my
room."

"Yeah," he said like it was the most natural thing in
the world. "You wanna get in your bed now? I've got
some homemade chicken soup for you." He held up an
oversized mug and a sleeve of crackers.

Tears gathered in her eyes. Embarrassed, she turned
her head and rapidly blinked.

"You're not...crying, are you?" He sounded horrified and slightly panicked.

"No," she sniffed, and wiped a finger under her eyes.
Then she looked up at him and lifted a shoulder. "So
maybe I am. You made me soup and cleaned my room
and took care of me. You're still taking care of me. It's
nice. Sweet. And it made me a little emotional, I guess."

"I am not sweet. I couldn't sleep and needed something to do. And I didn't make the soup. Caleb did. I
just bought it. Now move. Get your butt in bed."

"You know, you won't lose your alpha man card if
word gets out that you're sweet."

He gave her a look. "You want your soup?"

"Yes, but I have to get dressed first." She went to
her dresser and pulled a pair of black leggings and an
oversized T-shirt from the drawer. "I'll just be..." She

trailed off and slowly turned to look at the chair under the window, praying she was imagining what she'd seen out of the corner of her eye. But there, on the ottoman of the leather chair, sat her laptop. Open and on.

"I forgot to tell you. When I picked up your soup this afternoon, Caleb asked me to let you know that someone named Lenny came in, and he took care of him. Friend of yours?"

"Sorry, what?"

"Lenny, is he a friend of yours?"

"Yes," she said distractedly. She couldn't put it off; she had to know. As nonchalantly as she could with her heart pounding a frantic beat, she asked, "So, my laptop, were you using it for anything special?"

"Just, uh, you know, passing the time," he said, but before he'd turned away from her to put the sleeve of crackers down, she saw it. She saw the way his mouth quirked as though he'd just heard the best joke ever.

She rushed to the chair and picked up the laptop. She looked from the screen to him and slowly lowered herself onto the ottoman. "How could you? That was private."

He turned and scratched the back of his head. She would have admired his bulging biceps if she weren't fighting the urge to throw up.

"Look, you'd made a big deal with me and Finn about not being able to miss work, and there was no way I was letting you go in today. But no one knew how to get in touch with your staff. I searched your desk and came up empty. By the way, your phone didn't die. You forgot to pay the bill and were cut off."

She stared at him.

"I wasn't snooping. I looked on your computer for their contact info, and I found it."

"But you didn't stop there, did you?"

"No," he said, fighting a grin. Which disappeared when she glared at him. "Come on, give me a break. You don't have a TV."

"You have a phone."

"Look, I saw my name and thought—"

"You did not see your name. *Warrior's Touch* is not about you. It's about Adrian Greystone."

He walked over and sat on the chair and then reached around her to point at the screen. "Give me some credit. I make a living following the evidence. First, the name. Remove the *r* and what have we got? That's right, sugarplum, move the *i* and you have Aidan. And then we have his surname, Greystone. Greystone Manor ring any bells?" He leaned into her, so close his chest brushed against her back and his warm, minty breath fanned her cheek. "Another coincidence, he just happens to be a six-foot-three cop with blue eyes and black hair. Oh, and did I tell you? I don't believe in coincidences. But right here is where you gave yourself away." He scrolled through to what she'd written just before he kicked in her door.

She stared at the screen. *Aidan smiled that slow, sexy smile of his just before he lifted his gun and fired. The glass shattered, and the...*

He touched her hot cheek. "You don't have to be embarrassed. I'm flattered. And impressed. You're a great

writer, Julia. I usually can't sit still long enough to read
a book, and I couldn't put it down."

"You read the whole thing?"

"Yeah, every single word." He cleared his throat.
"You have quite the…imagination. I had no idea you
were so—"

She whipped around and covered his mouth. "Don't
say it."

He smiled into her hand and then removed it. "We're
adults. We can talk about sex."

"I don't want to talk about sex with you."

"I kinda want to talk about it with you."

Her inner hussy cheered until Julia reminded her—in
her head, of course—that he'd said *talk about it* not *do
it*. "I don't write about sex gratuitously or to titillate—"

"What's that saying? Sex sells…"

"So you're telling me that you read the entire book
just because of the sex? I don't know what that says
about your love life if that's true."

"No, I liked the story and all the action. And not to
blow my own horn, but I'm a pretty cool guy."

She buried her face in her hands. "The book isn't
about you."

"Are you Gillian?"

"No, and you're not Aidan."

"I kinda am."

Sweet Caroline, she'd said Aidan instead of Adrian.
Closing the laptop, she stood up with as much dignity
as she could muster after revealing her secret crush to
her crushee. "I'm going to bed."

"You forgot these."

She turned to see him holding up her black leggings and long-sleeve gray T-shirt. "Thank you," she said coolly, reaching out to take them. No way would she let him see her sweat.

"Jesus. Julia, you might want to, ah." He motioned at her with his finger.

She looked down and gave a strangled *eek*, whirling on her heel as she clutched her robe to her chest. She'd just flashed him.

* * *

Aidan stood in the middle of Julia's bedroom debating whether he should leave or not. She was ostensibly still changing in the bathroom. She'd been in there for more than half an hour.

So, yeah, he got that he'd embarrassed her by reading her book and insisting he was the hero, Adrian Greystone. Even though he had no doubt that he was—none whatsoever—he should have shut up about it. He wouldn't have said anything if she hadn't guessed he'd read her book. At first he hadn't realized she was the author. He'd been telling the truth. He'd started reading because he was bored and then he'd gotten into the story.

Admittedly, because he'd figured out by then who the writer was and thought he might learn her secrets. He'd discovered two, and they were mind-blowing. He just hadn't figured out if they were the good or bad kind of mind-blowing yet.

At the moment, he was leaning toward bad. If Julia had a crush on him as her book and her reaction seemed to imply, he probably shouldn't be hanging around her. He didn't want to give her the wrong idea. He liked her. She was adorable, and sweet. She was also vulnerable, and the last thing he wanted to do was hurt her. She was the type of woman who wanted the life Aidan had left behind. All he was up for now was hot sex, no strings, and no expectations.

And therein lay his problem. The woman he'd like to have a no-strings relationship with was the woman who'd written the hottest sex scenes he'd ever read and who had a body who rocked his world. The same woman who just then walked back into her bedroom with a dazed expression on her face.

"You didn't just clean my bedroom. You cleaned my entire apartment."

"Yeah, it only took me a couple of hours." She didn't pick up on his sarcasm. Her apartment had been a disaster. She was either a slob or her world was out of control. He'd bet on it being the latter. "You know, this is what Finn and I were talking to you about last night."

"When? I don't remember Finn saying anything about my apartment being a mess."

He didn't miss that she made no mention of him. "What about me telling you to cut back on your commitments before you burn out?"

"I've got everything under control," she said, retrieving her laptop from the ottoman.

"Is that right? So why did I practically need a shovel to clean out your living room? You have no real food in the place, your cell phone was cut off, and you're past due on your heat."

She frowned and sat on her bed. "I'm positive I paid my heating bill." She clicked through screens on her computer. "I don't understand. I...I guess I didn't pay it after all. I have two days before they put me into collection."

He sat beside her. She looked pale and forlorn. "Don't worry. I'll call and pay your bill for you." The mortgage and child support had already come out of his account, and so had the rent to his dad. So he was good. It ticked him off that he actually had to think before he'd made the offer. Maybe Julia had done him a favor suggesting to Harper that they sell the house. He couldn't continue living this way.

"Thank you. That's very kind of you to offer, but I have money. That's not the problem."

Last time he'd checked, she'd been scraping to get by. Granted, that had been in July, but still... "You don't have to be embarrassed, Julia. I can afford to—"

She tapped the screen and turned it to face him. He blinked at the amounts in her checking and saving accounts. "Okay, so you're right. Money isn't your problem."

"Why would you assume that it was?"

Yeah, not going there. He'd had a friend in the DEA run a search on her financials. "I don't know. I got the impression business was down. And you're not paying your bills."

"Business hasn't been great, but it's picking up. I depend on my holiday sales. My income from my writing has been good though."

"That's great. I'm happy for you." He dug out his

phone and handed it to her. "Get your bills straightened out, and I'll heat up your soup. You need to eat."

"I'll borrow your phone to make the calls, but you don't have to take care of me. I'm feeling better, honest. I feel bad enough that you obviously lost a day of work because of me."

"I'm suspended with pay for a week."

Her shoulders slumped. "I'm so sorry. I keep trying to help, and in the end, I just make things worse for you."

"You didn't do anything wrong. I overreacted. I need to work on that. But there's something you can help me with. I get bored easily, and you have too much on your plate, so put me to work."

What was his problem? He'd just decided he needed to keep his distance, and here he was offering to spend more time with her. It didn't matter that he wanted to. He knew what happened when he let his feelings over-rule his brain—nothing good. And Julia brought out his protective instincts. If she accepted his offer, she'd no doubt want him to help with the thing he wanted to avoid even more than her: holiday events. He'd seen her schedule for the next couple of weeks leading up to the big day, and it was staggering.

He was trying to come up with a way to renege on his offer without hurting her feelings when she said, "If you're serious, I could use some help with my book. It'll be a huge weight off my shoulders when I get *Warrior's Touch* off my plate and onto my editor's. I thought maybe you could give me some feedback and some advice on the fight scenes?"

"I guess," he said slowly, and then realized he could help her out without spending much time with her. He'd just ignore the part of his brain that had changed fight scenes to sex scenes. But first, he should probably clear something up. "Just so you know, I was teasing you about me being Adrian Greystone."

"It's okay. I was just embarrassed you figured it out."

"So you are in love with me?" he said, his voice rising an octave. After twenty years with the DEA, the past decade working undercover, it took a lot to rattle him. The thought that Julia might be in love with him did more than just rattle him; it terrified him. Because somehow she not only got *to* him, but she got him.

"Of course not. Some authors use actors and actresses as their inspiration for their characters, and I use people from town or that I know or have briefly met. Using you as inspiration for Adrian was a no-brainer. You're like every woman's bad-boy fantasy."

"But not yours?"

"No. I prefer a beta male to an alpha. No offense. It's just that I have three older brothers. I like a sensitive, artistic man. Quiet and gentle and a little geeky."

"Like Jack Summers, the guy with all the answers. Who was your inspiration for him? He seems to be carrying a lot of guilt for something that happened in the first book."

"I have a copy of *Warrior's Kiss* you can borrow. It might help if you read it before making suggestions for *Warrior's Touch*."

He thought there might be a story there. She'd purposefully avoided telling him who her inspiration for Jack was. "What about Gillian?"

"She's the kind of woman I aspire to be."

"Aspire harder. The woman has saying *no* down to a science. The sooner you learn that particular trait the better. The White Witch is an interesting character. I can't tell if she's good or evil. Who was your inspiration for her?"

"My mom. She died when I was twelve. She was bipolar."

"I'm sorry. That must have been tough."

"Tougher for my dad and brothers than me, I think. They tried to protect me. I didn't know she was bipolar until a few weeks before she died. In my eyes, she was the most amazing mom on the planet."

"Do you wish they'd told you?"

"Yes... it would have been better if they had."

There was a story there. Something that left a mark. He could tell by the hesitation in her voice, the shadow that crossed her face.

With a faint smile, she lifted a shoulder. "That's what happens when you're the youngest and have three brothers. I suppose it didn't help that I looked a lot like my mom and had a vivid imagination."

No, he imagined it didn't. It must have been tough for them to let Julia move halfway across the country too. The over-the-top alarm system made sense now.

Her stomach growled, and she self-consciously covered it with a pillow. He moved to the nightstand to retrieve the cold cup of soup. "I'll heat this up. We can work on those fight scenes while you eat."

He turned and walked straight into the chief. "Where the hell did you come from?" he snapped. His anger was more at himself than at Benson. Aidan had been so caught up in Julia that he hadn't heard his boss come in. That had never happened to him before. Ever.

"I think the better question would be, what are you doing here, Gallagher?"

Chapter Thirteen

♥

It was just like old times. Colleen and Kitty were in the study at the manor with a tea tray between them listening to the Christmas carols playing in the background. There were some differences though. Namely, Kitty didn't know Colleen was there. Her daughter-in-law was also the one sitting behind Colleen's formidable desk while Colleen sat in Kitty's old chair.

Feeling a tad resentful, Colleen watched as her daughter-in-law plucked away at the computer keys while nibbling on a scone. They were Colleen's favorite. The ones with the raisins. And the real reason for her resentment. She could smell them but couldn't taste them.

"Peck, peck, peck, you'll get nowhere typing like that. What the bejasus are you working on anyway?" Colleen moved to stand behind Kitty. Looking over her daughter-in-law's shoulder, she perused the names on the screen. "You consider Owen O'Malley an eligible bachelor, do you? The man's ninety if he's a day. And what's Kyle Bishop doing on your list? I thought you and Rosa had come to your senses. Obviously you haven't if you've got Charlie Angel on there too." She didn't fail to notice Kitty's name beside the owner of the Salty Dog. There were several names Colleen didn't recognize, but the ones that she did made her nervous. They were a disreputable lot. Not all of them, mind you. Owen O'Malley was a good sort. Just a little old, to her way of thinking.

"Now let's try this again," Kitty murmured to herself as she leaned in to the screen. She moved the mouse, clicked File, and then clicked Print. Her brow furrowed as she turned to the printer. When the green light continued flashing and nothing happened, she reached over to press buttons.

There was a rap on the study door. Jasper opened it and stuck his head inside. "The Widows Club have arrived for your meeting, Miss Kitty."

"Thank you." She made a moue that was guaranteed to have Jasper running to her side. Kitty had a way about her. Even when she was younger, men were inspired to protect her due to her fragile, helpless air. "Would you mind giving me a hand? I can't seem to get the printer to work."

"Certainly, miss."

"How can you not see that he'd give you the world if you but asked, Kitty?" Colleen prayed that he simply printed off the paper without reading it. Jasper had been more like himself since Kitty had publicly dumped Kyle Bishop. And now, after reading the books they'd bought from Julia's store, Kitty and Rosa had come up with a plan to match not only themselves but the entire Widows Club.

Colleen moved around to the front of the desk—the better to observe the two.

Jasper leaned around Kitty, taking his time moving the cursor on the screen. From the blissful expression on his angular face, he appeared to be inhaling her daughter-in-law's French perfume.

"I've made a mess of it, haven't I?"

He blinked. "Quite. But it's nothing I can't..." His eyes narrowed on the screen, and his movements suddenly became brisk and abrupt.

Kitty gave a delighted clap when the printer began spitting out the pages. "Thank you. I don't know what I'd do without you."

Colleen winced at the wounded expression that came over Jasper's face. The man who rarely showed emotion was an open book right now. Only Kitty didn't see it. She was too busy gathering up her papers. "Oh, Jasper, do you remember where Mother Gallagher hid the Ouija board? Rosa and I can't get everyone to agree with their suggested matches, so I think what we need is some spiritual guidance to confirm our choices."

Without saying a word, Jasper turned to unlock the bottom drawer of the filing cabinet. He pulled out the Ouija board that Colleen had locked away years before. She'd found her great-grandchildren playing with it and had meant to throw the thing away the next day.

He set the dusty spirit board by Kitty's elbow, muttering, "You've lived your entire life in Harmony Harbor. It seems to me you shouldn't require a Ouija board to tell you that half the men on your list are too young for all of you and the other half are reprobates. I may not have lived here as long as you, but I'm well aware of their reputations."

Kitty released a soft gasp, no doubt shocked by the way Jasper had spoken to her. He was never short or angry with Kitty. He'd only ever treated her with deference and devotion.

Poor lad. He'd loved Kitty from afar for years, and now it sounded like once again she'd picked someone else. And as far as Jasper would be concerned, she couldn't have made a worse choice. Jasper and the owner of the Salty Dog, Charlie Angel, had a long and unpleasant past.

"If you don't believe me, all you have to do is consult Madame's—"

"For the love of all that is holy, what's gotten into you, my boy?" Before he spilled the beans and ruined everything, Colleen knocked a book to the floor.

Both Kitty and Jasper startled, but it didn't stop him from finishing his remark. "Book."

Looking confused, Kitty stared after Jasper as he strode from the study. Colleen hoped her daughter-in-law's perplexed expression indicated that she was more concerned by Jasper's abrupt demeanor and departure than what he'd said. To ensure that was the case, Colleen followed Kitty to the sitting room where the members of the Widows Club had gathered.

At first, everything seemed fine. The women exchanged pleasantries, talking about their upcoming choral performance at the manor as they slowly lowered themselves onto the carpet in the middle of the wood-paneled room.

"What in the name of all that's holy do they think they're doing? They'll never be able to get back up," Colleen muttered, and then refocused on Kitty, watching with trepidation as she set the Ouija board in the center of the Oriental rug. The fact the women were about to open a portal to the spirit world bothered her almost as much as Kitty realizing that *The Secret Keeper of Harmony Harbor* had been found.

"Jasper said something rather worrisome to me when I asked him if he knew where the Ouija board was," Kitty confided to her friends.

Colleen bowed her head. She should have known Jasper's remark hadn't escaped her daughter-in-law's notice.

"If the bag of bones told you this is not a good idea then, *sì*, I agree with him."

"You never agree with Jasper about anything, Rosa. Why would you start now?" Kitty said.

"Because it's dangerous to call on the spirits, *capisce*?"

"I agree with Jasper and Rosa, Kitty," Ida Fitzgerald said. "What if our husbands are listening in from heaven when we ask for advice about which men we should be dating?"

"Pssh, I hope mine is, the good for nothing. Running off without a word and leaving me to raise three *bambinos* on my own," Rosa said.

Rosa would be in for a shock if the spirit of her husband came through. And Jasper would be in serious trouble. Sometimes Colleen thought she should have Jasper burn her memoirs. But there were as many people who could be helped by them as could be hurt. In the right hands, the book wasn't dangerous. In the wrong hands...

"No, it wasn't about the Ouija board. It was about what we're using it for. I told him we were asking for spiritual guidance about the men on our list. He said..." She shivered. "Just the thought of what he said gives me goose bumps. It felt like someone had walked over my grave."

The women leaned forward, their eyes wide. "What did he say?" several of them asked at the same time.

"He said we didn't need a Ouija board to tell us that half the men on our list were reprobates and the other half were too young for us. If we don't believe him, he says all we have to do is consult *Madame's book*."

"Oh, *Madonna mia*, you think he has the book?" Rosa asked, the color leaching from her face. She'd be worried that the secret she'd told Colleen all these years before would come out. She had no idea that it had been discovered a long time ago.

Kitty shook her head. "No, I'm sure he would have told me if he did. Still, it was a worrisome admission. I'd come to believe the book was no longer a threat. That perhaps Mother Gallagher had gotten rid of it. Or that it was lost forever."

"Of course he has the book. He was Colleen's right-hand man. She rarely made a move without consulting him. We should have known it was Jasper all along. We have to get the book from him, Kitty," Ida said.

Oh yes, Ida had good reason to want the book too. She wouldn't want anyone to know about her grand-

daughters. She'd come to Colleen because she needed
help to hide one and protect the other.

"Kitty, while you distract Jasper, we'll search his
room," Rosa said, and all the women agreed. Except
Colleen's daughter-in-law, who looked nervous.

Colleen could work with that. She walked through
Ida's upper body, headed to the center of the circle, and
lay on her stomach by the board. She put all her energy
into her forefinger and touched the yellow planchette.
When the plastic heart began moving around the board,
the women gasped, some placing a hand over their
mouths while the others placed one at their throats. By
the time Colleen had spelled out *Touch. The. Book. And.
Die,* she was exhausted.

Ida, who'd been writing out the letters, read them
aloud.

Colleen managed a smile when Kitty looked about
ready to faint. Now all Colleen had to do was bring the
piece of paper in Ida's hands to Jasper's attention. He
needed to know the book was in danger.

* * *

Julia put two shots of expresso in a white mug with
MERRY AND BRIGHT stamped in gold on it. She then
added a dash of gingerbread syrup and a dollop of
gingerbread-flavored whipping cream, and topped it off
with crushed gingerbread cookies. Resting her elbows on
the counter in her coffee shop, she brought the mug to her
nose with a happy sigh. It smelled like Christmas in a cup.
The perfect way to end a perfect day.

Today's sales had doubled over last year's, and her throat was no longer sore thanks to another forty-eight hours of lounging in her jammies under the directive of Dr. Gallagher. Not the real one. Aidan, who'd apparently appointed himself her personal unlicensed physician, had insisted she take another couple of days off work. Since her staff were more than happy for the extra hours, she took advantage of the free time to work on *Warrior's Touch*.

It was the first holiday she'd had in years, and she'd never felt more relaxed and happy. No doubt sending off *Warrior's Touch* to her editor this morning was partially responsible for lifting the crushing weight from her shoulders.

She did a little shimmy-shake to celebrate and took another sip of her coffee. She didn't linger on the fact that her manuscript was still technically late. Her editor was thrilled, and so was she.

But it was Aidan who was truly responsible for the endorphins rushing through her body and lighting her up inside like a Christmas tree. If he hadn't read her manuscript, she'd still be stuck in revision hell, trying to find a way to disguise Adrian's likeness to Aidan. She didn't have to worry about that now. He was out there for all the world to see—her perfect crush.

Perfect might be stretching it a bit. Not on the outside, of course. There was no denying that physically the man was absolute, mouthwatering perfection. She knew this because she'd routinely had to check for drool just from sitting close to him and casting him sidelong glances.

She didn't have the same problem when he opened his mouth. He was a true alpha: bossy, broody, and bull-headed. And what was most annoying was that, after spending, like, a day with her characters, he thought he knew them better than she did, especially Adrian. Sometimes, even though Aidan could send her hormones off the charts with just one look, she wanted to send him home.

But then she'd catch a glimpse of her marshmallow man. Usually when he thought she was overdoing it or that she needed to eat, and then there were the times when she'd catch him watching her with a tender expression on his face.

And those were the times when she should have kicked him out. Because that's when she began playing the "what if" game. As she knew from experience, that was a very dangerous game to play. Especially when she found herself looking at him and "what if" became "I do." Like in, *Yes, I really do love you. Yes, I'll go to the chapel with you and say I do. Yes, I'll have your babies too.*

It was probably a good thing Aidan no longer had a reason to hang out at her apartment. Her strep throat had cleared up, she wouldn't receive revisions on her manuscript for at least another couple of weeks, and Aidan was back at work on Monday. Sadly, there was only a small part of her that seemed to agree that not being with Aidan every day was a good thing.

Julia took a sip of her coffee and glanced out the window. Her eyes went wide. "Snow!" she cried at the sight of the fluffy white flakes drifting lazily from cotton-candy clouds.

She hurried around the counter to the front door. The cars parked along Main Street were already lightly dusted with the white stuff. It looked like they were going to get their first real snowfall of the season.

It was just what Julia needed to return her to her happy place. There was nothing that put her in the holiday spirit faster than snowflakes falling from the sky. It pretty much guaranteed that tomorrow would be busier than today at the store. Snow seemed to signal the Christmas countdown alert in her customers' brains better than any advertising she had ever done.

But not everyone would be happy about the arrival of winter. She thought of Lenny, a vet who'd served in Iraq. She'd met Lenny last summer. She'd been picking up litter in the village green and had mistakenly put a bag of half-eaten potato chips in the trash. In Lenny's eyes, she'd stolen his dinner.

She wouldn't lie: Her heart had skipped a beat when he stormed out of the woods. All she saw was this big guy in tattered jeans and a grungy T-shirt, his dark blond hair as scraggly as his beard, coming at her. But she did what her brothers had taught her and visually checked him for weapons and intent, and then she stood her ground.

Actually, her two oldest brothers would have told her to get her butt out of there and fast. Her younger brother, he'd do the same as she had. Neither of them were the type to run scared. She was small, but she was no coward. She wasn't an idiot either. If she'd gotten even a hint that Lenny might harm her, she would have dropped the trash and left.

But she saw something in his soulful brown eyes that
made her stick around. She'd bought him hot dogs and
fries from the food stand nearby. She'd been checking
on him a few times a week ever since. He refused to go
to the VA or a shelter. As far as she knew, he didn't
have family.

Along with Julia, a couple of the guys from town
who were also vets looked out for him. The war had
broken Lenny. She thought maybe it had been worse for
him because, like Josh, Lenny had the soul of an artist.
When he'd moved from the village green to the fishermen's shacks in early November, she'd discovered that
he loved to paint.

In the spring and summer months, local artisans sold
their wares out of the brightly colored fishermen
shacks, and Lenny had found a brush and some old
paints that he'd been able to use. On the wall of the
shack, he'd painted a stark winter seascape. The true
extent of his talent wasn't revealed until Julia brought
him new brushes, paints, and canvas to work with. In
a week, he'd filled the shack with paintings so realistic
and haunting they made Julia's heart hurt. She wanted
to talk to Maggie about him, but he refused.

Julia hadn't seen Lenny since last week and decided
to pay him a visit. Caleb had been looking out for him
while she'd been sick. Lenny would sometimes stop by
for a coffee and muffin, but only when Julia was alone
at Books and Beans. She'd bring him both tonight, and
an extra sleeping bag, scarves, and mittens too.

If he was having a good day maybe she'd try to get
him to agree to go to a shelter. Knowing how low the

chances of that happening were, she played with the idea of setting up a place for him in her storage room—an idea she'd best keep to herself. Caleb and his friends would pitch a fit if she brought it up again. They'd shut her down when she suggested Lenny stay with her before. As much as she didn't like to admit it, they were probably right. She'd seen Lenny in a rage once before and didn't know what had set him off. Then again, she hadn't entirely understood what set her mother off that long-ago night. The night that had changed everything for both of them.

Not today, she told herself. She wasn't going to think anything but good thoughts today. It was a happy day, a day to celebrate. But her friends were busy. Unlike Julia, they were all in relationships at the moment. And Aidan and Harper were meeting with Julia's Realtor friend at their place in Newton. Aidan had been there last night too. Harper had invited him to Ella Rose's birthday.

Julia hadn't spoken to him since the party, so she wasn't sure how it had gone. Her Realtor friend was the one who'd told her about tonight's meeting when she'd called to thank Julia for the lead. She had an interested client already.

Which meant Julia should be over the moon. Her job as Aidan's fairy godmother was almost at an end. She was happy for him, she really was, and she was grateful too. Grateful that she'd been able to play a small part in helping him find his happily-ever-after. Even if that happily-ever-after didn't include her.

A small, depressing weight settled heavily on her

chest. Aidan not calling was bothering her more than she'd realized or wanted to acknowledge. Or maybe she just had time to think about it now that she was alone.

Suddenly the lyrics from "All by Myself" were playing in her head. *Nice. Thank you, brain, for pulling that oldie but goodie out of my memory bank. Oh well. What the heck. If you can't beat 'em, join 'em,* she thought, and belted out the lyrics to the song as she opened the bakery case to take out three muffins for Lenny. She added sugar cookies to the box and decided to bring him hot chocolate instead of coffee. She'd have her turning-in-the-manuscript celebration with Lenny.

The words *by myself* warbled in her throat as once again her thoughts turned to Aidan. He'd known she was sending off the manuscript this morning and hadn't bothered to call. Julia bowed her head. She'd been better off when the only interactions she had with Aidan Gallagher were in her dreams and within the pages of her books.

Chapter Fourteen

♥

T he end," Aidan said from where he lay half in and half out of Ella Rose's princess bed. He returned the book to the nightstand.

"No, Daddy, you're supposed to say *and they all lived happily ever after.*"

As he repeated the words back to her, his chest got tight. Along with the question in his little girl's eyes, he saw hope. He understood why. Things had been better with Harper over the past week. They hadn't fought, and Ella Rose had noticed.

Tonight, his ex had taken it a step further, acting as if they were back together. She'd said as much to the Realtor. Aidan had caught Ella Rose peeking around the hall corner and listening with a smile on her face when she was supposed to be in bed. He'd gotten her back to her room with the promise of a story, but obviously, the damage had been done.

He couldn't put the entire blame on Harper. After all, it was Julia who'd put the idea in his ex's head. Not that it had taken much effort on Julia's part. From the day

Aidan had left, Harper had been using whatever means at her disposal to win him back. He honestly didn't understand why. Though sometimes he'd wondered if it was because Harper had never failed at anything, and thanks to her doting older parents, she'd gotten everything she'd ever wanted and didn't handle disappointment or rejection well.

There was part of him that didn't want to rock the boat. Just the possibility that they'd sell the house had him feeling more hopeful for his future than he had in years. Yet he couldn't let Ella Rose start believing in a fantasy where they'd all live happily ever after. The last thing he wanted to do was hurt his little girl and damage the progress he'd made in the past couple of days, but it was important she knew the truth. He'd never lied to her before. He wasn't about to start now.

"You know, pumpkin, mommies and daddies and their kids don't have to live in the same house to have a happily-ever-after."

Her bottom lip quivered. "You're not going to live with us in the new house like Mommy said?"

"No, baby, I'm not." He put his arm around her and held her close. "I'm sorry. I don't like making you sad. Mommy and Daddy weren't happy together, pumpkin. It happens sometimes. It's no one's fault. And it doesn't mean we love you any less. You're the most important thing in our world. I know it'll be tough for you to move to Harmony Harbor and change schools, but I think it'll be good for all of us. I can see you more and help out Mommy."

Ella Rose played with the button on his shirt. "Sadie

is moving too. And George says her school is way more fun than mine. She's going to talk to her teacher and get us in the same class. We're going to have tea parties at the manor and go on treasure hunts too."

Leave it to George, he thought with an inward laugh. He owed the kid. Ella Rose was handling the idea of moving better than he could have hoped.

He was about to share a couple more selling points with her when she yawned and snuggled closer. "Can you sing to me, Daddy?"

"Sure, pumpkin." If only the conversation would go as well with her mother, he thought, as he began to sing "Over the Rainbow" to his little girl.

It might have, if Harper hadn't met him outside Ella Rose's room with tears shining in her eyes. She gave him a watery smile. "I've missed that. So has she."

He placed a hand at the small of Harper's back, guiding her away from Ella Rose's room. "That's why living close by is a good idea. Even when I'm working, I can drop in on my breaks. I can come by and tuck Ella Rose into bed at night, help her with her homework. It'll be better for you too. You won't feel like you're doing this on your own."

Her hand pressed to her chest, Harper stopped at the top of the stairs. "What do you mean? I thought the whole point of me moving to Harmony Harbor was so we could get back together."

"I'm not being a smart-ass, but we've been divorced for a couple of years now, Harper. I don't understand why you think anything has changed between us. And honestly, I have no idea why you'd even want to get back together. All we ever did was fight. It wasn't good for either of us. We weren't happy. The best thing that came out of our marriage was Ella Rose," he said as he reached the bottom of the stairs.

"You don't understand why I'd want to get back with you?" Harper asked as she came to stand in front of him, her voice tight, her cheeks flushed. "I'm forty and a single parent, Aidan. I don't want to be alone the rest of my life. But that little girl up there *is* my life. What if I meet someone, and I let him into our world, and he turns out to be a sociopath or a pedophile or a stalker or—"

That was the problem with Harper's job. As a psychiatrist, she'd dealt with a lot of unsavory characters, including the criminally insane. "I get it, okay. Our jobs put us in contact with some really bad people. But you're smart, Harper. You'd know if something was off with the guy, and if you had any worries, all you'd have to do is pick up the phone and call me. I'd check him out. Simple as that. And a lot simpler and safer if you live close by. I think moving to Harmony Harbor is a good idea for all of us. I really do. And to be completely honest, the mortgage payments here are killing me."

She twisted the strand of pearls she wore with her black sweater. "I understand what you're saying, I do, but I'm concerned about uprooting Ella Rose. Eventually, I'll be able to pay my share. Just not yet. Though you should know that I'll never agree to joint custody wherever we live."

"That's not fair. I love Ella Rose as much as you do. I'm a good father." He walked down the hall to the kitchen as he spoke, trying to keep his voice low and his anger under control.

"I'm not being a bitch," she said, following him into the kitchen. "I know that's what your family thinks, but they have no idea the psychological problems a child of divorce can develop. If you saw what I did in my practice, you'd understand. Ella Rose needs me, Aidan."

"Are you sure it isn't the other way around?" he asked quietly.

* * *

On his way back from Boston, Aidan drove down Main Street. His foot eased off the gas pedal when he spotted the sign for Books and Beans. Like the rest of the shops along the street, Julia's outdoor Christmas lights were on, but other than a faint glow from her security lights, the store was dark. His gaze lifted to her apartment. There was a soft pool of light in her bedroom window.

He knew her home intimately now. And he'd begun to feel like he knew her the same way. She ate peanut butter straight from the jar when she was trying to figure out something in her book. She wouldn't wear anything that wasn't soft to the touch. She talked to her plants and her fish. She was happiest when she was reading or writing or having deep conversations with her friends or walking in the snow. She was curious, and her mind never stopped. Sometimes in the middle of a conversation, she'd get this look on her face, and he'd know she was thinking about her story, writing in her head.

There was nothing fake about her. You got exactly what you saw, a funny, warm woman, who was kind and caring and a little quirky. He liked her passion and ambition, the joy she took in the simple things, the way her purple eyes darkened when she looked at him. If he was honest, he pretty much liked everything about her. It's why he'd vowed to keep his distance when he'd left her place yesterday afternoon. At least for a while.

He pressed on the gas and left her apartment in the rearview mirror. The temptation to check on her rode him hard all the way home. It was annoying and unnerving.

His dad looked up from the hockey game he was watching on TV when Aidan walked in the house. "How did it go?"

"The Realtor's clients loved the house. Supposedly they'll be coming in with an offer in the next twenty-four hours."

"That's fast. How do Harper and Ella Rose feel about it?"

Aidan hung up his jacket. "Now that it's looking like it might actually happen, I think Harper might be having second thoughts. Ella Rose just found out her best friend is moving, so it'll make it easier for her. She likes the idea of having the family close by and seeing more of George and Mia."

"How do you feel about it, son?"

"Honestly? I should have insisted we sell the house when we divorced. I let Harper know tonight that, one way or another, I'm done. Julia's right. I can't keep this up. And it's not like we could make a go of co-parenting with me here and them in Boston anyway." Though after his conversation with Harper tonight, he'd told his lawyer to withdraw his petition for joint custody for now. As long as Aidan could see his little girl whenever he wanted, he'd hold off until Harper was in a better place. He was hoping by then they could come to an agreement on their own.

"That Julia is as smart as she is sweet, isn't she?"

"Subtle, Dad, real subtle," he said as he walked into the kitchen and opened the fridge. "You want a beer?"

"No, I'm good, thanks."

Aidan used the edge of the counter to pop off the cap. "Hey, what's up with him?" he asked, lifting his chin at Miller, who was curled up in his red plaid bed by the fire. "It's not like him to not come greet me." He went over to give the retriever a rubdown.

"I think he's depressed."

Aidan didn't know if his dad realized it or not, but he'd looked in the direction of Maggie's when he diagnosed Miller. "Hey, boy, where's Maggie?"

The dog's head went up, and he leaped from the bed, nearly taking Aidan out to get to the window. With his nose pressed to the glass, he started to whine.

"Now, why did you go and do that?" his dad groused.

"He misses her. And I think you do too. Why don't you go over and make things right, Dad?"

His father crossed his arms and stared at the TV. "I can't. She's out with your boss tonight. Twice in a week. I guess it's serious."

"Buddy, come here. I'll take you for a walk," Aidan told the dog to get him to stop whining. He glanced at his dad, feeling bad for the part he'd played in Benson dating Maggie. Aidan looked down at his beer, picking at the label. "Was I the reason you ended things with her, Dad?"

"You? No, of course not. It's just"—he shrugged—"I don't know. It doesn't matter. I'm good with my life the way it is. I have you kids close by now, and the grandkids."

"If you're so good with your life, why are you sitting here looking all depressed and grumbling about your ex-girlfriend dating your best friend?"

"He's not my best friend. I'm not sure I'd even classify him as a good friend anymore." His father gave him a look. "Wipe the smirk off your face. I'm not jealous. I haven't been happy with how he's been treating you. I told you that."

"Yeah, and I told you I'd handle it. I'm a big boy, Dad. You don't have to worry about me."

"You don't have to worry about me either. I married my one and only, son. I wish I had her with me for another forty years. But I was blessed to have her as long as I did." His dad drew his gaze from the photos of Aidan's mother and sister that lined the mantel to smile. "Your brothers found their one and only, and I want that for you too."

"Been there, done that. I'm like you, Dad. I'm good with my life just the way it is. I've got my family close by, and if everything works out as planned, Ella Rose will be too."

"You think you're smart throwing my words back at me, don't you?"

Aidan took a pull on his beer and came to his feet. "Answer me this, and I won't bring it up again. Just remember that I'm a human lie detector, so give it to me straight. How will you feel if Maggie doesn't just go out on a couple of dates with Benson, but she ends up marrying him?" His father wasn't quick enough to hide his reaction. "I got my answer. Mom would want you to be happy, Dad. We do too. Why would you settle for being content with your life when you could have so much more?"

"Why would you?"

Aidan shook his head and called for the dog. "Come on, boy. We'll go for a walk and let the old man sit in his contentment."

"You always were a smart-ass," his father grumbled.

"You're mixing us up, Dad. That was Liam."

"You're right. He still is." His father gave a half laugh and then looked over his shoulder to where Aidan was getting ready to go out. "Your mother used to call you her sweet boy. Always making sure everyone was okay. Thing was, you managed to get into more mischief than all your brothers combined. But none of them could pour on the charm like you. You should think of using some of that charm on Julia. Because, son, Harper was never your one and only, and you weren't hers."

"You're as bad as Grams, you know. Maybe you should join the Widows Club. And I can't use something on Julia that I don't have. I must have used up all my charm when I was younger."

"No, it wasn't when you were younger. You lost it eight years ago on October seventeenth. Both your mother and sister would want you to be happy too. It's time for you to let go of the anger. Paul was right about that, you know. You should consider taking the course."

"Okay, this isn't exactly how I saw this conversation going. So whaddya say we stop here? See you in a bit." The minute Aidan closed the front door, Miller began panting and tugging on the lead.

"Hope you feel like a long walk tonight, buddy." He had no intention of going home until the old man was in bed. To distract Miller, Aidan scooped up some snow and made a hard-packed ball. He drilled it in the opposite direction of Maggie's house. The snowball disappeared in a flurry of flakes. The snow was coming down hard. If it continued, he figured the likelihood of his old man being called out to work was good.

As they reached the end of Breakwater Way, Aidan decided to head to the manor. Miller had other plans and tore down the road toward the harbor front. Anyone looking out their window would think Aidan was ski-ing. He'd forgotten how strong and determined Miller was when he'd made up his mind to go after something.

Aidan was wondering what that something was when Miller, practically frothing at the mouth, barreled through the snow. Aidan spotted the dog's prey. A woman twirling on the wharf with her head tipped back, catching snowflakes on her tongue. Off to the left, a man stood watching her. Julia was laughing, trying to get the guy to join her. Smiling, he shook his head. At the sound of Miller barking, the guy stiffened and turned. He said something to Julia and then hurried away with his head down and shoulders hunched.

The way Julia's friend took off put Aidan on alert. He let Miller's leash go before the dog ripped his arm out of his socket while he visually tracked the man. Aidan guessed him to be in his twenties, around six feet, and about a hundred and sixty pounds. The guy glanced over his shoulder, caught Aidan watching him, and broke into a run. Aidan stalked down the wharf to where Julia knelt in the snow, loving on his dog.

"Who was that guy?"

"Why are you acting all badass? It was just Lenny."

He crossed his arms and looked down at her, doing his best to ignore the way her violet eyes shone with laughter and her candy-apple-red lips glistened. "Just Lenny took off awful fast and looks like he has something to hide. What were you doing with the guy anyway?" Great. Now he sounded like a jealous boyfriend.

"Enjoying the first snowfall and celebrating sending off *Warrior's Touch* to my editor this morning," she said.

"That's great. You must be happy to check that off your list."

She stood up, smiling down at his dog, who was pushing his nose through the snow. "I thought you'd call," she said quietly. There was no anger or emotional manipulation to make him feel bad, just an honest admission of what her expectations had been.

After the four days they'd spent together, she had a right to be confused. He should have said something. Told her the truth. He couldn't give her what she wanted or deserved, so it was best he didn't spend time with her. Only he couldn't seem to get the words out.

Something was holding him back. "Sorry, I should have called. I had a lot on my plate."

"That's okay. But you were a big help, and I thought it would be nice to celebrate together." She gave him a playful grin. "I put you in the acknowledgments."

Now he felt really guilty. Though he doubted that had been her intention. "Thanks, but you didn't have to do that. I enjoyed myself," he said, keeping an eye on Miller, who was now rolling in the snow.

"Wait until you see what I wrote before you thank me."

"Let me guess. You got back at me for correcting you every time Adrian talked like a girl and fought like one." Her smile widened, and he figured he was right. But he'd let her distract him long enough. "So, tell me more about this Lenny guy."

She did, and the more she told him, the harder it was to keep his mouth closed until she finished. "You're unbelievable," he said once she did, his gut churning at the thought of all the time she'd spent on her own with this guy.

"Thank you," she said, knowing full well it wasn't a compliment. And he knew this because she rolled her eyes.

"I'm not joking around, Julia. I get you wanting to help Lenny. We should all be doing our part to help our vets when they come home. But this is the last time you're with him on your own."

She patted his arm. "That's very sweet of you to worry about me, and I do understand your concern. But I can take care of myself."

"He's a vet. You have no idea what he's capable of,

and it's obvious he has some mental health issues." He ducked to look her in the eyes. "You're five foot three and weigh a hundred and twenty-five pounds, Julia. You can't—"

She gasped. "I'm five three and three-quarters, and I don't... Didn't anyone ever tell you that you shouldn't guess a woman's weight? Out loud. To her face."

It wasn't all that hard to hold back the laugh rumbling in his chest at her outraged expression because he kept envisioning her down here all alone with a guy who could snap at any moment. "Okay, how is it that you're more concerned about me being three quarters of an inch off on your height and five pounds off on your weight when we're talking about you hanging out with a guy who unintentionally might hurt you? Please, enlighten me. I really want to hear you justify this."

"How about I show you that I can take care of myself, Mr. Sarcastic." She walked away and turned her back to him. "Okay, attack me."

He laughed. "You can't be serious?"

"As a heart attack. Come on. Give it your best shot."

"Julia, I'm not going to—"

"Is the big bad detective terrified of little old me?"

It was his turn to roll his eyes. He walked up behind her and carefully got her into a choke hold. Two seconds later, he was looking up at her from where he lay stunned on the snow-covered wharf.

She looked down at him with a smirk. "I have three extremely protective older brothers. Do you really think they'd let me move away from home without teaching me a thing or two?"

"Okay, I admit it. That was impressive." He reached out a hand, and she put hers in his to help him up. Instead, he yanked her down on top of him. Placing a hand behind her head, he rolled her beneath him and then encircled her wrists with his fingers. He held her arms over her head, positioning his body so she couldn't knee him. "Did your brothers happen to teach you how to get out of this hold?"

The moment her big eyes darkened and her lips curved in a provocative smile, he knew he was in trouble. It was the kind of trouble he'd been trying to avoid for the past few days. He was tired of fighting the attraction. He wanted her, and he wanted to keep her safe. She took advantage of his distraction by looping her arms over his head, forcing him to release her wrists. She drew him closer and he let her, his mouth now a whisper from hers.

She inched up, pressing her soft lips to his. He cradled her head with his hands and deepened the kiss. It was nothing like the one they'd shared under the mistletoe a year before. This kiss was hot and deep and so much more. She held nothing back. Neither did he. And as the snow fell around them, the moored boats rocked on the water that slapped gently against the wharf. Their kiss changed, slowing in time to the rhythm of the waves. As if no longer fueled by a desperate craving for each other, they tasted, teased, and—

A cold, wet nose shoved between them. "Miller," Aidan muttered.

Julia laughed. "He's feeling left out."

"Yeah, looks like," Aidan said, as he searched her

face, afraid of what he'd see. There'd been more to that kiss than simply heat and desire. He'd felt it just before Miller interrupted them. A tenderness, a want, a need that came with long-term hopes and dreams. At least that's how it felt. Yet as he looked into her sparkling eyes, all he saw was amusement. Still, he couldn't take the risk she'd think this would lead to something else. He'd come to care about her. He had to be honest. "Julia, you need to know that, if you want more than this, I can't give it to you."

"Oh, so we can only kiss? We can't have sex?"

Chapter Fifteen

♥

Julia didn't really mean to ask whether they could only kiss. That made it sound like he hadn't just rocked her world again. The kiss had been perfectly wonderful, and she would have been perfectly content to spend the rest of the night with his mouth on hers and his big body keeping her warm.

The sex question? Well, that sort of popped out before she could stop it. Because no matter how much she wanted to have sex with Aidan—and she really, really wanted to—she wouldn't. Actually, she couldn't. He'd been honest with her, and she respected him for that. He didn't want anything more than a physical relationship. And she did.

She knew herself. She didn't have sex; she made love. She didn't want to complain or feel sorry for herself, but she thought she deserved, had maybe even earned, some pain-free, drama-free happiness. So had Aidan. But she knew if they took their relationship, or whatever this was, to the next level, her feelings would get tangled up with love and marriage and babies in a carriage.

It wasn't that she'd expect a ring on her finger before she made love with him. She'd been in a relationship with Josh for more than two years before he'd popped the question. But Julia had known from the beginning that he was committed, that he loved her and wanted to be with her... forever.

"Hey, you okay? Do you want to talk about it?" Aidan asked as he reattached Miller's leash.

She would have laughed if she wasn't reeling from the painful reminder that sometimes men made promises they didn't keep. Men like Josh, who promised you forever and then swallowed a bottle of pills and left you to pay the price for their sins. And then there were men like Aidan, who were honest and didn't make any promises at all... Maybe men who promised nothing were the safest men of all.

He took her mittened hand in his. "Julia?"

She smiled up at him as they walked along the harbor front. "You, the man of few words wants to talk about it?"

"Honestly? No. But I will if you want to. You weren't really expecting an answer to your question, were you? Because I don't know any guy who would say no to sex, specifically sex with you."

"Um, I'm not sure if that was a compliment or not."

"Compliment," he said, his eyes scanning the area like the cop that he was. She hadn't realized until right then that he had an agenda.

"I'm not taking you to Lenny, Aidan. He's not comfortable with strangers. They make him nervous. You'll scare him away."

"I wasn't fooling around, Julia. I don't want you hanging around him without me or someone else there."

"I just proved to you that I can take care of myself. And I'm not stupid. I always tell someone where I'm going to be. If I'm not back by a certain time, they'll come looking for me."

"Are you telling me someone knew you were down here with Lenny tonight?" There was more than a hint of skepticism in his voice.

"Yes, I am, and there he is." She pointed to Caleb, who walked their way, and then winced, apologizing to the owner of Jolly Rogers when he reached them. "I'm so sorry. I should have called."

"Yeah, you should have." He bent down to pet Miller, lifting his chin at Aidan. "How's it going?"

"Been better. I just found out about Julia's homeless friend. You think it's safe for her to hang out with him on her own?"

"Of course he does. Caleb trusts me to take care of myself," Julia said, tugging on Aidan's hand to get him to start walking again. "Thanks for checking on me. I'll make it up to you."

"Doesn't look like you'll have much luck moving or distracting him, Julia. Though I probably should warn you, Aidan, she's really good at diversionary tactics," Caleb said, and then glanced at the fishermen shacks. "Kidding aside, for the most part, I think she is safe with Lenny, or I would have put a stop to the visits myself. He's more relaxed around Julia than he is with any of us. He trusts her. He's calmer since he's started painting too."

"We need to find him somewhere to live, Caleb. He hasn't been able to paint for the past week." She glanced at Aidan. "You can't hold this against me, or I'll stop telling you things. Agreed?"

His lips flattened, and then he gave her a clipped nod.

"Lenny was more agitated tonight than he has been for months. I'm sure it's because he no longer has a creative outlet. I've been thinking he could stay in the storage room at my..." She clamped her mouth shut when both men stared her down. "Fine. I'll talk to Father O'Malley and see if he can help."

"That's a good idea, actually. We need to get Lenny used to other people. Start reintegrating him back into society," Caleb said.

"My ex is a psychiatrist. I'll talk to her about Lenny. See if she has any advice for you on how best to go about it."

"That would be great. I finally got him to agree to let Maggie see his paintings. I told him that if he did, she might let him work out of her studio during the day. I think the only reason he agreed is that he's desperate to paint."

"Okay, looks like we have a plan. I'll fill in the rest of the guys. Until Lenny's painting again, you let us know when you're seeing him, and one of us will go with you, Julia."

"Thanks for the offer, but I'm—"

Aidan cut her off. "If she doesn't let you know, I will. Thanks, Caleb."

They said their goodbyes and continued down the harbor front. Julia imagined Lenny would have stayed away from the shack until he knew the coast was clear. Still, she hurried her pace when they were two down from the lemon-yellow shack where Lenny lived.

"You can slow down. I'm not going to raid his place. He isn't there."

"How do you know?"

He gestured at the footprints in the snow. "Feel better now?"

She smiled, letting go of his hand to loop her arm through his. "Yes, I do. Now I can relax and enjoy this beautiful night. There's something magical about the first snowfall, don't you think?"

"Never thought of it as magical before, but it's nice. Miller seems to like it as much as you." He nodded at the dog tossing snow in the air with his nose and then barking as he tried to catch it. Aidan kicked a small mountain of the white stuff, and snow sprayed in a wide arc, ensuring that Miller went crazy.

She smiled at the man and his dog. She couldn't have asked for a more perfect night to share her first *real* kiss with Aidan. There was nothing more romantic than walking in the winter wonderland with the heavy snow falling around them. Snuggled up against him, she was warm despite the cold.

As they turned to walk up Main Street, she saw the Christmas lights for the first time from that vantage point at night. She stopped and took them in, awed by the sight. "Do you see it now? Do you feel it?"

"What am I supposed to be seeing and feeling?"

"The magic. Look at the lights."

He turned his head. "I'd rather look at you."

She brought a hand to her chest. There was no teasing laughter on his face or in his voice. Her smile wobbled a little and she wondered if he knew what those five words did to her. "See, proof that there really is magic in the air tonight."

"Why do you say that?"

"Because a week ago you threatened to arrest me, and now you want to look at me. And don't forget, you kissed me too."

"No, I let you kiss me."

"You say to-may-to, and I say to-mah-to."

He gave his head a slight shake and then laughed. "You're a little crazy, you know. You're lucky you're cute."

"Okay, that's the second time tonight that I'm left wondering if you're complimenting me or not." She sighed. She'd gone from thinking he might be falling for her to thinking...No, she wouldn't let his *cute and crazy* comment derail her perfect night. Time for a subject change. "How was Ella Rose's birthday party?"

"It was a princess party with eight seven-year-olds on sugar highs. How do you think it went? You could have taught the princess Harper hired a thing or two though."

"Let me guess, princess for hire was more interested in partying with the prince than performing for the little princesses?" He made a noncommittal sound in his throat that told her everything she needed to know. "Next time Harper is looking to hire someone for Ella Rose's party, tell her to give me a call. I'd be more than happy to do it for free."

His mouth lifted at the corner. "So, you're telling me you'd be more interested in performing for the kids than partying with the prince?"

"Yes, because I have my priorities straight. Work first, party later. That's what happens when you're in your thirties versus your late teens and early twenties."

"I doubt you were ever much of partier, sugarplum," he said with one of those slow smiles that made her melt.

When she finally managed to pull her gaze from the warmth in his, she admitted, "You wouldn't be wrong. I didn't have much of a social life thanks to those same brothers who taught me to protect myself." She scooped up some snow and tossed it at Miller. "But other than the persistent princess and sugar-high seven-year-olds, everything went well? Ella Rose had fun and was happy you were there?" Since she'd used Aidan to tempt Harper into selling the house and moving to Harmony Harbor, Julia had been a little curious—okay, a lot curious—as to whether it had changed the dynamics of their relationship. As innocently as possible, she slid the question in. "And Harper, how are you two getting along?"

"Good. Everything's good."

She looked at him, waiting for more. "Really? That's all you're giving me? You might want to remember who you have to thank for being this close"—she held her thumb and mittened fingers an inch apart—"to selling your house, to getting rid of the albatross around your neck, and, lest you forget, standing a much better chance of gaining custody of your daughter."

"And how would you know I'm this close"—he held his gloved thumb and forefinger an inch apart—"to selling my house?"

"Of course that's what you'd focus on. Despite what you're implying, I wasn't sticking my nose in your business. But for the record, you should be grateful that I have, once, well, more like a few times, stuck my nose in your business."

"I'm waiting."

She sighed. "My friend called to thank me for the lead and mentioned her buyer was very interested. Just so you know, the offer will be conditional on a quick close. They want in before Christmas."

"Come on, you can't be serious. Harper's already starting to balk. I can't see her accepting on that timeline."

"You're the one paying the mortgage. Shouldn't it be up to you and not Harper?"

"I guess it'll depend on what they offer," he said as they stopped outside her store. A horn beeped, and they turned. It was Paul and Maggie. "Jesus," Aidan grunted when Miller took off like a shot after the SUV, dragging Aidan along for the ride.

"Watch out for the snowplow!" Julia cried, but Aidan was already diving for Miller, rolling them both safely out of the way.

The snow-covered man and dog made their way back to the sidewalk with Miller looking suitably chastened.

"Are you okay? Come in and dry off. I'll get Miller some water, and you something hot to drink."

"Appreciate the offer, but your place will smell like

wet dog for a week." Miller looked up at him with sad
eyes, and Aidan sighed, giving the dog a quick rub.
"I get it, buddy. We'll stop by Maggie's on our way
home." He returned his attention to Julia and rubbed the
back of his neck with a self-conscious look on his face.
"So, you know how I suggested you get Paul and Maggie together? I was wrong. I want you to break them up
and get Maggie back with my dad."

"You're serious? You're not just teasing me, are
you?"

"No. I'll even give you a hand. Just tell me what you
need me to do."

There it was, proof there really was something
magical about the first snowfall of the season. Because all the evidence was pointing to the Gallaghers
finding their happily-ever-afters by New Year's Eve.
"Okay, I'll call Paul first thing tomorrow morning
and...hmm, I don't think it's a good idea if I fake-
date him again," she mused, and then she realized
she'd been talking out loud and Aidan was staring at
her.

"Tell me you didn't just say what I think you did?"

"I didn't. I was...thinking out loud. Ruminating.
Storyboarding. Just, you know, doing my usual thing."

He put his hands on her waist and drew her toward
him. "I kissed you tonight and plan on kissing you a
whole lot more. So that means no dating other men, especially one old enough to be your father. That goes for
fake-dating too."

And that would go down as the very first time mistakenly talking out loud instead of in her head had a

positive outcome. She wondered if Aidan realized what his response to her slip-up seemed to say. She reached up to brush the snow off his hair and his shoulders, using any excuse to touch him. "So, you're saying we're dating? As in you and me are exclusive? No Paul or Harper or anyone else?"

"I...yeah, I guess I am. Just you and me. Dating... each other."

"Wow, I bet you sound more enthusiastic when you tell the dentist to go ahead and pull your tooth without novocaine."

He laughed. "I'm not sure. I've never had a tooth pulled."

"Of course you haven't. Your teeth are perfect."

"Doesn't sound like you plan on following that up with *and so are you*," he said dryly as he tugged her against him. "Less than twenty minutes ago, I basically told you I wasn't interested in anything more than a physical relationship. And now we're *dating*."

"Okay, now you sound like I'm holding a gun to your head, and I'd like to remind you that the dating thing was your idea, not mine. And the only reason you suggested we date is because you don't like the idea of me seeing anyone else while we're working through this thing between us. Whatever this thing is."

"Yeah, you're...Hang on a sec. I have to take this." He stepped back to pull his vibrating cell from the pocket of his leather jacket. "Hey, Harper. Tonight? All right. Yeah, I can be there in about an hour. You know what, better make it two to be on the safe side. Snow's still coming down pretty hard."

"They're making an offer?" Julia asked when he ended the call.

"Yeah. The Realtor is bringing it over to the house. Probably better if I'm there rather than on speakerphone. Especially if you're right and they want a quick close."

She stared at him, her heart in her throat. "I don't know what I was thinking. We can't date. Not until Harper agrees to sell the house and move here. If she thinks she doesn't have a chance to win you back, she has no reason—"

Aidan shut her up with a kiss, which she would've had a problem with at any other time. But when she was basically suggesting he woo his ex and he stopped her... Well, she didn't really mind. It also helped that the man could kiss. She may have even groaned her disappointment when he drew away. Only he didn't get far because Miller had wrapped his leash around them.

Once they'd finally gotten Miller to go back the other way so they could free themselves, Aidan said, "Harper knows exactly where our relationship stands. I cleared things up earlier tonight. Even though I wasn't happy about what you pulled the other night, it ended up being a good thing. We talked about what went wrong with our marriage, civilly. Something we've never been able to do in the past. It was cathartic, for both of us, I think."

"I really am good, aren't I?"

"I was hoping I'd find that out tonight. But it looks like that'll have to wait."

* * *

Twenty hours later, Julia carried a tray of coffee and cookies to the sitting area beside the electric fireplace at the front of the bookstore. Today she wasn't feeling quite so good about herself and the choices she'd made. She owed Paul the truth about her and Aidan.

When Paul had discovered Aidan at her apartment the other night, he'd grudgingly accepted the explanation that Aidan had stopped by and found Julia burning up with fever. Not only did she have to tell him about her and Aidan, but she had to confess why she'd steered him in Maggie's direction and then ask him to please stop dating the artist.

Covering her nerves with a smile, Julia walked to where Paul sat on the cozy two-seater. As she did, she thought about how often she'd had to fake a smile, fake being the happy, cheerful optimist whose life was wonderful. She didn't recall the exact date or the exact moment or the reason why she'd begun having to pretend to feel something she didn't, but she thought it may have been around the time she realized she couldn't go through with her marriage to Josh.

The changes in him had been gradual yet devastating nonetheless. It had felt like their relationship had died a day at a time, slowly and painfully. She hadn't thought anything could be more excruciating...Eight months before he took his own life, he'd become unrecognizable to her.

He'd turned sullen, growing increasingly frustrated and irritated at the smallest of things, real or imagined. He'd lost interest in both her and the bookstore and spent the majority of his time alone at his writer's shed.

When she questioned him, he'd have an excuse at the ready. His work on his new play was either going too well to stop or too horribly to do the same. He didn't seek her advice or ask her to read his screenplays like he used to. He had no time for her writing either. Within months, she'd lost not only the man she'd loved but her best friend and business partner too.

Those stark reminders of what her life had been like made it harder to keep the fake smile in place for Paul. Soon, she told herself, soon she would have paid her debt and all the plotting and scheming would end. But until then... "I appreciate your stopping by, Paul."

"I'd like to think I'd have called you up this morning if you hadn't called me first, but I never did like to be the bearer of bad news."

She sat on the edge of the chair across from him, an uncomfortable tightness growing in her chest. As much as Paul didn't like to be the bearer of bad news, she was getting tired of receiving it. "Mrs. Bradford isn't trying to stop the lobster tree lighting or the parade this weekend, is she?"

"No, it's me. There's no way to sugarcoat this, so I'll give you the straight-up truth. I've been stepping out on you with Maggie, darlin'. I knew you'd be wondering what I was up to after last night. I figured, if I honked the horn, you'd assume it was just an innocent meeting between the two of us, but you deserve better." He reached across the low table to take her hands. "You're a sweetheart, and the last thing I want to do is hurt you, but I'm too old for you anyway. Can you forgive me?"

"There's nothing to forgive, Paul." She gave his

hands a gentle squeeze before releasing them. "I enjoyed spending time with you too. But you didn't do anything wrong. We never said we were exclusive. Besides, I have a confession of my own, and I hope you won't be upset. I've started dating Aidan."

His brow furrowed. "I guess I was so frazzled about seeing you when I was with Maggie that I didn't pay close enough attention to what you were up to last night. I have to be honest. I'm not sure he's a choice your father would approve of any more than me. You're too tenderhearted for a man like Aidan Gallagher, darlin'."

"Why don't you like him, Paul? I've never really understood what your problem with Aidan is. I mean, I know you didn't appreciate Kitty trying to bribe you to retire so Aidan could take your job. Or that he basically hijacked your investigation into Olivia's disappearance and hauled me down to the station to interrogate me, but it seems like there's something more."

"You're right, none of that went over well with me. But I've known the Gallagher family a long time. I consider Colin a friend. So I was willing to give Aidan a chance despite my misgivings. With some convincing from you, I might add."

"Yes, and just so you know, we weren't dating at the time. We weren't even friends. Olivia had told me he needed a job to convince the judge to grant him shared custody of his little girl. I'd heard he had an excellent reputation as a DEA agent, so I thought—"

"He did. And if he could get a handle on his issues, I doubt there'd be a better cop than Aidan Gallagher in the entire state. But he has an attitude problem, he doesn't like or respect authority, and he's a ticking time bomb. He's a dangerous man. Has he talked to you about his last undercover assignment with the DEA?"

Her fingers tightened around her mug of coffee, afraid of what he was about to say.

Paul searched her face and nodded. "I thought not. He was an undercover agent for almost a decade and had a reputation as one of the best. Up until his last assignment, that is. He was undercover with a motorcycle gang for more than a year. Things started heating up last March, and Aidan disappeared off everyone's radar, no communication. They learned later that his cover had been compromised. He's lucky to be alive. He held out against them, didn't give them the information they were looking for. It takes a different breed of man to be able to do that, Julia. I'm not exaggerating or trying to frighten you off when I say he's dangerous. I'm just stating a fact."

"You implied the assignment tarnished his reputation. I don't understand how."

"There's no doubt that in some circles he's revered as a hero. Just not by the powers that be. Aidan had help on the inside and managed to save the op and take the gang down. But from what I've heard, he didn't trust the authorities to protect the man who helped him."

"Who was it?" As far as Julia was concerned, both Aidan and the man deserved a medal.

"The younger brother of the leader of the gang. Aidan let him go." Paul looked at her and slowly nodded. "I see you're in the hero camp. Boys at the station would agree with you. But it won't be only Aidan who suffers the consequences if he loses control one day on the job. It will be all of us at HHPD." He considered her carefully. "Maybe I'm selling you short, darlin'. Maybe you're the one who can get him to deal with his issues, get him into a good anger management program."

"I can. I can totally do that." She thought about how stubborn he could be. "If I can't, I promise to help him find a way to deal with his anger. He'll be one of the best officers you've ever had, Paul. I promise. You won't be sorry you hired him."

"If he ever hurts you, he's the one who'll be sorry."

"You're a sweet man." He was, and now she had to hurt his feelings. This fairy godmother gig was hard. "You deserve a woman who will love you unconditionally, Paul, and, um, that's not Maggie."

Chapter Sixteen

♥

Lately, it seemed like Colleen couldn't relax and simply enjoy a special event at the manor. There was always a crisis of some sort that she was trying to manage. She supposed it hadn't been much different when she'd been alive. Though after the loss of Mary, Riley, and Ronan—Kitty's husband and Colleen's son—there hadn't been much celebrating of any kind at the manor. Especially Christmas.

Because of their grief, she and Kitty had let Greystone fall into disrepair, and business had suffered. So had the town. But Sophie, as manager of the manor, had turned things around. She'd also reinstated a long-held Gallagher tradition.

Once the parade had made its way from the harbor to the town hall, the parade goers were invited back to the manor for free hot chocolate, baked goods, and a visit with Santa. The Widows Club provided the entertainment.

It was the only time Colleen questioned Sophie's judgment, because there wasn't one member of the

Widows Club who could carry a tune. If Sophie wanted entertainment that would draw a crowd, she should be getting her husband and his brothers to sing, Colleen thought as she looked to where the Widows Club were gathering on the grand staircase.

They were trying to keep their full skirts from knocking over the gold pots of poinsettias lining either side of the red runner. This year, their long dresses were green velvet and paired with white fake fur shawls and wide-brimmed bonnets.

So far the women hadn't managed to break into Jasper's room. Not for lack of trying though. As soon as Kitty had recovered from her near-faint that day in the sitting room, the women had been on her like dirty shirts. Colleen knew she had to figure out something soon. Her plan to get Jasper's eyes on Ida's paper hadn't worked as planned. Jasper was completely ignoring Simon's attempts to get his attention these days. She'd thought by now the lad would have learned his lesson.

At least the Widows Club would be occupied while the children were paying their visit to Santa. Colleen didn't want to miss out on that. It was the first Christmas for Griffin and Liam's sons, and neither George nor Ella Rose had attended the event before either: George because she'd lived in Kenya and Ella Rose because her parents were daft. Who in their right mind wouldn't want their wee one to believe in Santa Claus? Colleen chuckled at the sight of Julia entering the manor in her red coat and hat. She'd like to be in the room when Aidan tried to explain Harper's no-Santa rule to Julia.

Colleen had heard through the manor grapevine that the couple were dating. She would have done a jig if not for the Widows Club's determination to find her book. Aidan and Julia might not need any help from her in the matchmaking department, but Julia needed Colleen to protect her secret.

She felt a little better when Julia handed her coat to Jasper. Sometimes Colleen thought she was all alone in her schemes, but it appeared her great-granddaughters-in-law were on the job today. Last year's cute elf costume had been replaced by a sexy one. Julia wore black knee-high boots, red and white stockings, and a flared green velvet dress with a shiny black belt and a hood trimmed in white fur.

Colleen walked to the entrance to try to gain Jasper's attention before the parade goers arrived. Julia was admiring the display Jasper had created on the pedestal table. He'd made a red poinsettia tree with white poinsettias serving as the base. Colleen usually picked apart his floral arrangement to capture his attention but didn't feel right doing so on such a special day.

Instead, she moved to Julia's side and tugged on the white pom-poms that hung on the strings from her hood.

Jasper's eyebrow went up, and then he looked around, presumably for Simon, his first clue that Colleen was around. "Perhaps you'd like to give Master Colin a hand with his costume. He's playing Santa this year," he said to Julia.

"Yes, I know. It's a shame that Fergus had to bail at the last minute, isn't it?" Julia said with a grin, turning as the stately front door opened and Maggie walked in.

"Yay!" She hugged the other woman. "I can't tell you how much I appreciate you helping out."

"How could I say no after you introduced me to Lenny and helped me organize my wine and cheese party?"

"Is he as talented as I think, Maggie?"

"Incredibly so. His work reminds me a little of Andrew Wyeth. I just wish he'd see someone. Get some help."

"I know it probably doesn't seem like much to you, but yesterday was a really big step for him. A month ago, he never would have gone to the studio on his own. We'll talk later though." Julia picked up a bag from the floor. "Right now, you have to get into your costume. You can change in the study like we all did."

"But, Miss Julia..." Jasper trailed off at the look Julia shot him before she hustled Maggie down the hall to the study. "Well, Madame, it appears the last of the Harmony Harbor Gallaghers will find their happily-ever-afters this year." He smiled, watching Julia shove Maggie into the study and shut the door. "I must say Miss Julia and Miss Maggie will round out the family nicely."

From down the hall, they heard Maggie call out, "Julia, there's been a mistake. Can you please let me out?"

"Julia, open this door right now," came Colin's voice.

"Sorry, it's stuck," Julia said, pulling so hard on the doorknob that she was practically sitting on the floor. "Jasper, help!" she half-whispered, half-yelled.

"Coming, miss." He chuckled. "I wonder if Master Aidan has any idea what he's gotten himself into."

"We'll soon find out," Colleen said when Aidan pushed open the manor's front door. *Yes, indeed, we will,* she thought, noting Ella Rose's absence.

Colin and Maggie's shouts from the study drew Aidan's attention. He turned his head, and a smile spread across his face.

"Well, isn't that a sight for sore eyes, laddie. If I didn't already know Julia was the one for you, that smile would have decided it for me."

A small measure of her happiness disappeared at the thought of what would happen should Julia's secret be revealed. Colleen had to find a way to warn Jasper.

* * *

"Well, that didn't go as well as I had hoped," Julia said, watching with a disheartened expression on her face when Aidan's dad, dressed as Santa, scowled at the three of them and stalked from the study.

"You forgot your beard and hat, Colin, um, Santa," Jasper corrected as parade goers started to arrive at the manor.

His dad *harrumph*ed, turned around, and stalked back to the study. But he didn't have to go inside to retrieve the rest of his costume. Maggie tossed him his hat and beard and then slammed the door.

Julia hid her face on Aidan's shoulder as Jasper helped a grumbling Santa on with his beard and hat.

"It seemed like such a great idea when I first came up with it," she said, her voice muffled.

"You never know. Something good still might come of it," he said, stroking her hair. "At least Maggie didn't leave."

Julia lifted her head and smiled. "You're right. There's still lots of time to turn things around." Stretching up on her toes, she gave him a quick kiss. "Thanks for trying to help." She looked around. "Where's Ella Rose?"

"Uh, with Harper." He had to distract her fast or his father wouldn't be the only one ticked at him. "So you're an elf again. Great-looking costume, sugarplum. Maybe after your shift we can—"

"Why are you trying to distract me?" Her eyes widened. "Oh no, is Harper playing hardball with you again? She wouldn't let Ella Rose come today?"

For a brief moment, he considered throwing Harper under the bus. But sooner or later the truth would come out; it always did. "It's not a big deal, okay? It's just that Harper and I don't believe in lying to kids, so..."

Julia crossed her arms, and one of her sexy boots began to tap on the slate floor.

"Ella Rose knows there's no such thing as Santa Claus," he finished quickly.

"Oh no, that's so sad. She's only seven. I hate when that happens. Who told her? Someone at..." She stared at him. "No, you didn't. Please tell me it wasn't you."

"Okay, don't go all angry elf on me. We had our reasons—"

She raised her hand. "I can't even." And stomped off.

An hour later, Julia's mood obviously hadn't improved.

"Whoa, that is one ticked-off elf," Liam said, leaning against the bar as he gently bounced his seven-week-old baby boy in his arms. He smiled at his wife, who was standing in line with Mia.

"Okay, boys, raise your hand if you've ever seen Julia Landon without a smile on her face," Griffin said, grinning at Ava, who was making Gabriel giggle while she and Lexi stood in the long line with the baby.

No one raised their hand but Aidan. His brothers laughed at him.

"If it makes you feel better, bro, Olivia says I'm the only one who ever got mad at her, and look at us now." Finn smiled, winking at his wife, who stood in line with George.

To prove his brothers wrong, Aidan smiled and winked at Julia, who was talking to the kids and his brothers' wives. She looked at him and gently knocked a fist to the side of her head with her thumb out.

"Okay, I don't read sign language, but I don't think she's telling you that she loves you," Liam said.

"Nope, she told him he's a jerk," Finn said, trying not to laugh, but Aidan heard the chuckle in his voice.

"All right, it's obvious you need our help. How badly did you screw up?" Griffin asked.

"Leave it to me to get involved with Santa's little helper," Aidan grumbled, crossing his arms. His brothers waited him out. "Okay, Harper and I have never gone all out at Christmas. We keep it low-key. No Santa and—"

"Wait. What did you just mumble?" Griffin asked.

"No Santa. He said *no Santa*." Finn glowered at Aidan.

"Jeez, Finn, keep it down." Liam covered the baby's ears. "Uh-oh, you're in real trouble now. Here comes George."

Aidan groaned when she bypassed Finn and walked straight to him. She looked up at him with her big blue eyes and said in her raspy little voice, "Julia says you're not the Beast anymore. You're the Grinch. If you let her, she'll make your heart grow twice its size, and you'll believe in Santa again."

"You're so smart, sweetheart. If anyone can make your uncle Aidan's heart get big, it's Julia. I bet you that by Christmas Eve, he'll be putting out snacks for Santa just like us," Finn said.

"He better or Julia won't marry him. She can't. You gotta have Christmas spirit if you marry Santa's helper, you know."

He glared at his brothers, who were trying to keep straight faces. "Thanks for the advice, George. But I'm not—"

Liam shut up Aidan with an elbow in his ribs.

"Yes, you will. Me and Mia are talking to Santa about you. And Julia too." George skipped off.

"Looks like you better start picking out your wedding song, bro. Everyone knows a wish whispered in Santa's ear comes true. Just look at me and Soph. We're living proof that they do," his baby brother said.

Aidan rolled his eyes. "You do know that the man in the red suit and fake beard is Dad, right?"

"Ah yeah, and it looks like his wish just came true," Griffin said.

They looked over to see Maggie sprawled on Santa's lap.

"How did that happen?" Aidan asked.

"Julia stuck her foot out and tripped her."

* * *

Colleen followed Jasper to his room. It had taken more than four hours to get his attention.

"Given the mess you made of the library, I'm assuming this is what you were getting at, Madame. I still have the cleanup to take care of, so I hope it doesn't take all evening for you to convey what it is you wish me to see in the book."

And there it was, her conundrum. She still had no idea how to warn him about Kitty and the Widows Club's plan. She looked around his room as he went to the far wall to remove the landscape over his safe.

Spotting a copy of the *Harmony Harbor Gazette*, she scanned the front-page articles for words that she could point out and then realized that wouldn't do a whole heck a lot of good since he couldn't see her finger.

If only she had someone…George! Up until a week ago, the little girl had still been able to see Colleen. She should have thought of George before. Colleen rushed from Jasper's room, down the stairs and into lobby, or the great room, as she thought of it. There were a few stragglers about, but she didn't see any evidence of Finn, Olivia, and George. Or the Widows Club. She wasn't sure whether that was a good sign or a bad one.

She was on her way to the study when she came upon Aidan and Julia in the hall. They were kissing under the mistletoe. Now, that did her body good. And reminded her of how important it was that she found a way to convey the danger to Jasper. She walked into the study and almost walked through Maggie and Colin, who were kissing on the other side of the door.

She didn't need any more signs about the importance of somehow communicating to Jasper that the Widows Club were on the hunt for her book. That's it, she had her answer. She called for Simon and had to wait for what felt like an eternity for Colin to let him in the study. She would have been amused to see her grandson so flustered by being interrupted by a cat if she didn't have a job to do.

"All right, Simon." She pointed to a small photo on her desk. It had been taken more than a decade before when they'd started the Widows Club. "When I knock this onto the floor, you pick it up and scoot out the door as soon as Maggie leaves."

Colleen would have been overjoyed that the couple couldn't seem to stop kissing if not for the gravity of the situation. She knocked the photo on the floor, and they jumped apart like a pair of guilty teenagers. It was only last year that she'd pulled the same trick on Liam and Sophie.

"I should probably leave," Maggie said, looking both flustered and pleased. "Would you and Miller like to come for dinner tonight?"

"There's nowhere we'd rather be."

"Oh, for the love of all that's holy. You'll see each other in an hour. Give it a rest," Colleen said when they kissed again.

Finally, Maggie opened the door, and Simon scampered by with the photograph in his mouth. Aidan and Julia were no longer in the hallway, and Colleen noticed the mistletoe had disappeared too. The journey to Jasper's room wasn't as fast as she'd hoped. Every so often, Simon had to rest, the photograph weighing him down. Then it took another five minutes for Jasper to answer Simon's cries at the door.

"Did I not make it clear, Madame, that I had things to do? I don't have time for this." He frowned and picked up the photo of the Widows Club that Simon had dropped at his feet.

"Okay, now tug on Jasper's trousers and make like you're hunting a mouse, Simon."

The cat did what he was told. Jasper looked from the photo to Simon. "The Widows Club found a mouse?"

"I don't know, lad. You're usually much sharper than this. Lovesick, that's what his problem is, Simon. Until he gets over it, he won't be much use to us, I'm afraid."

Erin, one of the manor's waitresses, appeared. "Sorry to disturb you, sir. But we have a problem with one of the dinner guests. Mrs. Gallagher told me to get you."

Colleen went on high alert.

Jasper didn't. He slid the photo into his breast pocket and closed the door to follow after Erin.

"Simon, stop him!" Colleen cried, hurrying through

the door and into Jasper's room. If she had a heart, it would have stopped. Jasper's safe was open, and the book was on the bed.

At the beep of the passkey, Colleen sighed in relief. "What were you thinking leaving the book out in the open, you daft lad?" She turned.

It wasn't Jasper. It was Kitty.

Chapter Seventeen

♥

The Thursday after the parade, Julia was turning her sign in the window to CLOSED when Lenny appeared at her door. He had the hood of his olive-green puffy jacket pulled low, a knitted gray hat pulled lower, and a gray wool scarf wrapped around his neck and face. Pretty much the only things visible were the bridge of his nose and his eyes.

She opened the door and smiled. "Come on in."

"Nah, you're closing."

"That's okay. I'm always open for friends. Besides, I'm closed earlier than usual. It's Girls' Night Out."

"Yeah? What's that?" he asked as he came in, taking a seat at the counter.

"It's a shopping night for ladies only. And because a lot of the business owners are women, we're opening in shifts so we can all enjoy the evening and get some shopping done too. We have temporary liquor licenses so each store can serve a signature drink. Mine is a Hot Chocolate Martini with vanilla vodka and Baileys."

He'd lowered his scarf and taken off his gloves.

"You better be careful. You don't want someone drinking at your store and then driving. You might get charged or sued if they're in an accident."

"No one will be driving tonight. We've hired several horse-drawn sleighs to provide transportation, and there are drop-off and pick-up points all over town. Main Street will close in about an hour until midnight." It was the one time Julia wished she lived somewhere other than Main Street. Maybe she'd walk to one of the pick-up points just so she could go for a sleigh ride. "Now, what can I get you? How about a hot chocolate and a double chocolate cupcake? Mackenzie made them, and they're awesome."

"Sure. Thanks." He reached in his pocket and put a twenty-dollar bill on the counter. She could tell by the way he did it and the expression on his face that this was a proud moment for him.

"Hey, what's this? Have you been holding out on me?" she asked, taking a cupcake from the bakery case.

"Maggie sold one of my paintings."

"Lenny!" Julia dropped the cupcake and launched herself across the counter to hug him. "That is the most amazing news. I'm so proud of you. You must be over the moon. Tell me you're over the moon."

His soulful brown eyes were warm and shiny. "Yeah, I think I'm almost as happy about it as you are." He laughed and then sobered. "It wouldn't have happened without you, Julia. I owe everything to you. And one day, I'm going to repay you."

"This is all the payback I need, Lenny. Truly." She tilted her head. "Okay, maybe there's one other thing that you could do for me. I want this to be the start of a wonderful new life for you. But I think, for that to happen, you need to talk to someone."

"I talk to you and the guys. And Maggie."

She sensed him shutting down and didn't want to ruin his day. "I know, and you're doing amazing. Just promise you'll think about it, okay?" She turned to get him his hot chocolate. "This is definitely a triple whip-and-sprinkles kind of day, wouldn't you agree?"

He smiled and nodded. "Yeah. And I didn't tell you the rest of my news. Maggie's going to let me rent a room at her place."

"Wow, that so great. Maggie's the best, isn't she? And talk about talented." She turned to hand him his hot chocolate. He was off the stool and at the door. "Lenny, what's wrong?"

"Gotta go. I'll see you around," he said, and slipped outside. Head bent and shoulders bowed, he disappeared past her shop window. She was staring after him when her door chimed.

"What was he doing in here? And why did he take off as soon as he saw me coming?"

"Maybe because you're in uniform and you look a little intimidating when you scowl like that."

"Yeah, you look terrified." Aidan leaned across the counter and wrapped his cold hand around her neck, drawing her in for a kiss. "You taste good."

"You look good. I love a man in uniform." It was true, but she probably should have kept it to herself. The uniform was a sore spot for Aidan. He'd figured Paul would forget about putting him in a patrol car once he'd served his suspension. He didn't, and Julia knew why. She'd yet to fill in Aidan though.

"Sorry, babe. I don't plan to be wearing one for long."

She debated whether or not to tell him about her conversation with Paul. They had so little time together that she hated to bring it up. But…"Have you asked Paul when he plans to reinstate you as a detective?"

His eyes narrowed. "No, have you?"

"Not exactly. But you know the day he came in and I talked to him about your dad and Maggie, and he so graciously agreed to back off because he's a nice man and friends with your father?"

Aidan bowed his head and took a deep breath before giving her a long and drawn-out "Yes."

"Okay, so he told me why he has a problem with you."

"That was a week ago tomorrow, and you're just telling me about it now?"

"It's not exactly the kind of thing you tell someone over the phone or when they stop by on their break or for a quick lunch, and we haven't had any more time than that."

"Because, thanks to you, we sold our house, and I have two weeks to take care of the concerns listed in the inspector's report. You know the only way I can get everything done is to work after my shifts and on weekends. We could have spent last Saturday together, but you were busy playing Santa's little helper and giving me a hard time for not bringing Ella Rose."

"Yes, and rightly so. She missed out on a special day

with her family. Talk about stealing the joy out of the holidays. Do the three of you walk around saying *bah humbug* for the entire month of December?"

"We've talked about this, and it didn't go well, so maybe we should just agree to disagree, okay?"

"Fine. Here." She handed him the hot chocolate. "We've been dating for a whole week. We should celebrate."

His mouth twitched, and he put the cup on the counter. Leaning in, he framed her face with his hands. "Happy anniversary, sugarplum," he said, and kissed her.

Five minutes later, she came up for air. "Keep kissing me like that and I might forgive you for spending all your free time with your ex." She winced. "That sounded like I'm jealous of Harper, and I'm not. I just wish we had more time together. Are you sure you're not just using getting the house ready as an excuse? I'd rather you be honest if—" He shut her up with a kiss that wasn't soft and tender. It was demanding and deep.

"Was that honest enough for you? I'm thirty-seven, Julia. I don't play games. If I don't want to date you, I'll tell you. I expect you to do the same."

"You're mad at me."

"Yeah, I am. Look, I'm as frustrated as you are. I thought we'd have last Saturday and Sunday together. I didn't know Harper planned to break the news to Ella Rose on Saturday or that she expected me to check out every house for sale in Harmony Harbor and the adjoining counties on Sunday. But we should be good for this Saturday."

She caught her bottom lip between her teeth.

"You've got to be kidding me. You have another Christmas thing?"

"You could come with me. We're going caroling."

"Nice try." He checked his watch. "Break's almost over. Are you going to tell me what Benson said?"

She gave him the skinny on the conversation, minus the promise she'd made Paul. "It's just a thought, but if he thinks you need to learn to control your temper, how about taking an anger management course? You know, I've been thinking about taking one lately. Hey, I have a great idea. Why don't we take the class together?"

"You, taking an anger management course?" She could tell he was trying not to laugh, but he was only able to hold out for so long.

"I don't know why you find it so unbelievable that I get angry, Aidan. I've gotten angry at you."

"Right, you get in a snit, tell me I'm a jerk in ASL, and then less than an hour later, you're kissing me under the mistletoe. You don't have anger issues, babe."

"But you do?"

"I dealt with violent people when I was undercover. Sometimes, that's the only thing they respect. But that part of my life is over. I'm good, Julia. If I didn't think I was, I'd talk to someone about it."

"Paul thinks you keep your anger contained, and one day it's going to explode."

"Benson doesn't know what he's talking about. I'm no different from half the guys you know. When I need a release, I work out."

She smiled and leaned over the counter to squeeze

his biceps through his jacket. "Do you work out at Fun Fitness?"

He laughed. "No, I work out at the Y with a couple of guys. We do MMA. Mixed Martial Arts," he clarified.

"I was going to suggest we work out together, but that sounds a little hard-core for me. Maybe you could change it up once in a while and do yoga with me. We could work on alleviating our stress together."

"As much fun as that sounds, sugarplum, I have a better idea." He leaned in and whispered in her ear. She shivered not only because his warm breath tickled but because his idea involved them naked and in a bed and in other interesting locations she hadn't thought about. It sounded like he was going to be an adventurous lover. Maybe she should have had him advise her on other parts of her manuscript.

"I think we need to be in the same room for longer than ten minutes for that to happen," she told him, fanning her warm face. There were other parts of her that were warm, but fanning them probably wasn't a good idea.

"Definitely need all day and all night for what I have planned. What do you say we work on that?"

Enthusiastically nodding in response to his question while at the same time imagining exactly what that day and night might entail, she must have missed whatever he said given that he was frowning at her and repeating her name. She glanced at the twenty in his hand. "Lenny left it," she said, and then told Aidan his news. "Isn't that fantastic?"

"Yeah, but I can almost guarantee my dad won't be happy to hear Maggie's renting him a room."

"Please don't say anything. I don't want this to come between Maggie and your dad."

"I don't see that happening. They're in a pretty good place right now. I overheard him on the phone with Maggie this morning. He told her he loved her *too*."

"Wow, I thought it would take longer. This is…this is the most amazing news." She pressed her hands to her chest, rapidly blinking back the tears welling in her eyes. She couldn't cry in front of Aidan. He'd want to know why the news affected her so deeply. "Your dad got another happily-ever-after."

"I guess he did."

"Are you happy?"

"About my dad and Maggie? Yeah."

"Well, yes, but I was thinking more about you personally. Are *you* happy?"

He seemed to have to think about it a minute, and then he gave her one of his slow smiles that curled her toes. "Yeah, I'm happy, sugarplum. And you played a part in that. So thanks. Now I really do need to go or someone will rat me out to the chief. Don't get rowdy tonight. I wouldn't want to have to arrest you."

She smiled and mentally hung up her fairy godmother wings. She'd done it. She'd fulfilled her vow to Josh with three weeks to spare.

* * *

"Patrol car six, there's been a disturbance reported at Books and Beans."

Aidan bowed his head. "Copy that." If it'd been a call for any place other than Julia's, he would have been more than happy to hear the dispatcher's voice. There hadn't been much action in town, and his shift was dragging. It would have been worse if he hadn't brought his notes along.

Unbeknownst to the chief or Aidan's family, he was looking deeper into his mother and sister's accident. He'd found something he hadn't seen before. Probably because he'd been grief-stricken when he'd asked to see the evidence within days of the accident.

Looking through the file with fresh eyes, he'd found a notation that blue paint had been found on the rear bumper of his mom's white car. But more promising was a new eyewitness.

The officer at the scene had taken the man's contact information, but from what Aidan could tell, they'd never been able to reach him. After trying several times over the course of two years, they appeared to have given up. Aidan had finally gotten a lead on the man yesterday. Within a week of the accident, the witness had received an offer for a new job and moved from Boston to LA. He'd left no forwarding address. And over the intervening years, he had changed companies and moved two more times. Aidan had worked his contacts to get the information he needed. Now he just hoped it paid off. He'd left a message on the guy's voice mail earlier today.

Aidan passed two horse-drawn sleighs at the bottom

of the hill as he drove to Books and Beans. He pulled into a spot at the end of Main Street, which was closed to traffic for another hour. Obviously, he could park his patrol car wherever he wanted, but he didn't trust the groups of women weaving along the street not to walk into or in front of his vehicle. He'd forgotten about the signature drinks.

"This should be fun," he said as he got out of the patrol car.

"You may want to call for backup, son," said one of the older men sitting in a sleigh. "Anyone who says men are hard to handle when they get liquored up hasn't spent much time with those gals."

"I should be good, thanks." Aidan questioned the validity of that statement two doors down from Books and Beans when raised voices filtered onto the street. If they sounded raised out here, it meant there was screaming going on inside. He briefly wondered if he should radio in for backup. But he didn't want to do anything that might reflect badly on Julia and her business. The woman worked too hard to have him making the wrong call and messing things up for her.

As soon as he opened the door to Books and Beans, he knew someone was already trying to do just that. He recognized Old Lady Bradford yelling, "I'm telling you, my daughter just bought this book, and it's pornography pure and simple. The only reason you're defending her, Ava DiRossi, is because you're married to a Gallagher and the hussy is dating one."

A group of women, including the two baristas, were watching the show from under the arch between the

coffee shop and bookstore. He remembered the older
barista from when she filled in for Julia. "Donna." He
had to raise his voice to be heard over the mayor, who,
at that moment, was doing a good job of defending Julia
against Mrs. Bradford's charges. "Donna."

The woman turned, and he nodded at the cash register.

"Oh, sorry, Officer. I wasn't thinking. I shouldn't
have left the cash unattended." She hurried back around
the counter. "I'm so glad you're here. Poor Julia. They
were all having such a wonderful time until Mrs. Bradford and her posse showed up. She's just looking for
an excuse to get Julia kicked off as head of the Christmas committee, you know. Jealous old battle-ax." She
flushed. "I know that's not very Christian, but she's a
mean-spirited old woman."

"It's all right. I'll go——" There were several loud
thuds followed by shocked gasps. So much for thinking
Hazel had it handled. He'd been hanging back in hopes
they wouldn't need him. He was pretty sure that as soon
as Mrs. Bradford saw a uniform, the situation would go
from bad to worse.

Delaney pushed past the women crowded under the
archway. "Donna, try calling the police again——" She
spotted Aidan. "What are you doing standing out here?
Get in there before the fight between Hazel and Mrs.
Bradford gets physical." She grabbed him by the arm.

He peeled her fingers from his forearm as they made
their way through the throng of women.

"I swear to God, I'm going to strangle Julia. It's as
if she's determined to ruin Hazel's reputation. How am

I supposed to explain the videos of Hazel defending a woman who sells porn?"

"She doesn't sell porn, Delaney."

On the other side of the shop, near the electric fireplace hanging on the wall, he spotted Hazel facing down Old Lady Bradford and her friends. His sisters-in-law and the owners of the bakery, flower shop, and bridal store were helping Julia pick up books from the floor.

Julia stood with a bunch of paperbacks in her arms. She wore a red dress and black boots and had her hair in a messy knot. It didn't matter that the dress clinging to her curves was as sexy as her high-heeled boots; she still managed to project an air of innocence.

He was thinking she was too sweet for her own good when she said, "Mrs. Bradford, this is the last time I'll ask you and your friends to leave. If you refuse, I'll have you charged with defamation of character, destruction of private property, and ruining a perfectly lovely evening with your petty vindictiveness. If this is all because I was named chair of the Christmas committee, then I quit. I don't need a silly title or position."

Mrs. Bradford looked torn until ninety percent of the women in attendance loudly begged Julia not to quit. Then she spotted him. "Officer, arrest her! She's selling pornography."

He ignored Mrs. Bradford and walked to Julia's side. "You okay?"

She nodded, but the disheartened expression on her face said she was far from okay.

"Mrs. Bradford, leave quietly as Julia asked, or I

will charge you with destruction of private property."
He took one of the books—*Warrior's Kiss* by J. L.
Winters—from Julia and held it up. The cover had been
damaged.

"Don't think you can intimidate me, young man.
This time I will not only ask that you be suspended,
but I'll have your badge. There are laws against selling...smut." She grabbed the book from Aidan's hand
and went to rip it up.

He closed his hand over her wrist and brought her
arm behind her back as he loudly read Mrs. Bradford
her rights. Since she was yelling for her friends to take
pictures for evidence in court, he had a feeling she
didn't hear him.

"Ma'am, don't worry about it," Lexi, his ex-sister-
in-law and a former military cop, said, holding up her
phone. "I've been recording the entire time. I even got
you pushing Julia out of the way just before you threw
the books off the shelf."

"You'll see. You'll all see. When I'm done with her,
she'll be behind bars for selling pornography."

"Mrs. Bradford, a judge will laugh this out of court.
Julia doesn't write porn. I read the second book in
her series, and it was great. Steamy, but definitely not
porn." He glanced at Julia. "What did you call it? An
urban fantasy romance?" Her mouth opened and closed.
He imagined she was surprised that he'd just admitted
not only to his sisters-in-law but at least forty-five other
women that he'd read a romance. He was kind of surprised himself, but he was tired of Old Lady Bradford
besmirching Julia's reputation. This was a small town

with old-fashioned values, and this needed to be cleared up ASAP.

It was like the oxygen had been sucked out of the room. The women were all staring at him without making a sound. It was so quiet he could hear his heart beat, and it was starting to beat louder and faster because, as he caught the expressions on the faces of Julia and his sisters-in-law, he realized what he'd done.

* * *

Thirty minutes later, after hauling Mrs. Bradford to the station, Aidan returned to Main Street. He got out of the patrol car and walked to where the old man was sitting on the sleigh. "Any chance I can borrow your horse and sleigh for half an hour? I'll give you a hundred bucks." It ended up costing him two hundred.

Aidan brought the horse to a stop in front of Books and Beans, the jingle of its bells loud in the still night air. He texted Julia. *Will you come for a ride in my sleigh tonight?*

He watched the screen for what felt like an hour but was probably only a couple of minutes. His phone kept dinging with incoming texts. They weren't from Julia. His brothers were having a laugh at his expense. Lexi had gotten his romance-reading confession on video.

The door to Books and Beans opened. Julia had her head bent looking at her keys and then her back to him as she locked the door.

He didn't realize he'd been holding his breath until she turned to walk to the sleigh with a sweet smile on her face. "How did you know this is exactly what I needed?"

It would have been worth a thousand bucks just to see that smile on her face and know she'd forgiven him for outing her as author J. L. Winters.

"You organized the event, so I figured it was something you'd like," he said as he helped her into the sleigh.

When he got in beside her, she snuggled against him. "Thank you for being so sweet." She laughed when he pressed his lips together. "I'm not mad, you know. You were just trying to help."

"And I managed to make everything a whole lot worse. I really am sorry, babe. The last thing I wanted to do is hurt you and your business."

"Hazel loved that I used J. L. Winters as my pen name. She's always thought of me as her daughter-in-law, and this made it seem real. In the end, your reputation probably took a bigger hit than mine. I sold every single copy of *Warrior's Kiss* except the one Mrs. Bradford ripped."

"I'll buy that one."

"Don't be silly. I'll give it to you." She looked up at the night sky. "It's starting to snow," she said, her voice tinged with wonder. "Ever since I was a little girl, I've dreamed of going for a sleigh ride in the snow." She lifted up to kiss his cheek. "Thank you for making my dreams come true, Aidan Gallagher."

Chapter Eighteen

♥

It was the Tuesday after Aidan had outed Julia as J. L. Winters, and Books and Beans had never been busier. She already had a wait list for *Warrior's Touch*. And just like she'd thought and worried incessantly about, everyone correctly suspected that Aidan was the inspiration for Adrian.

But even though she'd known that was likely to happen, she'd gone ahead and pulled the copies out of the storage room and put them out on the shelf just before opening her doors for Girl's Night Out. She'd needed an outward sign that she'd moved on from her job as the Gallaghers' fairy godmother. Something that symbolized she was moving on with her own future. That she was no longer stuck in the past and righting Josh's wrongs. She looked down at the new shipment of *Warrior's Kiss* that she was unpacking. The past could still come back and bite her in the butt.

She'd worked out some of her anger and grief over Josh's suicide by writing *Warrior's Kiss*. Like Josh, the character Jack Summers hides his involvement in the death of a prominent member of the village.

For a man like Aidan, it wouldn't take much for him to figure out the connection. She wondered if subconsciously that's why she'd given him a copy. Even though she'd convinced herself that she could live with the lie, maybe she couldn't. Maybe deep down she worried that hiding the truth would not only hurt her but hurt their relationship.

It was at times like this that she didn't think she'd ever be able to forgive Josh for putting her in this position. Then, like always, she remembered how much Hazel loved her son and how much she loved Julia, and understanding replaced anger. And unlike Aidan, it would never cross Hazel's mind that her son was the inspiration for Jack Summers. Because unlike Josh, Jack Summers makes amends for what he does. And he doesn't kill himself.

"I can put these on the shelf, Julia. Why don't you call it a day? Donna said you've been on the floor since nine this morning. It's almost seven. We can close."

"Really? I didn't realize it was that late. Thanks, Tammy," she said to her new hire. Byron and Poppy had insisted they interview Julia after the brouhaha with Mrs. Bradford, and Tammy, an aspiring YA author from Bridgeport, the next town over, applied the following day. Until she'd read the article, Tammy hadn't known there was a bookstore close by. "I wouldn't mind heading up. But you know what? I should probably sign these first."

"Do it tomorrow. If someone buys one tonight, I'll text you to come down."

She lifted an eyebrow at the eighteen-year-old with blue streaks in her curly dark hair. "Is there a reason why you're trying to get rid of me?"

"No, but if I had what was waiting for you upstairs waiting for me, I'd have been gone like ten minutes ago."

It couldn't be her dad. It had to be Aidan for Tammy to go all starry-eyed...Unless it was Julia's brothers. They'd been taking turns calling her once a day. Julia didn't know for sure, but she'd bet good money that Paul had called to have a little chat with her father and mentioned his concerns about Aidan. Not that she'd share that with Aidan. Things weren't going well for him at the station after the kerfuffle with Mrs. Bradford.

Julia brushed dust from the knees of her black leggings and picked some lint off her hot-pink sweater, though it was somewhat of a miracle that she could see it given the brightly colored Christmas lights that decorated the sweater. She'd completed the outfit with a matching headband.

She might have gone with something sexier rather than ugly sweaterish if she'd known Aidan didn't have to work a double shift. If someone was sick or wanted to switch, he was always the first to offer. Julia hadn't shared her opinion with him, but she had a feeling he was trying to prove to his boss that he was a team player.

"You look great. Now go," Tammy said.

Julia didn't have to be told twice and fast-walked

to the back of the children's section to disappear up the stairs to her apartment. The smell of basil, garlic, and tomato sauce wafted past her nose as soon as she opened the door. Yesterday, she'd mentioned to Aidan that she'd been craving Rosa's lasagna and garlic bread, and if her nose didn't deceive her, that's exactly what the man had brought home.

He met her at the door with a glass of red wine in his hand and laughter on his lips. "Cute headband. One of your lights is out."

She took off the headband and tossed it in the direction of her bedroom and then kissed him. "You are the best boyfriend ever," she said, once she'd reluctantly stepped back to accept the glass of wine.

"And you're still the messiest girlfriend ever."

She toed off her shoes. "I'm not cleaning tonight. I can't. I'm too tired. I had to get up at four to get the revisions back to my editor before she leaves for the holidays."

He pulled a face. "You forgot, didn't you?"

She sagged against him. "Please don't tell me I have to go out tonight. I can't remember the last time I didn't have something to do."

"Hang on to your glass," he said, right before he swept her off her feet.

"Perfect. You can carry me around like this anytime. All the time would be good. At least until the Christmas rush is over."

He sat on the couch with her still in his arms. "Scooch over and lie back"—he gave his head a slight shake—"on the pile of clothes. Leave your feet on my lap."

As she complied with his order, he raised his hip to pull out his cell phone. He started to knead her tired feet while he waited for whoever to pick up, grinning when she moaned.

"Hey, Finn, do me a favor and tell—"

Julia made a grab for the phone when she realized what she'd forgotten. "No, no, I promised Olivia I'd help with the decorations for the Snow Ball. I'll just be a little late."

"You heard her? Don't listen to her. She's exhausted. Tell Olivia to blame me. The Sugar Plum Fairy won't be helping out tonight or any other night. She won't be performing at the Snow Ball either. She's hung up her tutu for the season."

"Finn, don't listen—"

Aidan leaned over and covered her mouth. "Yeah, I know. Agreed. Thanks, bro." He removed his hand, set her glass of wine on the coffee table, and then stretched out beside her. "Tell me the truth. And, Julia, I will know if you lie to me, and I won't be happy. I might even take back Rosa's lasagna and garlic bread."

"That's just cruel and unusual punishment."

"Then don't lie when I ask you if you really wanted to help out with the Snow Ball or if you were just doing it because you can't say no." He raised an eyebrow.

"You want me to answer now?" He gave her a *seriously?* look. "Fine. They're my friends, and it's a written rule you don't say no to friends." *Or half the other people in town,* she thought glumly.

"Okay, from now on, do me a favor. Unless it's something you really want to do, say no. You can't keep going like this, Julia. You'll get sick and be stuck in bed for Christmas. Now, is there anyone else I need to call?"

"No, I'm good. What about you? How did I get so lucky to get you to myself tonight?"

"I'm done with the house. We sign the papers on Thursday. And I'm tired of not getting time with you, so I decided to let someone else take the extra shifts."

"Now, you be honest with me. Is it any better between you and Paul?"

"No. I can't seem to do anything right in his eyes. Probably doesn't help that Mrs. Bradford is suing HHPD because of me."

"Hopefully she'll get Judge Monahan, and he'll put her in jail like he promised to if she ever tied up his courts again." She tilted her head and gave the idea some serious consideration. "You know, talking to Judge Monahan might not be a bad idea. I'll mention it to Paul. And, um, I have another idea. Don't get offended though."

He trailed his finger down her cheek to her neck. "I was having some ideas of my own, but I doubt they'll offend you. Maybe you should go first."

"Okay, so Paul has gotten it into his head that you're a dangerous rebel without a cause. I think the problem is he can't see past your hair and beard."

"You're not suggesting I get rid of my beard, are you? Because that is not hap—"

"Wait. Before you rule it out, think about this. When I kissed you under the mistletoe a year ago, you were clean-shaven, and your hair was a lot shorter than this."

"And your point is?"

"I know your relationship with Ella Rose is much better than it was, but you said it's still not the same as before. You and Harper have been separated for a few years, so maybe it's as simple as you not looking like the dad Ella Rose remembers."

He rubbed his hand over his beard. "That actually makes some sense."

"I think I'm offended. When have any of my ideas not made sense?" She didn't wait for his answer. She had a feeling this was the solution to his problems with both Paul and Ella Rose, and she didn't want to give him a chance to change his mind. "Come on," she said, and half-rolled off the couch. "I used to cut my brothers' hair all the time, and I'm sure there's a beard shaving video on YouTube."

"You know how you just asked when one of your ideas didn't make sense? This is one of them."

"It'll be fun. I promise," she said as she pulled a chair into the center of her living room. "While I get my scissors and stuff, you take off your shirt." She laughed when his eyes lit up with interest.

He stood up, his hands curling at the bottom of his long-sleeve navy HHPD T-shirt. "I'll take off mine if you take off yours."

"I can do that," she said, happy to accept his challenge. "I'll be right back." She hurried into her bedroom and closed the door to quickly change into a black and lilac yoga top and pants. Just in case the evening went the way she hoped it would, she tidied her room. Which meant she shoved a bunch of stuff in her closet and under her bed, checked on Eric and Ariel, and then brought up a beard shaving tutorial on her phone. It looked simple enough.

She left her room to head to the bathroom to collect what she needed and stopped short, frozen at the sight of Aidan in the living room. Shirtless, he stretched as he looked out the window. "That, that's exactly what I want."

He glanced over his shoulder and looked her up and down, a wolfish grin appearing on his face. "I feel the same way."

"No, that's not what I meant. I mean, I'm glad you want me, but I was talking about your back." She motioned for him to turn around. "Now flex like you were. Sweet Caroline, you're beautiful. Don't move," she said, and lifted her phone to take some candid shots.

"Do you mind telling me what you're planning to do with those pictures of me?" he called out to her as she headed for the bathroom.

After rummaging through drawers in the vanity, she came back with everything she needed and placed them on the coffee table. "I'm hoping my editor agrees, and we can use your back for the cover of *Warrior's Touch*." She patted the chair. "Now come sit down."

Though she hated to cover his broad shoulders and sculpted back from view, she placed a towel around his shoulders. "Do you want anything before I get started?" she asked as she picked up a glass of warm water and a tail comb.

"A promise that you know what you're doing."

"I wouldn't have offered if I didn't. You seem a little tense. I'll put on some music."

He groaned when Christmas carols came through the speakers of her docking station.

"If you don't want to listen to holiday music, you'll have to sing."

Aidan and his brothers had a boy band back in the day. Supposedly they'd been pretty popular on the local circuit. She'd heard them sing at Olivia and Finn's wedding and wasn't surprised. Now that she thought about it though, Aidan had played the harmonica more than he'd sung.

"Nice try. I don't like to perform. Never really did. I just went along with it to keep the family happy."

"You must have sung to Ella Rose when she was a baby," Julia said, drawing the comb through his thick, dark hair. She leaned over and picked up the scissors.

"I did. I sang 'Danny Boy' to get her to stop crying and 'Over the Rainbow' to put her to sleep. They were the same songs my mom used to sing to Riley."

The scissors jerked, and she cut off more than she'd planned to. "Crap," she murmured under her breath.

He lifted his hand protectively to his head. "Julia, what did you just do?"

"Nothing. Relax. I'll fix it." *And please, please don't talk about your mom and sister anymore.* But if she planned to have a long-term relationship with this man, that was not something she could ask of him. And she did plan to. The past few weeks together had proven to her that she'd been right the day he'd first touched his lips to hers under the mistletoe. He was her soul mate. The man she was meant to spend the rest of her life with.

"Yeah, *nothing* and *I'll fix it* kind of cancel each other out."

"I'll make everything better. I promise." She leaned in to kiss him just below his ear.

It's what she wanted to do for him. She didn't want to hurt him or remind him of all that he and his family had lost. Colleen hadn't wanted her to tell the family that it had been Josh who'd been behind the wheel that night. He'd been out drinking with friends when he'd gotten a call from Hazel. There'd been a big rally scheduled early the next day, and her campaign manager had forgotten to pick up the signs from the printer. She'd told the owner of the signage company that Josh would be there within the hour. Josh was a good son. He wouldn't have wanted to disappoint his mom. They'd had a lot riding on the election. And then Josh had made the fatal mistake of thinking that, after five beers, he wasn't drunk. And then he'd made the mistake of thinking he could cover up the accident and live with himself for taking the lives of Riley and Mary Gallagher.

On the day he died, he'd called her from the writer's shed. She'd been busy in the store and had let the call go to voice mail. She'd made her decision that day to tell him it was over between them. She'd always wondered if he'd somehow suspected that she meant to leave him. There was no way of knowing. He'd made no mention of it in his letter.

He'd left a letter for the Gallaghers. It was to be given to them only after Hazel had died. He didn't want his mother shamed by what he'd done. All he'd shared in his letter to Julia were his last wishes and how to carry them out. He didn't apologize or tell her he loved her. All he'd told her was to use his life insurance to see to it that the Gallaghers had happy lives. Only his term life insurance policy had been canceled the year before. He'd defaulted on the payments.

When Josh hadn't come home by midnight, Julia had gotten worried and thought to listen to his message. It was hard to understand him. His speech was slurred and little more than a whisper. She had to listen to the message several times before what he'd done had sunk in. He was insistent that she get to the writer's shed before his mother to retrieve the letters. Hazel had been out of town at a conference and was expected home that morning.

Julia had raced to the house on Mulberry Lane. A light had been on in the shed. From the window, she could see Josh curled up on the floor. He was cold, his fingernails and lips blue. Still, she'd checked for a pulse, her own hammering. He was gone. She'd gathered up the letters and ran to her car and went home. She erased his message, afraid if Hazel knew he'd called and Julia hadn't answered, hadn't gone to him right away, she'd blame her for her son's death. Julia had lost Josh, and she hadn't wanted to lose the love of the woman who'd become a mother to her too.

In that moment, she knew she couldn't tell Aidan either. Not only for Hazel's sake but for her own. If the truth came out she'd lose both the man and woman she loved.

"You've gone awful quiet, Julia. You're making me nervous."

Feeling the need to be close to him, she wrapped her arms around his neck. He tipped his head back and frowned. "Are you okay?"

She nodded, focusing on his mouth. She couldn't look in his eyes, afraid he'd see the shadows in hers from reliving that night. "Don't panic, but I've just realized that I'm in love with you." At least this was a truth she could share. She had enough to hide. She didn't want to hide that too. Not anymore.

"What was it? My naked back?" he teased, but there was a gruffness in his voice.

She'd surprised him. She wondered if he was ready for this. "That and your new haircut." She picked up the hand mirror and, keeping her voice light, asked, "What do you think?" He held the mirror in his hand, but he wasn't looking at his hair; he was looking at her.

He put the mirror down and took her hand, drawing her around to face him. She sat, straddling his lap. "I told you this wasn't something I wanted." He held up a finger to stop her from interrupting him. "I didn't think it was. I may not be in exactly the same place as you are right now, but I'm getting there. So don't give up on me, okay?"

She nodded, smiling as she gathered his beard in her hands. "This is going to be fun."

And it was for the first twenty minutes, but then, as she began to reveal the man beneath the beard, his sensuous mouth, his hard, rugged jawline, the cleft in his strong chin, she was overcome with desire. "I think we're in trouble. Maybe I should glue your beard back on."

"What are you talking about now? Or do I even want to know?"

"I don't think I'll be able to keep my hands off you."

"Now, that's the kind of trouble I'm totally on board with. If I'd known how you'd feel, I would have shaved it off weeks ago." He put his hands on her hips. "You almost done? Never mind." He took the razor from her hand and tossed it on the coffee table. "I'll finish up later."

Chapter Nineteen

♥

This isn't good. This isn't good at all, Simon. Kitty's looking at Aidan like she's about to turn his world upside down." Colleen stood with her sidekick at the elevators near the atrium watching as her daughter-in-law welcomed Harper and Ella Rose to the manor.

Aidan and his ex-wife were just back from signing the papers on the sale of their marital home. Harper had yet to buy one of her own. She'd always been the picky sort. One of those mansions on Ocean Drive would be her style.

But for now, they'd be living in Colleen's old suite of rooms in the tower. The thought of having Aidan's little one here for the holidays made Colleen's heart sing. Well, it would have been singing if it were still beating.

Colleen thought it quite a feat that Ella Rose being at the manor was able to cheer her up even for a few moments. A cloud of impending doom had been hanging over her head ever since Kitty had absconded with the book. Jasper wasn't himself either. He'd been in a right panic from the second he'd returned to his room to discover *The Secret Keeper of Harmony Harbor* was missing.

After tearing his room and the manor apart, he'd begun interrogating the staff and guests and any outside tradespeople who'd been working at Greystone. But not once had he thought to question the thief. Beside himself as he was, Jasper apparently didn't notice that Kitty had barely left her room for the entire week. She'd been holed up in her tower room reading each and every page of Colleen's memoirs.

Colleen knew this because she'd been by Kitty's side practically the entire time. But no matter how hard Colleen tried, she couldn't come up with a way to get the book out of Kitty's possession. Nor did she have a clue what her daughter-in-law meant to do with her newfound knowledge.

Well, she hadn't until this very moment. It was the sorrowful look on Kitty's lightly lined face and the comforting way she rubbed her grandson's arm for no foreseeable reason that gave Colleen's daughter-in-law's intentions away.

"Does she not think that the knowledge bedeviled me? That I didn't weigh the consequences of the truth coming out to all those involved and choose to remain silent for a reason?" Colleen gave her head a frustrated shake before saying to Simon, "Here they come. Find Jasper and see if you can get him to follow you to Kitty's room. If he does, make a right fuss. Go spastic cat so he'll go against his moral code and use his master key to invade Kitty's privacy."

Meow.

"Don't worry about me. I'll be standing guard, waiting for Kitty to strike." Because bejaysus, after going on near five decades, she could read her daughter-in-law's body language and expressions, and everything pointed to her telling Aidan that Josh Winters was the one responsible for his mother and sister's deaths.

Meow.

"Stop nagging me. That's all I've got so far. If I... What's the matter with you?" she asked when Simon bumped her leg with his head. Once he had her attention, he padded over to sit at Ella Rose's feet. Colleen looked up to find the little girl's baby-blue eyes focused directly upon her.

Simon gave her a smug *meow.*

Colleen smiled and mouthed, *You can see your GG?*

Her great-great-granddaughter smiled and nodded with not so much as a hint of fear in her eyes. Unlike Mia and George, Ella Rose had spent a fair amount of time with Colleen, so it stood to reason she wasn't troubled by the sight of her. Then again, the child had her father's genes. He'd been the fearless one. Except in matters of the heart. Even more so now after having it broken. "Oh, but you're the spitting image of your auntie Riley, poppet," Colleen said, feeling choked up and hopeful at the same time. She had another partner in crime.

Harper looked down at her daughter, following the direction of her gaze. "Darling, what is it? What do you see?"

Colleen touched a finger to her lips and then mouthed, *Our secret.*

Ella Rose smiled and nodded and then looked up at her mother. "I thought I saw an elf peeking in the window."

"An elf? You thought you saw an elf? You mean like a leprechaun or a—"

"Not an Irish elf, Mommy, a North Pole elf. One of Santa's helpers."

"Do you hear that, Aidan? Our daughter is seeing elves peeking through windows. I agreed to allow Ella Rose to spend an hour with your girlfriend at her bookstore while we were at the lawyer's office, and look what happens." Harper grabbed Aidan's arm and dragged him out of Ella Rose's hearing. "In an hour, your girlfriend has managed to undermine everything we've tried to instill in our child. Ella Rose believes in Santa Claus, Aidan! Santa Claus for godsakes."

"Just relax. Julia wouldn't do that. She knows we keep the holiday low-key and Santa-free."

Harper might not have caught Aidan's grimace, but Colleen did. No one had celebrated Christmas like Mary Gallagher. Colleen had known it would be only a matter of time before Aidan embraced the holiday like he used to. None of this Santa-free nonsense. He couldn't help but celebrate the age-old Gallagher holiday traditions when he was in love with Julia Landon, a Christmas elf herself.

Colleen felt a twinge where her heart used to be. Couldn't Kitty see the love shining in Aidan's eyes every time he mentioned Julia? Why couldn't...? Colleen stopped abruptly in the middle of her inner rant as the truth smacked her right between the eyes.

Her daughter-in-law wasn't intentionally trying to hurt Julia or Aidan or tear the couple apart. Kitty knew how high a price Julia would pay for keeping a secret from the man she loved because she'd kept a secret from her husband and suffered mightily for it. She still did. Colleen had tried to ease the burden Kitty had carried for all these years, but nothing she said ever helped.

"Really, you think someone whose store has more fake snow and glitter than a snow globe and dresses as an elf is going to be able to keep the holidays low-key? Because unless this is just a fling..." Harper's eyes rounded in surprise. "It's not just a fling, is it? Oh God, please tell me you are not in love with a woman who believes in Santa Claus!"

Aidan rubbed his jaw and then looked at his hand as though just remembering he was beardless. Colleen was glad of it. He looked more like the great-grandson she knew and loved. "Come on, Julia doesn't really believe in Santa Claus."

"You didn't answer my question, Aidan. I deserve to know and have some say as to who will be spending time with our daughter. If I find someone else, I'd respect your right to have a say too."

Aidan opened his mouth and then closed it. Turning his head, he appeared to be looking at the twinkling Christmas tree outside the atrium before he admitted, "Yeah, I'm in love with Julia. But you don't have to worry about Ella Rose spending time with her. She's incredible with kids. Look how easily Ella Rose went with her today, and she barely knows Julia. We had to practically drag her out of the store."

"Of course we did, because Julia was playing dress-up with her and plying her with hot chocolate and cupcakes. Plural, as in cupcake*s*, Aidan."

"Big deal. It's more important that Ella Rose is happy, isn't it? You said so yourself. She has some major adjustments to make. Can't we just let her enjoy the holidays like every other kid? Celebrate—"

"Oh, you've gone and done it now, my boy. I can practically see the steam coming out of Harper's ears." Colleen glanced back at Ella Rose and caught the worried expression on the child's face. Colleen had to put a stop to this before Aidan and Harper exchanged heated words as they were wont to do when they fought. The couple were hot blooded and hot tempered. It's how Colleen had known they weren't a good match.

Thankfully, Kitty must have sensed the same thing and called out, "I'm going to take Ella Rose to the kitchen to get her some snacks for the room. Do either of you want anything?"

"Snacks? No. No snacks. She's already had more than enough treats at Books and Beans," Harper said, and returned to her daughter's side with Aidan following behind, rolling his eyes.

Colleen didn't miss the sad smile Kitty shot her grandson at the mention of Julia's shop, before she said, "All right then. I have something I need to take care of." She bent and kissed the top of Ella Rose's head. "I'm so glad you're spending the holidays with us. I'll see you all later."

"Do you need a ride to the thing at Maggie's gallery tonight, Grams?" Aidan asked Kitty.

"Thank you, dear, but I won't be attending. I'm a bit under the weather."

Colleen prayed that was so and that she'd earned a reprieve. If Jasper found the book and realized what Kitty was up to, maybe he could talk some sense into her.

* * *

Aidan sat on the end of the canopied bed in the tower room beside his daughter, who was educating him and his ex on all things Santa Claus.

"Now, darling, we've had this talk before. Santa doesn't exist."

"I'm sorry, Mommy, but he does too."

Harper gave him an *I told you so* look. "And who told you Santa is real, Ella Rose? Did Julia?" his ex asked in a smoothly persuasive voice, ready to pounce on any evidence that proved Julia had gone against their wishes.

Aidan was trying to figure out a way to come to Julia's defense if—who was he kidding, *when*—his daughter confirmed her mother's belief. The last thing he wanted was to give Harper any reason to stand in the way of his relationship with Julia. It had shocked the hell out of him, terrified him if he was honest, because he'd not only fallen in love with Julia, but he adored the woman. But if Harper made him choose between the woman he loved and his daughter...

Ella Rose shook her head. "No, George did. Uncle Finn, Aunt Olivia, and George are leaving for Kenya in the morning, so she came to Books and Beans to say goodbye to Julia. All the kids love Julia."

"They sure do, don't they, pumpkin? Julia's a special lady," Aidan said, unable to keep the smug pride from his voice.

"Yes, well, children typically respond well to someone who gives them everything they ask for."

"How come she didn't give me another cupcake when I asked?"

"Because Julia respects Mommy and Daddy's rule of not too many sweets before dinnertime," Aidan said.

Harper snorted. "Would that be before or after she gave her two?" She patted Ella Rose's knee. "So, darling, tell me why George was discussing Santa with you."

"All the kids were. Julia made a special party for George and the storytime kids. It was supposed to be Saturday, but George won't be here." Ella Rose's happy smile fell, and she swung her feet. "They were talking about Santa, and I told them he wasn't real. Derek got mad at me and pushed me. George told him to stop being a bully. She said it wasn't my fault my parents brainwashed me against Santa." She looked up at them. "Why did you do that?"

Harper ignored the question and snapped, "Where was Julia when this was happening?" Aidan wasn't happy about his daughter being bullied either, but he knew Julia would have intervened had she'd been there.

"She was at the coffee bar getting our snacks. That's why I got two cupcakes."

"And did she also take George and Derek to task?"

Ella Rose shook her head and smiled. "No, she told us a story about Millie the Mermaid. I like Millie. The other mermaids didn't like her because she was different. They made fun of her, too, and it hurt her feelings. So she tried to be the same as everyone else, but she wasn't happy anymore. Then one day she met a shy fish who wore glasses, and he told Millie she had to find the courage to be different. Every day Millie and the fish worked on finding her courage. And when the big shark came, Millie found her courage and saved the school of fishes." She made a *ta-da* motion with her hands.

"That's a very good story, darling."

Ella Rose nodded. "Julia's going to give me my own copy when it gets published. She's really smart, you know. She writes books. George said she wrote one about you, Daddy. But we can't read it be—"

Aidan didn't think this would be a good time for his ex to hear about Julia's sexy books. "Okay, so who wants to grab a bite to eat before I have to leave?"

Harper frowned at Aidan and then said, "I hope Julia told Derek to apologize to you."

"Yes, she did. And she said that just because someone doesn't believe what you do doesn't make you right and them wrong. We have to respect each other's differences."

Harper gave him an apologetic *I guess I overreacted* look. "I appreciate that Julia doesn't talk down to you because you're children. That's why Mommy told you that Santa isn't real and neither are the Easter Bunny and the Tooth Fairy. I respect you too much to lie to you, darling. And now, you see, I'm not the only one. Julia doesn't believe in—"

"Oh, yes, she does, Mommy," Ella Rose said, her eyes shining. "Julia believes in Santa Claus, and the Easter Bunny, and fairies too. She believes in everything magical, and I do too!"

Aidan covered his laugh with a cough.

"Don't you dare. This is your fault for getting involved with a woman who is delusional. Who in their right mind believes in fairy tales and—"

"It's okay, Mommy. Julia says not everyone can see the magic."

"All right, Ella Rose, I think I've heard just about enough about Julia for—"

"She says why be ordinary when you can be extraordinary?" Ella Rose jumped off the bed and did a pirouette. "I'm going to be extraordinary just like Julia when I grow up."

* * *

"I never should have doubted you, my boy," Colleen said as she moved across Kitty's suite to where Jasper stood holding *The Secret Keeper of Harmony Harbor*. "Now you'd best skedaddle before Kitty comes back. She—" Colleen broke off at the sound of a beep.

Jasper muttered a curse that would have singed Colleen's ears had she not used the word plenty of times herself. The situation called for it. There was no time for him to hide.

Kitty entered the room. Her head snapped up, her

gaze shooting to Jasper and the book in his hands. "What are you doing in my...? Oh," she said as though realizing she couldn't rightly call Jasper out for invading her privacy when she had done the same.

With a woebegone expression on her face, Kitty walked to the sitting area. Her pretty ruffled white blouse, black leggings, and boots somehow managed to make her look stylish and fragile at the same time.

"You must hate me now that you know what I did," she murmured as she lowered herself onto a blue-and-white-striped wingback chair.

Jasper took a seat across from her. Setting the book on the coffee table, he tapped the leather-bound cover. "I didn't read the book in its entirety. Only the parts that referred to Ava and Olivia. But even if I had, I could never hate you, Miss...Kitty."

"I don't understand. Why, if you've had the book this whole time, wouldn't you read it all?"

"Because I respect the privacy of others. I wouldn't want anyone to know my secrets, so why should I know theirs?"

"If you're trying to shame me, my boy, you're wasting your breath. You're not saying anything I haven't said to myself before. I've paid a price and have no doubt, before this is over, I'll pay some more," Colleen said, taking the wingback chair nearest Kitty.

"But as I've learned," he continued, "sometimes knowing what someone is hiding is the only way to help them."

Colleen smiled. So maybe he wasn't trying to shame her after all.

"I'm afraid I'm not so honorable as you, Jasper. I know your secret now."

He nodded. "I thought as much."

"I don't understand why you never came forward. You are the true heir of Greystone Manor. Your father was the firstborn, not Ronan's. I can't believe how you and your mother were made to suffer because Niall Gallagher refused to recognize you as his child. Just because your mother was his mistress didn't..." Kitty trailed off, turning her head to look at the winter seascape beyond the French doors. "I have no right to judge. I'm as bad as your father."

"Surely not," Jasper said, the hint of a tender smile touching his lips.

"You don't know what I did."

"No, I don't. As I told you, I only read a few pages of the book. But perhaps you'd feel better if you told me. And it only seems fair. You know all of my secrets after all."

"I... You're right, I do." She looked down at her hands. "I had no idea you had feelings for me, Jasper. I feel like I should—"

"Please, don't say anything. I never meant for you to know. I apologize if it's caused you any undue distress."

"But what if I'm flattered? What if I'm happy to know that you do?"

He raised a skeptical eyebrow. "You forget I've seen your list of Harmony Harbor's most eligible bachelors. I wasn't on it."

She gave him an impish grin. "Yes, you were. Only

you wouldn't know it. Since there's nothing that gets past you, I call you Christopher, as in Christopher Plummer. The actor?" His brow furrowed, and she lifted a shoulder. "You remind me of him."

"Oh, I...I'm not sure what to say to that," he said, looking disconcerted.

"You don't have to say anything. And you must know, I won't say anything about what really happened to Antonio DiRossi. Rosa will never hear it from me. No one will, Jasper. I'll take your secret to my grave."

"These things have a way of coming out. But perhaps I'd feel more confident if you were to share your secret with me, Kitty."

Colleen snorted. She knew Jasper better than anyone. There was only one reason he wanted Kitty to share her secret. He could see that it weighed heavy on her, and he wanted to help. She doubted Kitty would share her secret with him. If Colleen hadn't overheard her at the hospital, Kitty would have taken it to her grave.

To her surprise, Kitty told him of the letter that had arrived for Ronan only days after they had wed. It was from a woman, Bridgette Green. Ronan had briefly dated the woman while on holiday in Ireland. He hadn't cheated on Kitty in the true sense of the word. After Colleen had accidently let it slip that Ronan had once been in love with Rosa, Kitty had temporarily broken their engagement a few months before their wedding. So, as insecure as she was at that time, when Kitty learned this Bridgette Green was pregnant with Ronan's child, she burned the letter instead of sharing it with her husband.

"At the beginning of every year, I vowed I'd tell Ronan, and then another year passed and then another. I thought if I told him that night, as he lay dying in the hospital, that it would give him a reason to live. But he was already gone. Colleen heard me though." Her gaze moved over Jasper's face. "You hate me now, don't you?"

"No, as I told you before, I could never hate you. I can see this still weighs heavily on you. With your permission, I'd like to try and track down Ronan's son."

"Would you?"

"I would do anything for you, Kitty. Surely you know that by now."

Her cheeks flushed becomingly. "Yes, I think deep down I've always known." She smiled and then grew pensive.

"What is it?"

"I've discovered the identity of the drunk driver that killed Mary, Riley, and indirectly Ronan. I'm torn, Jasper. Torn between sharing the information with my family and protecting two women who were as dear to Mother Gallagher as they are to me. My grandson and son have only now found their way to happiness, and if I tell—"

Jasper nodded and briefly closed his eyes. "Josh Winters." He frowned. "But what does he have to do with Maggie?"

"She's his biological mother. And Julia has known since Josh died that he was behind the wheel that night. In her defense, Mother Gallagher asked her to keep it to herself. To protect Maggie, I think. And as I understand it, Josh asked that Julia keep the truth from us until Hazel died."

"Oh, the webs we weave," Jasper murmured, and then lifted his gaze to Kitty. "We've both lived with our own secrets for far too long. The rest of the family needs to know about Josh. It may take time, but in the end, I believe Master Aidan will forgive Miss Julia, and Colin will find his way back to Maggie."

They'd made up their minds. There was nothing Colleen could do now. Nothing to do but pray.

Chapter Twenty

♥

Ella Rose had no idea that she'd just landed the killing blow by telling Harper she wanted to be just like Julia. Aidan knew his ex well; her sense of self-esteem and self-worth were tied to her job and her looks. She hadn't practiced since they'd separated, and she'd always believed, no matter how often Aidan had told her otherwise, that he'd left her because she'd gotten older and was no longer attractive in his eyes.

"Hey, you know what? I'm starved. Let's go down to the dining room and get something to eat." He glanced at his watch. He'd be cutting it close—the party at the gallery was at seven—but he wanted to make sure Ella Rose was okay, and that meant ensuring her mother was too.

"Yay, and then can I write my letter to Santa and tell him I moved?"

It looked like Aidan might be here all night. He didn't dare look Harper's way as he followed a skipping Ella Rose to the door. She bent over and picked up an envelope. "Look, Daddy, you got a letter. Maybe it's from Santa. Open it. Open it."

"Okay, settle down. I'll open it." He didn't recognize the handwriting on the envelope. Noting it wasn't sealed, he slid the flap open. There were three sheaves of lined journal paper inside. He took them out to examine. They appeared to have been photocopied from a book. The writing was oddly familiar. He knew why as soon as he read the first line. Someone had found his great-grandmother Colleen's memoir, *The Secret Keeper of Harmony Harbor*. It felt like he'd been gut-punched when he read the next line. It got worse the farther along he read. He'd gotten the answer he'd thought would bring some kind of closure. Instead, it ripped the wound wide open. And killed any hope of a future with the woman he loved. Julia had known all along that her fiancé had been responsible for the death of Aidan's mother and sister.

If his little girl hadn't been looking up at him with a worried expression on her face, Aidan would have put his fist through the door. His concerns from the beginning about Julia had been warranted. He'd known all along that she'd been hiding something, interfering in their lives for a reason. But instead of working on her until he got the truth, he'd fallen in love with her. He'd made the same mistake that had cost him so much in the past—he'd let his heart overrule his brain.

* * *

Julia stood toward the back of Impressions, Maggie's high-end art gallery, which overlooked the harbor front. The building was modern with lots of natural light.

There was a cool wire Christmas tree in the entrance decorated with stunning blown-glass balls. Maggie, looking gorgeous in a beaded black dress, rejoined Julia where they'd been admiring one of Lenny's paintings before an older couple had pulled the gallery owner aside.

"So, are they interested?" Julia asked, barely able to control her excitement. The painting of Lenny's that the couple had been interested in was gallery size and priced as such. In Lenny's eyes, it would amount to a small fortune.

Maggie discreetly crossed her fingers. "I almost guarantee it's sold."

"I wish he was here to be a part of this. Wait. I have an idea. Hold this for a sec, please." She handed Maggie her wineglass and took out her cell phone from her clutch. "I gave him a phone the other day." She motioned for Maggie to stand in front of the painting with her, facing the gallery floor. "Selfie time." They smiled and gave a thumbs-up to the camera.

Once they'd finished taking the photo, a caterer gestured for Maggie.

"Everything okay?" Julia asked when Maggie returned to her side.

"He just wanted to reconfirm numbers. I think he expected more people to be here by now."

"He does realize the doors don't officially open for another twenty minutes, doesn't he? And unlike me, most people prefer to be fashionably late."

Maggie smiled. "I appreciated you coming early to help me set up. Aidan's coming, isn't he?"

"He better be." She'd gone all out and bought a gorgeous red velvet dress with a fitted bodice and wide flared skirt. Her shoes were red and sequined and made her feel like a fairy princess.

"I'm so happy for you both, Julia. You're good for Aidan. Colin thinks so too. He's glad you'll be there for Aidan when he finally breaks the case."

Julia frowned. "What case is that?"

"Sorry. I thought Aidan would have mentioned it. I wouldn't have known anything about it if Colin hadn't told me last night. I don't think Aidan's even told his brothers. He probably doesn't want to get their hopes up. But Colin's positive that Aidan is days away from finding out who was behind Mary and Riley's death. He found a new witness, you know. He finally spoke to him yesterday. The man agreed to work with a sketch artist. Aidan's setting up . . . Julia, are you all right?"

"Yes, I, um, I'm sorry, Maggie, but I have to go. I think I left the stove on. I'll be right back."

Maggie's lips twitched as though she held back a laugh. Of course no one would be surprised that Julia Landon left the stove on. If only that was all it was. It felt like her world was coming apart. She had to tell Aidan before he found out from someone else. But first, she had to break the news to Hazel. She wouldn't let her be blindsided by this.

As Julia set the wineglass on a table, Aidan walked into the gallery and glanced her way. Butterflies fluttered in her stomach at the intent expression on his face. She still wasn't used to seeing him without his beard, and she wondered if that's why he looked so fierce. Or maybe it was his reaction to her dress.

He didn't say anything as he approached, and her welcoming smile faltered. "Aidan, are you all right?"

"I need to speak with you. Not here. Do you have a coat?"

"Yes, but I have to go—"

"This won't take long." He walked away.

She gave Maggie an apologetic smile before following Aidan from the gallery. When she caught up with him in the lobby, everything became clear. He looked fiercely intense because he was furious. And his anger was directed at her. As she glanced at the harsh angles of his face and the rigid lines of his body, her heartbeat quickened. It was too soon for him to have discovered the truth about the accident. The witness hadn't seen the sketch artist yet. The only thing she could think of that would draw this strong a reaction from him was what happened to Ella Rose today.

She was a precious little girl, and Julia had been devastated that she'd been hurt on her watch. But she'd thought everything was okay by the time Ella Rose left. "I'm sorry. I should have told you about Derek when you picked up Ella Rose. I planned to—"

"This has nothing to do with my daughter." He gestured to the cloakroom. "Get your coat. I'll meet you outside."

She'd never been frightened of Aidan before. Paul's warnings about how dangerous Aidan was, that he was a ticking time bomb, she'd never taken them seriously. Until now. "No, I'm not going anywhere with you until

you tell me why you're so mad at me. What did I do
wrong, Aidan?"

He didn't answer, looking around as though to check
and see if they were alone. Then he lifted his hand.
She gasped, and took a step back. A flash of emotion
flared in his eyes before it went out, leaving them cold
and hard again. He reached into the inner pocket of his
jacket and removed what looked to be three pages from
a book. Everything became clear in that moment. *The
Secret Keeper of Harmony Harbor* had been found.

"I'm sorry," she whispered, her throat tight, her eyes
burning. "I had no idea until the night Josh committed
suicide that he'd been the one behind the wheel." She
waited for him to say something, to lash out at her, but
he just stared at her, waiting. "I told Colleen. She asked
that I not tell your family. She must have had her reasons, but I never knew why."

"I do. What was your reason? It wasn't just because
GG asked you not to. Something else was holding you
back."

"Josh asked me not to." She knew as soon as the
words were out of her mouth it was the wrong thing to
say. Aidan had gone completely and utterly still.

"Hazel. Hazel was the reason I didn't say anything.
I couldn't do that to her. She would have been devastated."

His lip curled.

"Don't...don't judge me and look at me like I'm
evil. Your mother and sister had been gone six years by
then, and Hazel had just lost her only son."

"Why didn't you tell me?"

She stared at the gold veins in the white marble floor, swallowing hard before she raised her gaze to his. "Because I love you. I didn't want you to look at me like you are now. I didn't want to lose you." She held up her hand. "I'll go." As she walked to the cloakroom, a hot tear rolled down her cheek. She dashed it away and then turned back. He hadn't moved. "I have a letter for your family from Josh. He asked that it be given to you upon Hazel's death. Where should I—"

"Do what you want with it. There's nothing he could say that any of us want to hear."

"You're wrong." She lifted her chin. "I know it doesn't make up for what he did or what you and your family lost. But Josh wasn't a monster. He made a horrible, horrible mistake that night. And he paid for it with his life."

"Julia, w-what are you saying? What mistake? What mistake did Josh make?"

She whirled around to see Hazel and Delaney standing a few feet away. They'd come in through the side door. In the state she'd been in, Julia hadn't noticed. She wondered if Aidan had known they were there all along and turned to look at him.

He held her gaze as though surprised she'd think him capable of such cruelty. As if him wanting nothing to do with her wasn't enough evidence that he could be.

"You need to tell her. Someone sent me the pages. Word will get out," he said, and then walked away.

Chapter Twenty-One

♥

Two days before Christmas, the sidewalks outside Books and Beans were crowded with holiday shoppers bundled up against the bitter cold, a typical sight with only two shopping days left before the big day. What wasn't typical was how quiet her shop had been. The downturn started the day after Aidan had confronted her at the gallery. He'd been right. Word had gotten out, though through no fault of the Gallaghers. The blame lay entirely at the feet of Delaney Davis.

Determined to get ahead of the story, Delaney had called Byron and Poppy Harte first thing the next morning. After the interview, they'd come directly to Julia. They didn't want to run the piece. They were upset about how Hazel—directed by Delaney—had portrayed Julia. Afraid of what it could mean for Books and Beans. They'd been right; she'd been wrong. But Delaney would have gone to their competition anyway. Julia wouldn't have Byron and Poppy lose out on a story and revenue from Hazel's campaign ads because they were trying to protect her.

Julia's biggest mistake had been telling the complete truth to Hazel. After what had happened with Aidan, she hadn't wanted to hold anything back. She should have. She shouldn't have told Hazel that she'd been going to end her relationship with Josh and that she hadn't answered her phone that day.

Hazel, no doubt with extensive coaching from Delaney, had all but asked for an investigation to be opened into her son's death. She blamed Julia for Josh taking his own life and for the night he'd run Mary and Riley off the road. It didn't seem to matter that Julia hadn't known Josh then. Though Bryon had run a correction the next day.

Still, even with Hazel destroying Julia's business and reputation, she felt sorry for the woman who'd once been like a mother to her. Hazel had done nothing wrong. She'd been a wonderful mother, and she'd lost her only son. Over the past year, Hazel seemed to have come to terms with Josh's death. She could talk about him without crying and was in the planning stages of setting up a scholarship fund in his name—only to discover now that he'd taken his own life, and not only *his* life. He was responsible for Mary's and Riley's deaths too.

As if she hadn't suffered enough, Hazel had been dealt another blow. She'd learned that Maggie was Josh's biological mother. She'd had no idea that Josh had met Maggie only days before he'd died. Neither had Julia. After Maggie's two daughters had left the nest, the widow had searched for the child she'd given up as a teenager. Maggie had come to Harmony Harbor with the sole purpose of connecting with Josh.

The revelations that night had ended Maggie's relationship with Colin. Julia had been relieved to learn that Aidan hadn't been the one to tell his father, though she never really believed that he would. Maggie had come looking for Julia and confronted Aidan. His brothers and father had arrived at the gallery by then. As soon as she'd heard the truth about Josh's death, Maggie had broken down and told Colin that Josh was her son.

Julia hoped that one day the couple would find their way back to each other. But that wasn't her job anymore. Her fairy godmother wings were gone for good. Though there was one thing she had left to do. No matter what Aidan thought, in her heart she believed that they needed to read Josh's letter. She'd been carrying it around in her purse ever since the night at the gallery, hoping to be struck by inspiration as to whom to give it to and when to send it.

At the tinkle of bells from the front of the shop, Julia got out of the storytime chair. She didn't have to work to put a smile on her face. She welcomed the distraction of customers. At least she'd have someone to talk to instead of going over the events of the past week in her head. She started walking to the front of the store and realized she was barefoot.

"Julia?" Lenny peeked his head into the bookstore.

"Hi. Sorry, I'll be right there." She pulled on her reindeer slippers. For the two days leading up to Christmas, Julia and her staff wore pajamas. Because it had been so slow, she didn't have Tammy coming in until five. They were open until nine tonight.

"How come you don't have your Christmas music on?" Lenny asked, taking a seat at the coffee bar.

She tilted her head to listen. He was right. The store was eerily quiet. She'd been open two hours and had yet to turn on the Christmas carols. She wondered how many other things she'd missed, little signs that no matter how brave a face she put on things, not only was her relationship with Aidan over, but her business and reputation were damaged, maybe beyond repair, and there'd be no Christmas for her this year. She wouldn't be spending the holiday with Aidan as she'd hoped or with Hazel like she had for the past five years. Before she could stop it, a tear slid down her cheek.

"It hasn't been a good week, Lenny," she said, offering him a weak smile as she brushed the moisture away.

He got up and patted the stool. "Here, you sit, and I'll make you a hot chocolate. If that's okay. I've watched you do it enough. I won't hurt anything."

"I would love that. Thank you." She sat on the stool and then leaned around the bakery case. "Make yourself one, too, and we'll have some sugar cookies..." She trailed off at the sight of Delaney outside the store with two boxes in her arms. The woman moved her head, rolling her eyes when Julia just stared at her.

She must have yelled *Open the door* because Julia heard her in the store.

Before she got off the stool, Lenny was around the counter and at the door. He opened it for Delaney and took the boxes. "Thank you," Hazel's right-hand woman said to Lenny. Instead of immediately heading back to her car as Julia assumed she would, Delaney opened her purse. "Hazel boxed up everything you left at her place."

"Oh, okay." Julia didn't know the reason for the small, painful twinge in her chest. It seemed she still held out hope that she and Hazel would get past this.

Delaney handed her an official-looking letter. "You have two weeks to vacate the premises. Both the store and the apartment."

Julia stared at the eviction notice. "I...I don't understand. I haven't done anything wrong. My rent's paid up. What am I supposed to do? Where am I supposed to go?"

Lenny took the paper from her trembling fingers. "You can't evict her without cause. You have to give her thirty days."

"Not if the landlord needs the property for her own use. Which Hazel does. She's going to run her campaign from here."

"You put her up to this, didn't you, Delaney?" Julia asked, praying she was right. She didn't think she could take it if she was wrong.

The other woman shrugged. "So what if I did? You have nothing to tie you to Harmony Harbor now. Go home to Texas. Hazel might actually stand a chance of reelection without you here."

A man walked in with a registered letter. "Julia Landon?"

She nodded, and he handed her another official-looking envelope. "Thank you."

The man gave her a look that seemed to say she wouldn't be thanking him once she opened it. Which is why she waited for Delaney to leave before she did.

"Julia, what are you going to do? You're not moving to Texas, are you?" Lenny asked as the door closed behind Delaney.

Julia opened the envelope. "I don't know, Lenny. I honestly don't know. Hazel and I were close once. Maybe if I speak to her without Delaney around I..."

"Julia, what's wrong? What is it?"

The print on the registered letter blurred. "The bank just called in my loan. I have a week to pay it off."

Lenny slowly sank down on the stool beside her. "Why is this happening to you?"

She told him about Hazel and Josh and Mrs. Bradford, whose husband owned the bank. Now that she no longer had the Gallaghers or the mayor in her corner, Julia supposed she was easy prey.

Lenny stood up, his face flushed and angry. "Don't worry. I won't let them get away with this."

There was something in his eyes that concerned her. She put her hand on his arm. "It'll be okay, Lenny. I promise. If I can't come to some sort of agreement with Hazel, I can find another space to rent. My apartment's too small anyway. And the loan...There's other banks, right? I'll just...I'll figure it out," she said, trying to sound confident for Lenny's sake.

He shook his head. "They can't do this to you and get away with it."

"Lenny, don't do anything—" He stormed from the store, the wind catching the door and slamming it shut behind him. She ran to call out to him. But when she finally managed to get the door open, he'd disappeared on the crowded sidewalk.

Her mom used to tell Julia that something good always came out of something bad. She might not see it right away, especially when she was in the middle of the storm, but eventually she would. And that one day she'd look back on those bad times and know they had to happen to get her to where she needed to be.

As Julia tucked the letters inside one of the boxes, she wondered if the eviction and the bank calling in her loan were signs that she should move back to Texas. The one thing she could always count on was her family. She gathered up the boxes and carried them to the back of the store. She had a decision to make, and she had to make it today.

At the tinkle of the bells, she turned, praying it was Lenny. It wasn't. She bowed her head and put down the boxes beside the storytime chair. Her heart hurt as she walked back to the coffee shop, where Ava, Sophie, and Lexi were taking seats at the counter.

"If you've come to run me out of town, you'll have to get in line."

"What are you talking about, and why are you in your pajamas?" Lexi asked, and then added, "Before you explain that and also why you didn't at least confide in us, your friends, about Josh, could you get me a coffee, please?" She nudged her head at Sophie and Ava. "They dragged me from the manor before I could—" Lexi gave Julia an alarmed look and raised her hands. "No, do not start crying. They'll blame me."

Julia sniffed back tears. "I thought you all hated me. I didn't think any of you would ever speak to me again."

"That'd be a little hypocritical, don't you think? The

three of us have kept secrets, too, Julia. We just wish you had told us. You didn't have to deal with this on your own," Sophie said.

"I couldn't. I wouldn't put any of you in a position where you would have to lie for me to your husbands and Colin." Swallowing hard, trying to keep the tremor from her voice, she asked, "Does he hate me?"

Ava gave her a gentle smile. "No, of course he doesn't hate you. And neither do Griffin, Liam, or Finn. But this opened everything back up again. In the end, it'll be for the best. They're all just a little raw right now."

"H-how's Aidan?" It didn't escape her notice that Ava hadn't mentioned him along with his brothers.

The three women exchanged a glance, and then Lexi opened her mouth. Suddenly afraid the other woman would confirm what Julia already knew in her heart, she held up her hand. "It's probably better if you don't tell me. I honestly don't know how much more I can take today."

Lexi got off the stool, took Julia by the shoulders, and sat her down. "Talk. We're not leaving until you tell us everything."

By late that afternoon, Julia had decided to leave Harmony Harbor. Her friends hadn't made the decision easy for her. Several hours after Ava, Sophie, and Lexi left at eleven, half the owners on Main Street dropped in for a nip of Christmas cheer. When she told them about Hazel and the bank, they'd sprung into action.

Mackenzie, who owned Truly Scrumptious, didn't deal with Mr. Bradford. Her grandmother, who'd started the bakery, couldn't stand the man. Mackenzie called her bank manager and set up an appointment for Julia first thing the next morning.

Poppy and Byron, who rented from Hazel, too, called to tell the mayor they'd be giving their notice if she kicked Julia out and that the *Gazette* would back whoever ran against Hazel in the next election. Hazel told them she'd get back to them.

The Gallagher women must have been working the phones as well because Julia had received a call from Olivia to tell her she'd lend her the money if the bank wouldn't.

Still, sales at Books and Beans were way down. She'd be lucky if she rang up a hundred dollars today. And she didn't see that changing anytime soon. But the reason she'd decided to leave had nothing to do with her business. It was because she'd cause the two people she loved more pain by staying here. They'd made it clear they didn't want her around. Hazel had been more obvious than Aidan, but his silence spoke just as loudly.

As Julia walked through to the children's section, her eyes filled with tears. It wouldn't be easy to leave. She went to sit in her storytime chair and tripped over the boxes from Hazel, knocking one over. Papers, folders, and knickknacks spilled out. She frowned, kneeling down to pick everything up.

Just as she began to think that Delaney had brought her someone else's box, she recognized a yellow pen with a rubber emoji on the end, a sushi stapler, and the cheeseburger timer she'd given to Josh. She turned the box upright. It was his things from the writer's shed. She pressed her hand to her mouth to hold back a sob and then slowly began picking up each of the items, smiling at the memories they evoked. She drew a coiled purple notebook toward her and flipped through the pages. It was the screenplay Josh had been working on before he died.

She leaned against the chair and began to read. Like she'd done in *Warrior's Kiss*, some of the characters in Josh's screenplay were thinly disguised. It wasn't difficult to see the resemblance of Josh, Hazel, and herself to the three main characters. This was the man she'd been going to marry, the man she had loved. He'd loved her too. It was as if he knew that one day she'd stumble upon the notebook. It was his love letter to her, a goodbye and his blessing.

She didn't realize until that moment how much guilt she'd been carrying around. It was time to let it go. Time for her to finally forgive Josh. Because while she'd defended him to Aidan, she hadn't truly forgiven Josh herself. She saw that now, felt it deep inside. She picked up the emoji pen and flipped to the empty pages at the back of the purple notebook to write him a letter. Six pages later, she was finally able to write the words *I forgive you* and just as important, *I forgive myself. I did my best.* She put down the pen and closed the notebook, closed that chapter of her life. It was over now. She could move on.

Sitting with her back against her storytime chair, she looked around the bookstore. She'd worked so hard to make her dreams come true, and now she was leaving without a fight. When had everyone else's dreams become more important than her own? Was she really going to give up on the life she'd made for herself because the two people she loved no longer loved her? *No.* Julia thought, no she wasn't.

For once, she was putting herself first. She wasn't leaving Harmony Harbor. She'd convince Mackenzie's bank manager that she was a good risk. And if Hazel wouldn't back down, Julia would find somewhere else to live and set up shop. She smiled, feeling more like the person she used to be. A woman who wasn't weighed down by secrets.

* * *

It was after seven when Julia stood up from dusting the last of the shelves in the store. She took the buds from her ears. She'd been humming along to "Where Are You Christmas?" by Faith Hill.

"Tammy, why don't you go home early? I can…" She trailed off at the sight of Aidan standing behind her. "I didn't hear you."

It had been a week since she'd seen him, and she drank him in. He was still big and beautiful, and, like the other night, he wasn't smiling. She realized she was. It seemed she couldn't help herself where he was concerned. Hope was a horrible thing.

"Maybe because you were singing."

"Maybe." Her lips lifted the tiniest bit at what appeared to be a hint of amusement in his eyes. "Can I help you with something?"

He looked down at his boots and then raised his gaze. "I have to take you in for questioning, Julia."

"What? No. Why?" She backed into the shelf. "I know what Hazel's saying, but it's not true. I didn't let Josh die because I didn't love him anymore. I would never do something like that. He'd...he'd been drinking, and staying out all night, and not helping at the store. I was tired of it. Tired of being the only responsible adult in the relationship, and I let his call go to voice mail. That's it. Do you not think I haven't beaten myself up over it? Asked what would have happened if I had taken his call? Or listened to my messages earlier?"

Her knees went weak, and she sat on her storytime chair, wishing she could curl up and disappear into a make-believe world. Was this what she got for trying to take back her life? "I don't know why I took the letters like he asked and ran instead of calling the police. Maybe because I'd just seen the man I'd once loved lying dead on the floor and was in shock." Guilt weighed her down once more. She gave herself a mental shake and lifted her chin. "But there is something I'm sure of. Nothing I've done since that night was done to hurt anyone."

He crouched in front of her. "Julia, this isn't about Josh's death. No one is investigating you for that, okay?"

"Then I don't understand. Why are you taking me in for questioning?"

"Mrs. Bradford is missing, and her husband is pointing the finger at you."

No, no, no, Lenny, what did you do? Julia did her

best to keep any emotion from showing on her face. She didn't say anything and waited for Aidan to continue.

"Did you receive registered notification that your loan was called in this morning?"

"Yes, I did. I also received an eviction notice from Hazel. I have two weeks to clear out my store and apartment. She's not missing too, is she?" She was being half sarcastic and half serious.

"Don't, okay? This is serious. If I'm going to help you, you need to tell me the truth."

"Why would you want to help me? You made it pretty clear how you felt about me the other night."

"I can't do this now, Julia. And unless you have an alibi for between noon and one today, I'm going to have to bring you into the station."

"I don't. I was here by myself. No customers to vouch for me either. Business pretty much dried up when word got out about Josh."

A muscle flexed in his jaw. "I'm sorry. You don't deserve any of this."

"No, I don't. And I didn't deserve how you treated me at the gallery that night. And I don't deserve you taking me in for questioning either."

"Then give me something. Other than you, do you know of anyone who'd have reason to harm Mrs. Bradford?"

She pretended to be thinking, but what she was really doing was wiping any sign of guilt from her face when she said, "No, nobody."

He crossed his arms. "You're lying."

She lowered her hand from her Rudolph earring.

"No, I'm not. I'm also not going to the station with you." She didn't have any time to waste. She had to find Lenny.

"You don't have a choice."

"Yes, I do. I know my rights." She leaned over and picked up her phone from the floor.

"Julia, come on. It'll look better if you come in of your own accord. You don't need a lawyer. I'm not going to let anyone . . ."

"Hi, Daddy. I have a detective standing in front of me, and he's trying to force me to go to the police station with him for questioning. Okay." She smiled at Aidan. "My daddy would like to talk to you."

Chapter Twenty-Two

♥

"Are you awake, Daddy? It's Christmas Eve day," Ella Rose whispered in his ear.

He frowned, wondering what his little girl was doing at his dad's place. Aidan felt like he was hungover and pried his eyes open with his fingers. "Hey, pumpkin. What are you...?" He looked up at the canopy, and things started to click into place—storytime with Ella Rose at the manor. And a dream, one weird-ass dream that he'd been talking to GG. A chill ran up his spine at the memory of how real it had seemed. If he didn't know better, he'd think he'd been visited by her ghost.

"There's something wrong with daddy, Mommy," Ella Rose called out to her mother in the next room.

"Daddy's fine, pumpkin. I've just been working a lot of hours, and I guess I was more tired than I realized." It totally explained why he'd been talking to his dead great-grandmother about Julia. Or maybe it had nothing to do with how tired he'd been and everything to do with how much he missed Julia.

And maybe the GG in his dream was right. Learning

that Josh had been responsible for Aidan's mother's and sister's death had opened a wound that had never really healed. From the moment he'd read the pages from GG's journal, all the anguish and anger had oozed from the tear in his heart until now there was nothing left and it was slowly healing over. It wasn't fair that Julia had gotten caught in the backlash. Like GG said, she'd paid a horrible price for a sin that was not of her making. All she was guilty of was trying to make things right.

After seeing her yesterday at Books and Beans and learning what she'd suffered since the night at the art gallery, he had a feeling her forgiveness would be hard-won. But that was the least of his worries right now because, unless they'd found Mrs. Bradford in the middle of the night, Julia's legal problems were just beginning.

He ruffled Ella Rose's hair and sat up. He was fully dressed. Jesus, he felt for his gun. It wasn't there.

"Your daughter's right. You don't look well." Harper sat down beside him wearing tailored slacks and a cream mohair sweater. She handed him a cup of coffee and smiled at Ella Rose. "Darling, why don't you go to your bedroom and get dressed?"

"Can we go to the special brunch in the dining room?"

"Yes. Now give your daddy a kiss goodbye. He's going to be late for work."

"'Kay." Ella Rose gave him a hug and kiss and whispered in his ear, "Uncle Liam says we're going to track Santa on NORAD, so be sure to come back here tonight."

"Wouldn't miss it, pumpkin." He grinned at Harper when Ella Rose skipped to the other room. "You're being an awfully good sport. What's going on?"

"I don't know. Over the past couple of days, everyone's been talking a lot about your mother and sister and how much they loved the holidays. You rarely talked about them, you know." She gave her head a frustrated shake. "That's what I did for a living, help people deal with their pain. And once upon a time, I was very good at my job."

"I think you still are. You just let fear get in the way."

"Like you did with Julia?"

"Maybe in the beginning of our relationship. But this thing with Josh, that was anger, pure and simple."

"Anger is never simple, and yours had many layers you had to work through. You're a complicated man, Aidan. And while it's understandable that Julia was trying to protect a woman who had taken on the role of her mother, she hid the truth from you, a man she claimed to love. She hurt you, and it got conflated with the pain you were feeling at being forced to confront your mother's and sister's deaths again. But as painful as it's been for all of you, it's something you needed to go through. You even more than your brothers and father, I think."

He gulped back a mouthful of coffee. "You're right, Julia... Jesus, that's it." He kissed Harper's cheek. "Thanks. It's time for you to go back to work."

"I don't under—"

"My gun." When she got up and walked to the closet to get it off the upper shelf, he said, "You're good at what you do, Harper. You just helped me figure out the only other person who has motive to kidnap Mrs. Bradford. Julia lied to me yesterday, and the only time she lies is to protect someone she cares about. It's Lenny."

"I don't have a clue what you're talking about, but if I've been of some help, I'm glad."

"Hopefully we can wrap this up, and I'll be back by—" He broke off at a banging on the door. He opened it to Ava, Sophie, and Lexi, the three women glaring at him in varying degrees of severity.

"What are you doing here when Julia is in jail?"

"How could you let them put her in jail?"

"Why haven't you apologized to her for being such a jerk and breaking up with her?"

He wasn't sure which of the jail questions came from Sophie or Ava, but the jerk question definitely came from Lexi. "First of all, Julia isn't in jail. She refused to come in for questioning. And I got yelled at by her father. Secondly—" He felt a tug on his jacket.

"Daddy, you didn't break up with Julia, did you?"

"Yes, pumpkin, I did. But it was a mistake. A really big mistake, and Daddy's going to make it up to her."

His daughter wrinkled her nose like she didn't think he was up for the task. "Maybe I should help you."

"I have a feeling he's going to need all of our help, Ella Rose," Sophie said.

"I don't know if we're up for it, ladies. Sounds to me like this is a job for Santa Claus." Lexi held up her phone. "Because according to my source at HHPD, one Julia Landon was brought in by Mr. Bradford, who made a citizen's arrest when she was putting out her garbage at midnight."

As Aidan found out as soon as he arrived at HHPD, Lexi hadn't been joking. He walked into the chief's office without knocking. "Chief, what the hell's going on? Why is Julia in lockup?"

Focused as he was on Benson behind his desk, Aidan didn't notice the man sitting on the two-seater couch right away. He looked like Jeff Bridges in *Hell or High Water*, except bigger, a lot bigger.

Nodding an apology at the man, Aidan said to his boss, "Sorry. I didn't know you had someone in with you."

Aidan didn't understand why Benson appeared to be holding back a grin. "Detective *Gallagher*, this is Julia's father, Sheriff Beauregard Landon."

Okay, so that explained the grin. Benson was probably glad he wasn't in Aidan's shoes. Aidan wished he wasn't standing in them either when Julia's father rose from the couch. He was even bigger than Aidan had first thought, and he didn't look happy to see him.

As though the sheriff read his thoughts, he said, "We grow 'em big in Texas. You should see my three boys, all bigger than me. Fierce sons of a gun, rip a man in two for just giving their baby sister the side-eye." He hooked his thumbs in the belt loops of his jeans and rocked on his cowboy boots.

Aidan prepared himself as he stepped toward the man with his hand extended. Julia's father looked down, grinning as he took Aidan's hand and then proceded to crush it in his bear-size paw.

"Sir, Julia and I have had some problems..." Oh, Jesus, he forced himself to continue, his voice sounding like it did before it changed when he was twelve. "But I love your daughter. I'm going to make it up to her..."

He nearly fell to his knees when the sheriff released him. "I'll just, uh, take a seat here, I think," Aidan said, rubbing his throbbing hand as he pulled the chair in front of the chief's desk around.

Benson covered a laugh with a cough.

"Sheriff, I don't know what Julia's told you, but—"

"Everything. She told me everything." The man had taken a seat. Elbows resting on his knees, he leaned forward to skewer Aidan with a hard look. "My baby girl is just a bit of a thing, but me and my boys trained her well. She can shoot better than most men and take down someone even bigger than you."

"I've had personal experience with Julia's self-defense moves. No, no..." He raised his hands when her father's expression went nuclear. "It wasn't like that. I was worried about her, and she wanted to prove to me that she could take care of herself."

Aidan glanced at his boss, who was pretending to be looking at his computer screen but was silently laughing his ass off.

"My girl might be able to protect herself physically, but she's never been good at protecting her heart. She has a tender heart, and it's been broken twice already. Once when her mama died and next when Winters took his life." His eyes narrowed at Aidan.

"I know I hurt your daughter, and I will do whatever I have to to make it right between us. I should have handled it better, but Julia kept something from me." He could tell by her father's expression he was just making things worse by dancing around the issue, so he told him everything.

"I'm sorry for your loss, son. Things might have gone better between you and my daughter if you'd taken a day or two to think things through before you talked to her. I don't know if this helps, but Julia has had a thing about telling someone else's secret since she was twelve."

"When her mom died," Aidan said.

Her father nodded, looking at him differently now. "She told you about her mama, did she?"

"A little. I got the feeling she was holding something back though."

"My wife was bipolar. Up until Julia was twelve, we'd gotten by okay. Medication managed the mania..." The sheriff looked down at his big hands and twisted the gold band on his finger. "I was away. My oldest was staying with his mama and sister. He got called out, didn't think he'd be long. My wife decided to have a party. Julia saw things she shouldn't, and then Emmie decided they needed to go to the bar. Julia wouldn't let her go. Emmie lost it on Julia when she hid the keys to the truck, pretty much destroying the house looking for them. She'd worked herself into a frenzy and hit Julia." He gave his head a slight shake as though trying to clear the memory. "We'd kept my wife's illness from her. So you can imagine how terrified she'd been..." He cleared his throat. "Julia tried to hide it from us. But about a week later, she came to me and told me her secret. I loved my wife, but things were spiraling out of control. I'd heard about a facility a couple hundred miles from where we live and brought Emmie there. My wife never came home. She had a reaction to a new medication they tried and died."

Aidan rubbed his hand over his mouth, releasing a heavy breath. He understood why her dad had told him. It made perfect sense that the long-ago event had played a role in Julia keeping Josh's secret. She'd told her father her mother's secret and as a result of that Emmeline Landon had been sent away and then had tragically died. Julia might not have even realized that the past event had played a role in her need to keep Josh's secret. But you don't go through something like that without it leaving a mark. What she'd suffered as a little girl... Well, that just slayed him. He cleared the emotion from his voice. "I'm sorry for your loss, sir. Unbelievably sorry that Julia had to go through that, that you all did. I'm glad you told me though. I needed to know."

"I have a feeling she'll talk to you about it one day. She adored her mama. Everyone did. There was something special about Emmeline She was extraordinary, magical almost."

"Like her daughter."

The sheriff smiled and nodded. "We worried sometimes, me and her brothers, that she was too much like her mother. Probably stepped in it a time or two, making her feel bad about being a little different. But she just kept dancing to the beat of her own drum. She got only the best of her mama."

The chief, who'd been talking quietly on the phone throughout the rest of their conversation, disconnected.

"It looks like we might have a problem getting Julia out of jail. Mr. Bradford has gotten Hazel, the mayor," Benson said for the sheriff's benefit, "and Judge Monahan on his side."

"What they don't have is evidence. I know for a fact my daughter isn't involved."

Aidan narrowed his eyes at Julia's father. "Because you know who is, don't you?"

"No, sorry, can't help you there," the sheriff said, rubbing his earlobe between his thumb and forefinger.

Aidan snorted. "Now I know who she got it from. And I know why your daughter is lying, but I don't know why you are unless...One of your sons came with you, didn't they? He's looking for Lenny right now while you're stalling us."

Julia's father let loose a loud, rumbling laugh and slapped his own thigh. "You might just keep one step ahead of my baby girl after all." The sheriff looked over at Benson. "He's sharp. You probably shouldn't fire him."

There was a knock, and the office door opened. "Sorry to interrupt, but I need Aidan, Chief."

"What's going on?"

"Your grandmother and sisters-in-law are here demanding we release Julia. They're getting a little rowdy. And, um"—he glanced at the chief, his cheeks flushing—"Mrs. DiRossi brought cupcakes for the prisoner, I mean Julia, and we found a knife in one of them. Am I supposed to arrest Mrs. DiRossi for that? If I am, could someone else please do it?"

The sheriff chuckled. "I'm starting to see what my girl likes about this town."

He stopped laughing when another officer poked his head in the door. "The mayor just reported Delaney Davis missing. And, sir, a man by the name of Wyatt Landon has been taken to the hospital with a concussion and superficial injuries. You might want to talk to him. He says the man responsible for his injuries is the man we're looking for."

* * *

Her father, who sat in the passenger side of Aidan's black sedan, turned to look at Julia. She'd refused to sit in the front seat. "Now, little bit, Aidan is just trying to keep you safe."

"Lenny wouldn't hurt me."

Aidan looked at her in the rearview. "You don't know that. He hurt your brother."

She briefly closed her eyes, thankful that her brother's injuries weren't worse. She wouldn't have been able to forgive herself if something terrible had happened to him. Her father and brother had gotten on a plane almost the minute after her dad had spoken to Aidan yesterday. She was the one who'd told her brother all the places Lenny could be.

"Aidan's right. Your friend Lenny isn't just a homeless man with mental health issues. He's a former Ranger. He's dangerous."

"Don't talk about him like that. He's not just a homeless man with mental health issues. He's an amazingly talented artist who was wounded, maybe not physically, but here"—she touched her head—

"fighting for us. He's my friend, and he's a good person. The men out looking for him need to know that. You should let me help. I—"

"No," her father and Aidan said at almost the same time, and then smiled at each other.

She groaned at the evidence that the two men had bonded. "I'm beginning to think you shouldn't have come, Daddy."

He grinned over his shoulder, knowing exactly why. "I like this one, Little Bit. He'll take good care of you. Keep you from disappearing into your fairy-tale world."

"I make a living disappearing into my fairy-tale world, thank you very much."

He reached back and patted her knee. "We know you do. Me and your brothers are proud of you."

"Thank you. That's nice to hear. Now, does someone want to tell me where we're going?" She didn't ask Aidan directly because she wasn't speaking to him. He'd hurt her. Deeply. And she wasn't sure she wanted to risk being hurt by him again.

Aidan raised an eyebrow at her in the rearview mirror before saying, "Yes, *someone* would be happy to tell you if you asked them directly."

She pursed her lips and met his gaze.

Her father chuckled and looked out the window as they drove past clusters of snow-covered trees.

"We're meeting up with everyone at the old O'Hurley place."

Julia gasped. "I'm not staying there. That's where Paige died and..." She trailed off, leaving unsaid *the woman you shot.*

"We're not. We're meeting up with everyone there, and then my brothers will drive the vehicles back to the manor. Grams suggested an old house on the estate. It's about a mile in the woods. No one knows about it, so it's unlikely Lenny is aware of it."

Ten days ago, the thought of spending Christmas Eve in a house in the woods with Aidan would have had her dancing in the street. Now she wasn't sure how she felt. "You keep saying everyone. Who are you talking about?"

"We made a list of potential targets. People Lenny might go after because he believes that in some way they've hurt you."

"Aidan's grandmother and her friend Rosa were very helpful." Her father grinned. He was a bit of a flirt, and Julia had felt the need to warn him away from the two older women back at the station. She wasn't sure if her admonishment had worked.

She smiled at Aidan and asked him sweetly, "Are you on the top of the list?"

"Yeah, so that means I'm not taking any chances with Ella Rose's safety. Harper's coming too. Hazel refused. There's a detail on the town hall and her house. The chief is coming along for added backup. And for the same reason you're going into protection, so is Maggie. And my dad."

If she hadn't been sure how she felt about spending Christmas Eve in the woods before, she did now. "This is going to be the worst Christmas Eve ever."

Chapter Twenty-Three

♥

The only sound in the old, abandoned house was the wind whistling down the chimney and the fire crackling in the grate. William Gallagher, Aidan's great-grandfather many times over, had gifted the gray wooden two-story to his best friend and fellow mariner Francis Kavanagh. The house had remained in the Kavanagh family until a decade ago, when Aidan's grandfather Ronan reappropriated it.

The four-bedroom home was a simple box style. Its wide pine floors and fireplaces and mantels dated back to the seventeen hundreds. According to his Grams, no one had been out to the place in years, which was obvious from the amount of dust that had collected on the sheets that had been covering the overstuffed furniture in the living room. The old-fashioned harvest gold appliances in the good-sized kitchen were in working order. And after airing out the place for twenty minutes when they first arrived, the smell of dust and disuse had lifted.

Now it smelled like the wood smoke emitting from

the stone fireplace Aidan sat beside in the rocking chair with Ella Rose in his lap. She had on her pajamas, but he doubted she was going to bed anytime soon.

"It doesn't feel like Christmas, Daddy. We're missing all the fun at the manor."

"I know, pumpkin. I'm sorry. I'll make it up to you tomorrow, okay?" He felt the weight of someone's stare and looked to where Julia had curled up on the end of the couch. She was watching him and Ella Rose.

He could almost see her brain clicking, her imagination kicking in as she looked around. She glanced at their housemates. Everyone, other than Benson and Julia's dad, who were playing chess at the kitchen table, was sitting in their own corner. No one talking, no one exchanging glances. They were either on their phones or reading a book.

Julia rose from the couch and walked over. "You're right, Ella Rose. It doesn't feel like Christmas. But if you help me, I think we can fix that. What do you say?"

Ella Rose nodded enthusiastically. "Can my daddy help too?"

"Of course, and so can your mommy and your grandpa. In fact, everyone's going to help. Do you hear that, people? We have a Christmas to plan."

Harper groaned as loud as the men, but that didn't stop her from pitching in. Julia gave everyone a task. She broke them into groups. She put Aidan with Harper, but he took it upon himself to reorganize so that he ended up with his daughter and Julia instead. They were on the hunt for anything that resembled a Christmas decoration or could be made to look like one. A tree had been at the top of the list. His dad and Maggie were to look for anything that could be fashioned into Christmas gifts, specifically gifts that would appeal to a seven-year-old little girl. The chief, Harper, and the sheriff were in charge of food.

Aidan tried everything he could think of to win over Julia. He went out in the bitter cold with the wind whistling through the trees and chopped down an evergreen. He made decorations with paper and tinfoil plates. He complimented Julia on everything she did, and he was being sincere. She really did see magic in the little things, and if you looked long enough, she could make you believe that you saw it too. But she no longer believed or trusted him, and he was beginning to think she no longer loved him either.

Ella Rose did her best to help him. She praised everything he did, insisting that Julia do the same. When that didn't seem to be getting them anywhere, his daughter pulled a twig off the tree and held it over their heads, claiming it was mistletoe. Julia laughed and gave Ella Rose a kiss instead. At least that was something: He didn't have to worry about the woman he loved and his daughter getting along. He felt like a third wheel.

His dad, on the other hand, was batting a thousand. He and Maggie were supposedly in one of the bedrooms upstairs wrapping their presents. The squeak of bedsprings seemed to suggest otherwise.

At the sound of laughter coming from the kitchen, he looked over to see the chief gazing at Harper like he'd been given the best present ever. Harper was drinking in the attention, sparkling with laughter. Julia's dad looked at them like he'd been given a couple of duds as partners and went back to searching the cupboards. Aidan was beginning to think he should have partnered with the sheriff.

The ringing of the chief's cell broke up Benson and Harper's flirting session. The older man was grim-faced when he disconnected and motioned for Aidan.

"Mr. Bradford's missing. One of the officers who was watching his house is gone too. The other one is on the way to the hospital. Similar injuries to Wyatt Landon," the chief told Aidan.

"You two are needed in town. I can handle things here," Julia's dad said.

Aidan's father joined them, holding up his phone. "Just got word winds have brought down a couple of power lines. Station's overrun with calls. I have to get back. Liam's coming to get me on the snowmobile. Do you need a ride out?"

"Yeah." Aidan glanced at Ella Rose sitting between Harper and Julia, who were making up a Christmas story for his daughter. Julia caught his eye and rolled hers. Apparently, she didn't think Harper was holding up her end. "I don't know if I'm comfortable with this. It's just you and three women and my little girl."

"I'll take good care of her, son." The sheriff reached for the gun tucked in his waistband. "So will my girl. Julia's a crack shot. I'd trust her with my life."

"I have a feeling she is my life, sir. So I need your promise you'll keep her safe and won't let her do anything that puts her in danger."

"You've got it," he said and gave Aidan's shoulder

a firm squeeze. "You should tell her what you just told me. It might go a ways in winning her back."

"I've tried. I've struck out each and every time."

"She always was as stubborn as a Texas longhorn. Just ask her brothers."

That wasn't exactly welcome news, Aidan thought as he walked over to crouch in front of Ella Rose. "Daddy has to go with the chief into town."

"But what about Santa?"

"That's why I'm going, pumpkin. I have to make sure he knows where you are." He tucked the blanket around her. Kissing her forehead, he stood. "Julia, can I talk to you a minute?"

Without an argument, she got up and followed him to the laundry room, the only place they were guaranteed privacy on the main floor. He told her why they were really going into town. "I need to know, if Lenny finds you before we find him, that you won't put yourself in danger to protect him."

"No, that would mean putting Ella Rose at risk. I wouldn't do that. You don't have to worry. My dad and I will protect them."

He nodded, reaching out to tuck her hair behind her ear. "You know what else I'm worried about? I'm worried that you're working so hard to protect yourself from me that you won't be willing to take another chance on us."

She looked away.

He clasped her chin gently between his fingers and drew her gaze back to his. "What do I have to do to convince you that I love you?"

"Show me."

He took her in his arms and kissed her like his life depended on it. Because suddenly, it felt like it did.

"Gallagher, where are you?"

He reluctantly ended the kiss. At the sight of only a small softening in her eyes, he knew he hadn't completely won her back.

* * *

Two hours after Aidan and Paul had left, Julia was sitting on the floor with Ella Rose, Harper, and Maggie, hanging paper snowflakes on the Christmas tree. *Christmas tree* seemed an overblown title for the tiny, scraggly bush. Though she couldn't fault Aidan. All he'd had to work with was a butcher knife. He'd been out in the bitterly cold, dark night for almost an hour.

Her words in the laundry room came back to taunt her. *Show me.* Wasn't that what he'd been doing all night long? Yes, she had a right to be hurt. In her thirty-two years, two people she loved had broken her trust. Building it back up again hadn't been easy, but she had, only to have it broken by Aidan. But he'd just left to do his job. And it was a job, like life, that didn't offer any guarantees. What if he didn't come back? Would she regret for the rest of her days that she didn't tell him she still loved him because she was afraid to be hurt again? Because she was afraid he'd never feel for her what she felt for...

"Sweet Caroline, he told me he loved me." Maggie, Harper, and Ella Rose looked at her. She pulled a face. "Sorry. I thought that was in my head."

"Are you talking about my daddy?"

Julia's cheeks warmed. She glanced at Harper, unsure if this was something she should admit to. The other woman gave a small nod that was somewhat encouraging. "Yes, I was talking about your daddy. Do you mind?"

"No. He said he broke up with you, and it was a big mistake. But he's trying really hard to make it up to you. Did it work?"

"I think so." Harper and Maggie looked at her. "I mean, yes, of course it did."

"You should tell him. That can be his Christmas present."

"That's a good idea. I think I'll do that." She uncrossed her legs and pushed to her feet.

From where he sat on the couch, her father leaned forward. He picked up her cell phone and tossed it to her. "He's a good man. I like him. Reminds me a bit of your brothers."

"Just so you know, that doesn't actually play in his favor." Movement outside the kitchen window caught her attention. She narrowed her eyes at the shadow, positive it wasn't her imagination. Quietly, she cleared her throat. When her dad looked at her, she nudged her chin at the window.

He followed her gaze and then came to his feet. "It's getting late. Think I'll check on those snacks for Santa."

"Wow, it's already eight o'clock. What do you think, Harper? Maybe it's time for Ella Rose to go to bed?" Julia said.

"I think it's okay if..." Harper began, then looked

from Julia to her dad. Worry flashed in her eyes and then was gone just as quickly as it had appeared. "Julia's right. Santa won't come if you're awake, darling."

Ella Rose gasped. "You believe. Julia, Mommy believes!"

Despite her worry that Lenny had found them, Julia laughed at the disconcerted expression on Harper's face. "That's what we call a Christmas miracle, Ella Rose."

Julia's laughter faded as she glanced at her dad. He was by the kitchen door putting on his jacket and boots. "Maggie, you should probably go to bed too. We'll be up early tomorrow."

"Really early. Mia said she's getting up at five in the morning," Ella Rose piped in.

As soon as the others headed up the stairs, Julia hurried over to her dad. "What do you think you're doing?"

"Just going to do a walk around the house." He checked the sight on his Glock.

"I don't think that's a good idea. If Lenny's out there, it's safer to stay inside. Once we know for sure that he is, we can call Aidan and—"

"He's here, Little Bit. And he's not alone. The officer he took, I think he's got him with him. Probably how he found out where we were. Best I can tell, the boy's injured."

Breathing deep in an effort to slow her racing pulse, Julia reluctantly nodded and reached for the switch beside the door. "I'll shut off the lights. It'll make it harder for Lenny to see you. Take my scarf, and wrap it around your head."

He grinned. "You're not all your mother, are you?"

She reached up and kissed his cheek. "Be careful, Daddy. I'll let Aidan know."

"Took care of that already. They should be on their way. Keep your gun on you at all times," he said before opening the door a crack.

Julia held her breath as he slipped noiselessly outside, carefully closing the door behind him. She raced around the main floor, turning off lights and blowing out all but one candle. She left it on the fireplace mantel. At the sound of a drawn-out creak, she turned to see Harper tiptoeing down the stairs.

"Ella Rose went out like a light. Maggie's with her. What's going on?" she asked when she reached Julia's side.

"Lenny's here. He's got the police officer with him. My dad thinks he's hurt. He doesn't know how badly, but he's not the type of man who can just stay inside and do nothing."

"Do Aidan and Paul know?"

There was a heavy *thud* against the kitchen wall. The window shook with the weight of the blow. Julia's heart leaped to her throat. She crouched low and ran to the window. Harper did the same. Julia steeled herself to look outside.

Harper clung to her arm. "Do you see anything?" she whispered.

"No, I . . . Yes, oh, God, yes, it's the police officer. I have to get—" She broke off at the sound of gunfire. It was several yards from the house. If she acted now, she had time to get to the injured man. "Have you ever fired a gun before?" she asked Harper.

"Yes, Aidan taught me."

"Okay, good." She handed Harper the gun. "Cover me. I'm going to get him." Julia didn't waste time putting on her jacket or boots. She inched open the door. Keeping an eye on the surrounding woods, she stayed low and hurried to the man on the ground. He groaned when she lifted him to fit her hands under his arms. He was too heavy for her to carry, so she dragged him into the house. As soon as she reached the threshold, Harper helped her pull him inside.

It took almost ten minutes for them to get the injured officer onto the couch. He had an open wound on his head.

"Can you check and see if there's a first aid kit? Maybe in the bathroom upstairs," she said to Harper.

"I have one in my purse."

"You carry a first aid kit in your purse?"

"I like to be prepared."

Noting the flush spreading up the other woman's neck, Julia smiled. "You shouldn't be embarrassed about it. That's a good thing." She glanced at the kitchen window, growing more concerned about her dad with each passing minute. "I'm going to take another—"

"Julia, I've got him. You're safe now," a voice yelled from outside. It was Lenny.

She briefly closed her eyes. Somehow the situation must have triggered an episode. He was confused. Instead of seeking revenge like they'd assumed, he'd been trying to protect her. "I told Aidan I wouldn't leave Ella Rose unprotected, but I have to do something, Harper.

He's got my dad. I can't let Lenny hurt my dad. I couldn't live—"

Harper nodded, her face grim. "I know. I don't like it, but I know."

"Thank you," she said, relieved Aidan's ex wouldn't try to stop her. She moved to lift the wounded officer's coat. His gun was gone. Lenny must have taken it. It was probably better if she didn't approach him with a weapon anyway. She unclipped the handcuffs from the officer's belt. "Go upstairs. Stay with Ella Rose and Maggie. Don't come down unless I call all clear."

At the sound of Lenny shouting her name, his voice agitated, Julia ran to the door and opened it. "Here I am. I'm okay, Lenny." He stood a few yards to the left of the door with her dad on his knees in front of him. She couldn't tell for certain, but her father's hair looked like it was matted with blood. But he wasn't dazed; his eyes blazed with fury, no doubt angry that Lenny had gotten the jump on him and probably just as angry at her for opening the door.

"Lenny, that's my dad. He came all the way from Texas to protect me. I'm just going to come out and—"

Her dad growled, and she stepped back, giving him a *relax* look. She threw in a *don't try to be a hero* look for good measure. "Could you let him up, please?"

Lenny looked confused. "He's your dad? But he had a gun. He tried to shoot me."

"He didn't know you're my friend. He thought you were one of the people who were trying to hurt me."

"I got nearly them all. I just need to get the mayor. But I don't know who else is working with them, so it's better if you come with me. That way I can make sure you're safe."

"You got them all, Lenny. I'm safe. And so are you. You look cold. There's a fire inside. You can get warm. Just let my dad go, okay? And put down the gun." She smiled. "I'll make you hot chocolate."

"You're sure you're safe? It's all over? Everything's okay?"

"Everything's okay, Lenny," she said, her voice thick with emotion. "Can you put down the gun for me? It's making me nervous."

"Sure." He tossed the Glock in the snow and then hauled her father to his feet. "I'm sorry I hurt you, sir. You shoulda told me you were Julia's dad." Her father stumbled, and Lenny put him in a fireman's carry.

The cavalry arrived ten minutes later. Aidan was the first through the door, his face pale and anxious, but her brother Wyatt pushed him aside to get to her first. He picked her up. "Geez, Little Bit, you manage to cause a boatload of trouble wherever you go, don't you?"

Aidan tapped him on the shoulder. Her brother looked back and turned to hand her to Aidan. "You and me aren't done talking yet, Gallagher. My brothers want a word with you too."

Aidan didn't respond. He walked with her through the kitchen, past where Lenny sat at the table with her father and the chief. Lenny's gaze followed them, his eyes narrowing.

"It's okay. He's one of the good guys, Lenny," she called back to be on the safe side.

"I'm not so sure about that," she heard her brother say.

Aidan walked into the laundry room, placed her on the washing machine, and shut the door with his foot.

"Aidan, I can ex—"

He cut her off with a toe-melting, knee-knocking kiss.

And as much as she never wanted it to end, she felt it was past time she said something about his habit of shutting her up with a kiss. Reluctantly, she leaned back. "You can't keep kissing me to get me to stop talking."

His dark eyebrows pulled inward. "I don't. I kiss you because I'm going to yell at you. Once I have my mouth on yours, the last thing on my mind is yelling. Except today. After what you pulled with Lenny—"

She kissed him, and kept kissing him until someone pounded on the door. "There's a cute little girl looking for her daddy. Seriously can't believe she's yours, Gallagher," her brother Wyatt said though the door.

Aidan leaned his forehead against Julia's. "Are the other two as bad as him?"

"Worse."

"As far as you know, they have no plans to move east, do they?"

"Not that I know of. Why?"

"Because I love you, and I don't plan on going anywhere, so that means I'll have to put up with your brothers for a very long time."

"Does a very long time mean forever and always?"

"It's looking that way, sugarplum."

* * *

It was the strangest, but also possibly the best, Christmas Eve Aidan had ever known. Strange because Lenny, the man who'd kidnapped three people and wounded three others, was sitting on the couch in the house in the woods between Julia's father and her brother Wyatt, who was even bigger and slightly more terrifying than the sheriff.

Ella Rose knelt with Mia at the coffee table watching Lenny draw their portraits. The man would eventually go to jail, just not yet. He'd been Julia's Christmas wish. It was Harper who carried the swaying vote.

In her professional opinion, now that he knew Julia was safe, Lenny was no longer a threat to anyone. Harper had agreed to treat him. He'd be her first patient in the practice she was setting up in Harmony Harbor. Moments ago, Julia had whispered to Aidan that it was one more sign that Christmas magic really did exist.

To his mind, it wasn't a sign of Christmas magic but of Julia's. He looked to where she sat with his sisters-in-law, the four of them casting smiling glances at his father and Maggie, who were sitting together by the fire roasting chestnuts. The door banged open, and his brothers dragged in a *real* tree.

And there was the reason why it would possibly go down as the best Christmas ever. Not because of a tree. If anything, this Christmas had taught them that they didn't need the trappings of the holidays as long as they were with the people they loved.

Kitty and Jasper followed his brothers in with boxes of lights and decorations.

Julia jumped up. "Tree trimming time." She grinned

at Aidan. "And Christmas carols courtesy of the Gallagher boy band."

Her brother leaned back against the couch and crossed his arms. "This I gotta hear."

"Yeah, well, you'll be waiting a while," Aidan said. There was no way he was going to perform in front of...

Julia pressed her hands together. "Pretty please." She leaned over to nudge Ella Rose and Mia, who obediently took up the refrain. Which is how Aidan ended up standing beside the Christmas tree singing "All I Want for Christmas Is You."

Chapter Twenty-Four

♥

Julia woke up alone in the bed to an odd thumping sound. She, Aidan, Ella Rose, Harper, Paul, and her father and brother had all stayed at the house in the woods. She got out of bed and tiptoed downstairs to see Aidan kneeling near the fireplace with his hands in his boots, walking them around the area rug.

"What are you doing?" she whispered.

He grinned at her over his shoulder. "Resurrecting a Gallagher family tradition. My dad used to do this when we were kids."

"Santa's footprints. That's perfect." She wrapped her arms around his neck and hugged him from behind. "Ella Rose will be so excited."

Along with the decorations, Kitty and Jasper had brought Aidan's, Harper's, and Ella Rose's presents from the manor last night. They were all, including her brother and father, joining the Gallaghers for a Christmas lunch later today.

His gaze followed hers, and he briefly closed his eyes. "Jesus, babe. There's nothing for you under the tree."

"I don't need anything. It's already been an amazing Christmas. Better than I ever could have imagined."

"No, I have to give you something. I won't feel right if—"

"Okay, sing for me."

He laughed. "Didn't you hear enough of me earlier?"

"No, listening to you sing will never get old." She smiled and then thought of the one thing she really did want but was afraid to ask for. "I don't want to ruin your Christmas, so just pretend I didn't ask if—"

He sat back on his heels, his piercing blue gaze roaming her face. "You want me to read Josh's letter, don't you?"

She chewed on her bottom lip and nodded. If she didn't think it would help him, she would never have asked.

He turned to look at the smoldering embers in the grate for a long moment and then finally said, "Okay."

She could tell it wasn't easy for him to agree to her request and kissed his stubbled jaw. "Thank you." She straightened and went to the couch, where she'd left her purse.

"You brought the letter with you?"

"I've been carrying it around since the night at the gallery. You don't have to do it now if—"

He motioned with his fingers for her to bring him the letter.

"Do you want to read it on your own?" she asked, handing him the envelope.

He nodded, the muscle in his jaw flexing. "I'll come up after I'm finished."

In the bedroom on the second floor, she lay in the dark waiting, wondering if she'd made a mistake by giving him the letter, by leaving him to read it on his own. Just as she was about to get up and go to him, the door creaked open.

The mattress depressed under his weight and then he stretched out beside her. He drew her into his arms, pressing his face against hers. His cheek was damp. "Thank you. You were right. He wasn't a monster. I needed to read the letter. My dad and brothers do too. So do Hazel and Maggie. I forgive him."

Her eyes filled at the thought that maybe now Josh could rest in peace. "I'd say now that's truly a Christmas miracle."

"You're my miracle."

* * *

Aidan had just about given up on Hazel answering her door when it opened an inch. He did his best to hide his surprise at what little he could see of the woman. It was three in the afternoon on New Year's Eve, and Hazel was still in a robe, her hair unbrushed, her face pale and haggard. He hadn't believed the gossip going around town that Hazel hadn't been out of her house since the night at the gallery. Now he was beginning to think it was true.

"Hi, Mrs. Winters. I was hoping you had a minute."

"Some other time perhaps. I'm not up for visitors." She clutched her white robe at her neck, her gaze flitting to his face and then away. "I sent a note to your grandmother and father with my heartfelt apologies for what my son did to your family. I know it's not enough, but I don't know what else I can do."

"I think I might be able to help you with that, Mrs. Winters."

Her eyes widened. "Don't sue me, please. My house is all I have now. I don't have much in savings. My buildings down—"

"Calm down. We're not planning to sue you, Hazel. Let me come in and talk to you for a minute. I have something you need to see."

She glanced up at him and then nodded, opening the door. "Excuse the mess. I haven't been myself since... Well, you know."

"If you think this is messy," he said as he followed her into the spotless living room, "you've never been to Julia's apartment."

Hazel made a distressed sound in her throat, and Aidan realized he'd upset her by bringing up Julia. It hadn't been intentional. These days Julia was pretty much on his mind all the time, so it was only natural that he mentioned her. He bore no ill will toward Hazel. None of his family did, including Julia. In part, that's why he was here.

By the time Hazel lowered herself onto a cream love seat, there was no hint of the anguish he thought he'd heard and seen moments ago. "If you're here to ask me not to evict Julia, my attorney has already sent her a letter. She can stay in the apartment and continue running her business out of my building for as long as she wants." Hazel played with the tie on her robe. "I...I wasn't myself. If I had any hopes of being reelected, Delaney felt it best if Julia wasn't in town to remind people of what my son did. I was angry too. Angry that Julia kept everything from me."

"She did it to protect you, Hazel. You're the closest thing to a mother she has. She didn't want to lose you too. You do know that Josh asked her not to tell us until you had passed, right? She was fulfilling his wishes. Your son loved you."

"Loved me? He took his own life. How is that love? Knowing how much we'd...I'd suffer... That's not something—"

Aidan reached in the inner pocket of his jacket for Josh's letter. His brothers and father had read it, and so had Maggie. Knowing how deeply Josh had suffered for what he'd done had made it easier for them to forgive Hazel's son, easier for them to find closure and peace. No judge or jail time could have pronounced a stronger sentence than Josh had pronounced on himself.

"You need to read this, Hazel. Josh never wanted you to know that he'd taken his own life or that he was responsible for my mom and sister's accident. He asked Julia to keep that from you because he loved you. You'll see that when you read his letter. I think it'll help you understand how much he was suffering. He couldn't see another way to escape his pain and guilt."

"He could have told me. He could have told Julia. She did love him, you know. Once, she'd loved him very much." She hesitated and then took the letter from him.

Even if Josh had come forward and told Aidan's family, Julia, and his mother, Aidan had a feeling, in

the end, the outcome wouldn't have been much different. Josh Winters would never have been able to forgive
himself or live with what he'd done. "She did love him.
Just like she loves you."

The older woman nodded, ever so slightly, and then
grew quiet as she began reading the letter. There were
four pages from Josh trying to make them understand
that it had never been his intention to hurt anyone, least
of all the Gallagher family. He talked about how kind
Aidan's mom had been over the years to Josh and his
mother, especially when his dad had left them. How
much he liked and respected Aidan's father. How devastated he'd been knowing Aidan and his brothers had
lost their baby sister because of him.

Tears rolled down Hazel's face, and she hiccupped
a sob as she carefully refolded the letter. He stayed
quiet, giving her time, hoping that, in the end, she
would agree to Josh's final request. Somewhere in the
house he heard a clock ticking down the time. Ten
minutes later, he looked up at the rustle of paper. "If
you and your family think allowing Mothers Against
Drunk Driving to publish Josh's letter will make
someone think twice before they drink and drive, then
yes, I'll agree."

"Thank you. I know it won't be easy having all this
come out in the open, Hazel. But if Josh's letter can
save another family from going through what ours has,
it'll be worth it."

"Yes, yes, it will." She went to return the letter.

"No, that's yours. I made a copy," he said as he stood
up. "If you don't have any plans tonight, I thought you

might like to join us. I have a surprise planned for Julia. I know she'd want you there."

"Thank you, Aidan. After what..." She lifted a help-less shoulder, and her eyes filled once again. "It's very kind of you and your family, but I'm not feeling up to it just yet. I'm happy for you and Julia though. Please tell her so for me."

"I think she'd rather hear that from you."

"You're right, of course. We need to talk. I will call her."

It wasn't what Aidan had hoped for, but he thought knowing Hazel hadn't cut her out of her life for good would make Julia happy. Which made him happy be-cause he'd been working hard every night this week to give Julia a magical New Year's Eve.

* * *

Julia stood in the study at the manor with her arms crossed. She was one ticked-off fairy. Oliva—who'd arrived home with her family yesterday morning—fastened the wings to the back of Julia's Sugar Plum Fairy costume. "This is not how I pictured my first New Year's Eve with Aidan," Julia grumbled. This was the night she was supposed to lose the wings, not put them back on. She'd said no several times to her friends but couldn't hold out against Ella Rose, George, and Mia.

"It's really too bad he has to work tonight, but look on the bright side. You get to perform as the Sugar Plum Fairy and make everyone smile." Olivia handed her the fake-fur cape. "Finn and Liam are probably already out front with the snowmobiles."

The Snow Ball on Christmas Eve had been canceled due to Lenny being on the loose. As Julia understood it, the guests staying at the manor for the holidays had been disappointed, so the Gallagher women had come up with the brilliant idea—and yes, she was being sarcastic, which probably meant Aidan was rubbing off on her—of staging a performance of *The Nutcracker* in the woods on New Year's Eve.

And they wouldn't be wearing ballet slippers or boots. They would be wearing skates. Which was the real reason for her sarcasm. Apparently, the Gallagher men had spent the past week icing a path in the woods. Fireworks and a bonfire would follow. As lovely as that sounded, Julia planned to skip that part of the night and head home to tend to her bruised behind. And she had absolutely no doubt it would be bruised because she could barely skate. Something she'd repeatedly told her *friends* and they had repeatedly ignored.

Needless to say, all things considered, Julia was a tad grumpy tonight. The snowmobile ride did nothing to improve her mood. When they reached their destination, she could make out approximately fifty people sitting on benches around a bonfire at the outer edge of the woods.

Liam got off the snowmobile and looked down at her with a grin. "Instead of sugarplum, I think my brother should call you sourpatch."

"Ha-ha. See how you like it when your wife forces you to perform on New Year's Eve."

"I can pretty much guarantee she will, and I'll love

every minute of it," he said with a wink that told her exactly where his mind had gone.

She gave him a look. "I don't think you're funny." Then she got off the snowmobile to look around. "Olivia said the other people in the play would be here, but I don't see anyone else in costume."

Liam offered his arm. "They're probably waiting for you on the path."

"Maybe we're in the wrong place," she said as they reached the woods. No one was there, and she could barely see a foot in front of her.

"Nope. See? There's the sign." He shined the light of his phone on a hand-painted sign that read SUGARPLUM WAY and then texted someone.

"But there's...Oh," she gasped when all the trees lit up with white fairy lights. "How did you...It's so beautiful." The crowd *ooh*ed and *aah*ed along with her.

"You better take off your skate guards. Your fairy friends are coming to get you," Liam said, once again lending her his arm.

She drew her gaze from the trees to look at the iced path through the woods. Ella Rose, Mia, and George, dressed in fairy costumes, skated toward her. "Come on, sugarplum. We're going to take you to your prince," Ella Rose said.

The people from the bonfire had joined them near the path, clapping and smiling. Julia spotted Olivia, Ava, Sophie, Lexi, Mackenzie, and the rest of her friends. Their sentimental smiles and shiny eyes gave it away.

"Aidan did this, didn't he?" she asked Liam, trying not to cry.

"You're talking about my brother Aidan, right? The hardass?" he asked, but the smile in his eyes gave him away.

She didn't get a chance to respond. George skated over and tugged on Julia's hand, dragging her after her.

"Just a minute, George. I haven't been on skates in..." The blades flew out from under Julia, and she landed on her butt.

Behind her, she heard Liam say, "Hey, Prince Charming, your princess can't skate. You better come and get her before she breaks something."

Ella Rose, Mia, and George were trying to help her up when a familiar leather-clad arm reached past them. Julia looked up to see Aidan smiling down at her. "Up you go, sugarplum," he said, half lifting her to her feet to the sound of cheering and clapping.

"We tried to get him to wear his costume, but he wouldn't," George said, clearly perturbed.

Ella Rose quickly came to her father's defense. "That's okay, because he bought her a castle."

"You bought me a castle?" Julia said, her voice husky with unshed tears. She couldn't believe Aidan had done all of this for her.

"It's not exactly—" he began.

"It's the old house in the woods. But everyone's going to help fix it up. Me and—"

Aidan shook his head and yelled, "Finn, would you come and get your kid? She's ruining my proposal."

Everyone laughed, including George. She loved whenever anyone called her Finn's kid. Which Aidan knew, of course. Finn skated over to them and took

George's hand. "Come on, girls. Let's give the prince and princess some privacy. You can help your moms put on their skates." When they left them alone on the path, Aidan took her hand. "Hang on, and I'll drag you the rest of the way."

She stared up at him. "Did you say 'proposal'?"

"No, I..." He tilted his head as though thinking back to what he said, and then he blinked. "I guess I did."

"So you weren't actually proposing to me?"

"No, I bought the house, and I was hoping you'd move in with me..." He looked down at her and then smiled. "But you have to admit it's the perfect setting to propose to the Sugar Plum Fairy. What do you say?" he asked as he went down on one knee. "Will you marry me, Julia?"

"I've been half in love with you since you kissed me under the mistletoe last Christmas, Aidan. But I don't want you to propose just because it slipped out by accident. I'd be just as happy to accept your proposal to move in with you. Honestly, I would."

"I don't think it was an accident. I think it was fairy magic. Julia magic. Say yes, sugarplum."

"Yes, Aidan, I'll marry you. Nothing would make me happier than being your wife," she said, laughing when the Gallagher family and her friends skated toward them, cheering.

Later, with Aidan's hand in hers, Julia watched the fireworks lighting up the night sky. She reached back and touched her fairy wings with a grateful smile. The journey hadn't been easy, but if she hadn't accepted the role of the Gallaghers' fairy godmother, she wouldn't have found her own happily-ever-after.

In the spirit for another holiday story?

'Tis the season for love in Harmony Harbor, but it's the last place Sophie DiRossi wants to be. After fleeing many years ago, Sophie is forced to return to the town that harbors a million secrets. Firefighter Liam Gallagher still has some serious feelings for Sophie—and seeing her again sparks a desire so fierce it takes his breath away. Hoping for a little holiday magic, Liam sets out to show Sophie that they deserve a second chance at love.

Please turn the page for an excerpt from

Mistletoe Cottage.

Sirens wailed, the fire engines' red and white lights bouncing off the clapboard Colonials on Main Street. People strolling along the tree-lined sidewalk turned to watch the rigs careen around a corner while cars veered to the side of the road. Ladder Engine 1 and Engine 6 were headed west of Harmony Harbor to Greystone Manor.

Three hours earlier, Liam Gallagher had been heading home to Boston. He'd stopped by the station to say goodbye to his father, Fire Chief Colin Gallagher, on the way out of town. But, because he loved his old man, who had put up with Liam for the past month, he'd made his first mistake. He'd let his dad convince him to stay another day. Taking his father up on his challenge had been a bigger one. Under the watchful eyes of the three men who knew him about as well as he knew himself, Liam would be battling his first fire in more than five weeks. Built in the early nineteenth century and modeled after a medieval castle, Greystone Manor was a firefighter's worst nightmare. And over the last month, Liam had been battling one of his own.

The chief disconnected his cell phone call and shifted to face Liam and Marco DiRossi, Liam's childhood best friend. The rest of the crew followed behind in the ladder engine. Fergus MacLeod, a burly beast of a man with russet hair and beard who'd known Liam since he was in diapers, blasted the horn at three-second intervals to clear the intersection up ahead. Liam's father raised his voice to be heard. "Manor's full of smoke, but the sprinklers haven't kicked in. Lights went out, and the generator took longer than it should to come on. A couple of guests sustained minor injuries evacuating—"

"GG and Grams?" Liam asked, unable to conceal the anxiety in his voice. He wasn't worried his father would misconstrue the reason for it or reprimand him for interrupting his brief. Liam's great-grandmother Colleen owned and operated Greystone with the help of her daughter-in-law and Liam's grandmother, Kitty.

He'd never understood what had possessed his great-grandmother to turn the manor into a hotel. If it had been up to him, she would have sold out years ago. Especially now that his grandfather Ronan was no longer there to help run the place. Liam hoped she'd be more open to the idea after tonight.

"Jasper got GG out, but your grandmother, a woman, and a young child are still inside. They can't find the little girl. Kitty and the woman refuse to leave without her." His father looked at Marco. "Jasper says she's your sister, son. And the little girl is her daughter, your niece."

Liam blew out a silent whistle. Sophie DiRossi. He

hadn't thought about her in years, and there'd been a time when she'd been all he thought about. He glanced at Marco, who sat in the jump seat across from him.

Beneath an inch of dark scruff, Marco's jaw tightened. "Jasper's gotta be mistaken, Chief. Sophie and her kid live in LA. She hasn't been home since she left."

"Just wanted to give you a heads-up in case it's true," his father said, then glanced at Liam and lifted his chin at Marco before facing forward.

Everyone in Harmony Harbor knew how the DiRossis felt about Sophie and her mother's defection. Within six months of Sophie and her mother taking off, the oldest of the DiRossi siblings, Lucas, had left Harmony Harbor, and a year later, their father, Giovanni, remarried and moved to Italy.

"You okay?" Liam asked his best friend.

Marco took off his helmet to stab his fingers through his dark hair. "Jasper has to be wrong. There's no way it's Sophie."

If Jasper said it was Sophie, Liam had no doubt that it was. Nothing got past the old man—a fact Liam, his brothers, and cousins could attest to. Jasper, or Jeeves as the Gallagher grandchildren referred to him, had been at Greystone for as long as any of them could remember. A tall beanpole of a man with stiff, overly proper manners, he ruled the manor and the Gallagher family with an iron fist hidden inside a velvet glove.

Since Marco knew Jasper almost as well as Liam, either his friend was in denial or he held a grudge longer than Liam had given him credit for. Noting the angry bounce of Marco's right leg, he was going with the latter. Then again…"They'll be okay, buddy. We'll find your niece. Get them out of there."

"Yeah, yeah, I know. What I don't know is why the hell she's here. After eight years, she just shows up out of the blue…" With a white-knuckled grip on his helmet, Marco gave his head an angry shake.

So Liam had been right after all. "I don't get it. Aren't you happy she's finally come home?"

"Give me a break. You have no idea what her leaving did to my family. For two years, we never heard a word from her. Now we're lucky if she calls a couple times a year. And for the amount of time she talks, you'd think we were putting a trace on her phone calls."

"So, what, you don't believe in second chances? Don't be a hothead and blow it. At least you still have a sister." Liam sensed his father glancing his way and Fergus's eyes on him in the rearview mirror.

"You're right. Sorry, I didn't think."

Fergus blasted the horn as he drove beneath a vine-covered stone arch, past the iron gates leading into the estate. The headlights and emergency lights sliced through the gloom of the late-October night and Liam leaned forward. What got his attention wasn't the sprawling mansion built of local granite or the people scattering from where they'd been standing on the circular drive. It was the white smoke billowing from the manor's entrance. He opened the door as the engine rolled to a stop and smelled the air—chemicals, not burning wood. "There's no fire," Liam said to his father as he jumped onto the asphalt.

"Not yet, but could be electrical. Breathing apparatus on, Liam," his father called after him.

Liam raised his gloved hand, indicating he heard him, as he jogged to where Jasper was leading Kitty from the manor. "You okay, Grams?" he asked once he reached them.

She nodded through a coughing fit.

He rubbed her arm and looked at Jasper. "Sophie and the little girl still inside?"

Jasper gave him a clipped nod. "We'd gone through most of the upper and main floors before Miss Kitty was overcome."

"All right. Go let Dad check you both over," Liam said as he started into the building, then pivoted when it hit him what he was smelling. "Jasper, you didn't have the fog machine going, did you?"

"Certainly not, Master Liam. As your father directed, I expressly forbade Miss Kitty and Madame from using it this Halloween."

Since Madame didn't like to be told what she could or couldn't do, Liam didn't rule out the possibility that Colleen and a fog machine were behind the smoke. As he walked into the entryway, he tapped the switch on his helmet twice. The beam of light cut through the haze, providing him with a 180-degree view. He jogged across the lobby, calling for Sophie while trying to get an idea where the smoke originated from. He spotted what he believed was the point of origin at the same time he heard someone cough.

A woman with long dark hair stumbled out of one of

the sitting rooms. "Sophie, it's Liam." He tipped up his helmet as he closed the distance between them.

She lowered a denim jacket from where she'd held it over her mouth and nose. Her face was pale, her golden brown eyes red-rimmed. She looked exhausted and utterly terrified. "My little girl. I can't find my little girl. You have to help me—" She started coughing again.

"I'll find her, Sophie. But you need to—" He broke off as a second beam of light joined his. "Marco, get her out of here," he ordered his best friend.

Marco nodded, his expression unreadable as he reached for his sister.

She pulled away from her brother and frantically shook her head. "No, I can't go. I have to help you find her. You don't—"

Her brother cut her off. "Dammit, Soph, don't be stubborn. We'll find her, but you have to—"

"No, no, you don't understand. She's terrified of fire...of firemen. And she can't..." Her voice broke on a sob. Liam saw the herculean effort it took for her to regain control, but she did, and then she finished what she'd been about to say. "She can't talk."

He and Marco shared a glance. Their job just got a whole lot harder. "Sophie, I'll take off the breathing apparatus and my helm—"

"Like hell you will," his father said through his com. Marco said the same thing beside him.

Liam knew the reason for their concern and ignored them. He couldn't think about that now. Couldn't let the memory of the warehouse fire into his head. "I'm going to find your little girl. What's her name?"

She held his gaze as though she believed him and swiped at her eyes. "Mia. Her name's Mia." Overcome by another coughing fit, Sophie struggled to take the knapsack off her shoulder. Waving off his offer to help, she dug around inside and pulled out a pink pig with a singed ear. "We had a fire at our apartment in LA. Other than Mia, Peppa Pig is pretty much the only thing that survived. It might help if you show her..." Sophie bit her bottom lip, then handed him the stuffed animal. "Please, Liam, please find her. She's all I have."

He slipped the pink pig into his pocket. "Right now it doesn't look like we're dealing with a fire. She'll be okay, Sophie. I'll find her," he promised.

"Jesus, Soph. Why didn't you call us? Why didn't...?"

Liam didn't waste time waiting for Sophie to answer her brother. He jogged toward the door behind the grand staircase. It led to the basement, a place that had featured prominently in his nightmares as a little kid. Probably because his older brothers and cousins had traumatized him with stories about the long-dead pirates that haunted the narrow passageways and secret tunnels. If the upper floors had already been searched, it's possible he'd find Mia down here.

Smoke billowed through the partially open door, and Liam adjusted his breathing apparatus before opening it wide. As soon as he did, he was hit by a thick wall of smoke. The beam of light cut through the fog and illuminated the spiral staircase.

Liam started down the stairs and the stone walls closed in around him, transporting him to a wide-open space filled with movement and noise. Voices came over his radio—yelling, the rapid repeat of gunshots. Faint at first, and then the gunfire became louder. *Get down. Get down.* He belly-crawled to where Billy lay in the middle of the floor, laser beams zinging overhead from one side of the warehouse to the other. Shouting. Everyone shouting. A bullet shattered the concrete an inch from his head, and then another one...

Something repeatedly bumped his leg, getting harder with each jab, and the flashback started to fade. Liam looked down. A pair of small blue eyes stared up at him. It was a black cat. It took a moment for his head to clear and for him to get his bearings. He wasn't in Boston; he was on the stairs at Greystone.

Someone yelled over the radio. "Liam, are you all right? Liam, goddammit, answer me."

"Good. I'm good, Chief. I'm in the basement. Must have played havoc with the com," he lied to his father, who must already suspect what Liam had been denying. He was so far from good it wasn't funny. "Found the problem," he said as he reached the bottom of the stairs.

To his left, barely visible behind cardboard boxes piled recariously close, sat two overheating commercial fog machines. They were damn lucky the units hadn't caused a fire. He reported his findings to his father over the com at the same time Marco thundered down the stairs.

When he reached the bottom, Marco searched Liam's face and stabbed an angry, gloved finger in his chest. "Get your head out of your ass, Gallagher, before I do it for you."

"I know. I know. But now's not the time to—" He

broke off and frowned down at the cat head-butting his leg. For a second, Liam was afraid he'd zoned out again. But no, Marco would have seen it coming on and shook him out of it. The cat meowed and looked toward the tunnels. Liam didn't read minds, cat or human, but somehow he knew this was about Mia. As though the cat sensed he'd clued in, he took off. Liam ran after him.

"Where do you think you're going?" Marco called out.

"To find Mia," he shouted back. His voice sounded like he'd been hacking up a lung. Maybe he had been during the flashback. Though now wasn't the time to think about those missing minutes and what they would have meant had they been battling an actual blaze. He'd beat himself up over it later.

As he made his way deeper into the tunnels, the smoke wasn't as bad. He pulled off his breathing apparatus, stopping briefly to remove the tank and rest it carefully against the damp stone wall. He thought he'd lost the cat until he heard an impatient meow up ahead. The beam of light from Liam's helmet caught the end of the cat's tail just before it disappeared down a narrow passageway.

As soon as Liam rounded the corner, he spotted the little girl. Sophie's daughter sat with her back to the wall, her forehead resting on denim-clad knees that were pressed to her chest. She slowly raised her head and blinked into the bright light.

"Hey, Mia." He didn't want to frighten her and crouched a couple yards away. Then he took off his helmet and set it on the ground, angling it so the light didn't hit her in the eyes. He smiled. "I'm Liam Gallagher, a friend of your uncle Marco. Your mommy too. I've known her since she was a little girl not much older than you are."

She scuttled away from him, then came to her feet, her eyes darting from left to right. His chest tightened. He recognized the look on her face, the wide-eyed panic and fear of someone who'd suffered a trauma. He should know, since after tonight, he could no longer deny he'd suffered the same. "Your mommy gave me"—he racked his brain for the pig's name—"Porky." She looked at him. "Peppy the pig?"

The faintest hint of a smile touched her adorable heart-shaped face. "Do you want your pig?" he asked, reaching in his pocket.

She gave her head a quick shake, and Liam withdrew his hand from his pocket. He got it. The singed ear was a reminder of what she and her stuffed animal had been through. "You don't have to be frightened, sweetheart. There wasn't a fire, just a lot of smoke from the fog machines." Within minutes, there might have been a fire. But looking at Mia, he couldn't let his mind go there. Couldn't think of her down here trapped and alone. "I know you're scared, and you don't know me, but your mommy's worried about you, so whaddya say we get out of here?"

She looked down, her long dark hair shielding her face, but not enough to hide the slight flush pinking her cheeks. He frowned and followed her gaze, wondering what...He briefly closed his eyes. She'd wet her pants.

He cleared his throat. "Mia. Sweetheart." Her big blue eyes flitted to his face, then darted away. "If I tell you a secret, do you promise not to tell anyone?" She glanced at him, then gave him a hesitant nod. "Okay, I'm holding you to that. When I was around your age...Now that I think about it, I was way older. Like ten." He'd been five. "My brothers and cousins brought me down here to hunt for buried treasure. We had flashlights and shovels, and while we were digging, they told ghost stories. Really spooky ones. And then they turned the flashlights off. They left me down here for hours all by myself in the dark. I was so scared, I wet my pants." That part was true. "So you see, you have nothing to be embarrassed about. Happens to the best of us," he said with a smile, and shrugged out of his jacket, holding it open for her. "You can put this on, and no one will know. It'll be our secret. Sound good?" He'd find a way to tell Sophie without embarrassing Mia.

She took a couple hesitant steps toward him. "Thatta girl," he said, and leaned over to wrap the jacket around her tiny, delicate frame. "It's pretty long. Is it okay if I pick you up so you don't trip?" She nodded, and he lifted her into his arms. "You know what? You're as brave as any firefighter I know, so you should probably wear this." He put his helmet on her head, grinning when she disappeared beneath it. He tipped it up. "There you are."

She rewarded him with a smile that lit up her face and wrapped around his heart, squeezing tight.

"Mia DiRossi, you're going to be a heartbreaker just like your mother."

About the Author

Debbie Mason is the *USA Today* bestselling author of the Highland Falls, Harmony Harbor, and Christmas, Colorado series. The first book in her Christmas, Colorado series, *The Trouble with Christmas*, was the inspiration for the Hallmark movie *Welcome to Christmas*. Her books have been praised by *RT Book Reviews* for their "likable characters, clever dialogue, and juicy plots." When Debbie isn't writing, she enjoys spending time with her family in Ottawa, Canada.

You can learn more at:

AuthorDebbieMason.com
Twitter @AuthorDebMason
Facebook.com/DebbieMasonBooks
Instagram @AuthorDebMason

*Can't get enough of that small-town charm?
Forever has you covered with these heartwarming
contemporary romances!*

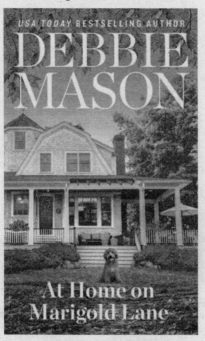

AT HOME ON MARIGOLD LANE
by Debbie Mason

For family and marriage therapist Brianna MacLeod, moving back home to Highland Falls after a disastrous divorce feels downright embarrassing. Bri blames herself for missing the red flags in her relationship and thus worries she's no longer qualified to do the job she loves. But helping others is second nature to Bri, and she soon finds herself counseling her roommate and her neighbor's daughter. Bri just wasn't expecting them to reunite her with her first love...

THE BEACHSIDE BED AND BREAKFAST
by Hope Ramsay

Ashley Howland Scott has no time for romance as she grieves the loss of her husband, cares for her young son, and runs Magnolia Harbor's only bed and breakfast. Ashley never imagined she'd notice—let alone have feelings for—another man after her husband was killed in Afghanistan. But slowly, softly, Rev. Micah St. Pierre has become a friend…and now maybe something more. Which is all the more reason to steer clear of him.

RETURN TO CHERRY BLOSSOM WAY
by Jeannie Chin

Han Leung always does the responsible thing, which is why he put aside his dreams of opening his own restaurant to run his family's business in Blue Cedar Falls, North Carolina. But when May Wu re-enters his life, he can no longer ignore his own wants and desires. Garden gnomes are stolen, old haunts are visited, and sparks fly between the pair, just as they always have. Han and May broke up because they wanted vastly different lives, and that hasn't changed—or has it?

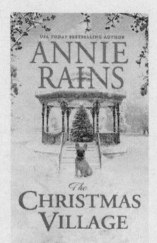

THE CHRISTMAS VILLAGE
by Annie Rains

As the competition heats up in the Merriest Lawn decorating contest, Lucy Hannigan can't help feeling like a Scrooge. Her mom had won the contest every year, but Lucy isn't sure she has it in her to deck the halls this first Christmas without her mother. But when Miles Bruno, her ex-fiancé, shows up with tons of tinsel, dozens of decorations, and lots and lots of lights, Lucy begins to wonder if maybe the spirit of the season can finally mend her broken heart.

DREAMING OF A HEART LAKE CHRISTMAS
by Sarah Robinson

To raise enough money to start her own business, Nola Bennett needs to sell "the Castle," her beloved grandmother's historic house, and get back to the city. But Heart Lake's most eligible bachelor, Tanner Dean, rudely objects. He may be the hottest, grumpiest man she's ever met, and Nola has no time to pine over her high school crush. But sizzling attraction flares the more time he spends convincing her the potential buyers are greedy developers. Will Nora finally realize that this is exactly where she belongs?

SUGARPLUM WAY
by Debbie Mason

Aidan's only priority is to be the best single dad ever, and this year he plans to make the holidays magical for his young daughter. But visions of stolen kisses under the mistletoe keep dancing in his head, and when he finds out Julia Landon has written him into her latest novel, he can't help imagining a future together. Little does he know that Julia has been keeping a secret that threatens all their dreams. Luckily, 'tis the season for a little Christmas magic.

A LITTLE BIT OF LUCK (2-IN-1 EDITION)
by Jill Shalvis

Enjoy a visit to Lucky Harbor in these two dazzling novels! In *It Had to Be You*, a woman's only shot at clearing her tarnished name is with the help of a sexy police detective. Is the chemistry between them a sizzling fling...or the start of something bigger? In *Always on My Mind*, a little white lie pulls two longtime friends into a fake relationship. But pretending to be hot and heavy starts bringing out feelings for each other that are all too real.

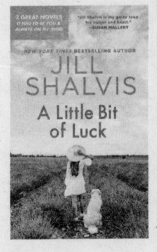